By the same author

The Novel of Worldliness

The Melodramatic Imagination

Reading for the Plot

Body Work

Psychoanalysis and Storytelling

Peter Brooks

WORLD
ELSEWHERE

Simon & Schuster

SIMON & SCHUSTER
Rockefeller Center
1230 Avenue of the Americas
New York, NY 10020

Designed by Sam Potts
Manufactured in the United States of America

1   3   5   7   9   10   8   6   4   2

Library of Congress Cataloging-in-Publication Data
Brooks, Peter, date.
World elsewhere / Peter Brooks.
p.   cm.
1. Tahiti—Discovery and exploration, French—
Fiction. 2. Bougainville, Louis-Antoine de, comte,
1729–1811—Fiction. I. Title.
PS3552.R657484W67   1999
813'.54—dc21   98-28230 CIP

ISBN 0-684-85333-7

Acknowledgments

My warm thanks to Lane Zachary and Todd Shuster for their persistent encouragement in this project; and to two readers of my manuscript whose tact and wisdom made it far better than it originally was: Chuck Adams, whose editorial experience and skill are exemplary; and Rosa Ehrenreich, exceptional reader and friend.

My thanks also to Preston, Kate, and Nat for their unstinting support and love.

I

Snow had begun falling at the close of that gray afternoon, gently settling on the cobblestones, whitening them for a moment before melting, leaving just a trace in the fissures between the stones. I was watching from the window of my third-storey room in my uncle's house in the rue de Bourgogne as night came on. Lejeune emerged from the porter's lodge and lit the two lamps that flanked the porte-cochère. The flames leapt and danced through the falling snow. It was magical, and the start of a magical evening. I was waiting for Frascati: Gianpaolo Sant'Angelo, Conte di Frascati, son of the Neapolitan ambassador to the Court of Versailles, perfect connoisseur of the opera, and my friend. We were going to the Opera to hear Sophie Arnould in *Eros and Psyche,* and then he had promised to take me to the divine Sophie's salon in the rue du Dauphin afterwards.

I'd never been to Sophie Arnould's. I'd known some actresses, to be sure; they were the first women I knew, and for the past two years—since my sixteenth birthday—the obsession of many of my evenings. But they were all bit players—on stage and in my life. Sophie Arnould was the toast of Paris and was destined to be something more in my life. Destined to determine my destiny, in fact, if you could put it that way. It's because of Sophie (though the Comtesse de Lesdiguières has something to do with this too) that I found myself four years later nearly naked on a beach in the South Pacific. And that is the real subject of this narrative: the voyage and what lay at its end. And maybe I should just start there, on that afternoon in Nantes in 1766 when I left the quay in the longboat and was rowed out to the shining black hull of the *Boudeuse*. But then you would know nothing about what set me on that voyage. Not that my motives were at all clear.

To the Opera, then, with Frascati. During the entr'acte, we strolled in the gardens of the Palais-Royal, Frascati filling me in on the plot of Rameau's opera while the ladies of the night came forth one by one from the shadows, insistently accosting us. My new dragoon captain's uniform was probably a magnet. Some of them were younger and more beautiful than Sophie Arnould, no doubt. But how to explain her peculiar charm? When she appeared as Psyche, her body at once full and lithe beneath her Greek tunic, her frail voice following the cadences of Rameau's sublime music, the whole house was swept up in the emotion. Her eyes. They were alive with a special liquid expressiveness. I kept reaching for Frascati's opera glasses so that I could focus on those remarkable eyes. I claim no originality in my sentiments here. All the men vying for Sophie's affections spoke of her eyes. Some even wrote verses to them, but that was never my strong suit.

I confess that I was weary of all this mythological business before the opera was over. I didn't fully share Frascati's enthusiasm for every phrase written by Rameau. The real point of the evening lay ahead, in the rue du Dauphin, where Sophie's friends and admirers gathered following the final curtain. Sophie's majordomo was passing wine and sorbet, and the Comte de Lauraguais—whom all recognized as Sophie's official protector and keeper—presided as host while we awaited her arrival. This was very new company for me, a far more mixed and interesting assortment of guests than I found at my uncle's or with my fellow officers. It ranged from the Prince de Conti, of royal blood, to such a scribbler as Denis Diderot—famous, to be sure, but not the kind of company I usually kept. There were other writers as well: Dorat, the sometime lawyer and sometime musketeer who could improvise verses on demand; the grave Helvétius; Diderot's friend and associate Marmontel; Poinsinet, who wrote Sophie's libretti. Already, there was a hubbub. It was the noisiest crowd I'd ever been among.

Sophie made her entrance, two lapdogs in her arms, and the evening was truly under way. I stayed close to Frascati, waiting for an opportune moment for him to introduce me to the queen of our revels. But in fact, Frascati did not have to do anything. Not more than half an hour had gone by before Sophie spotted the new face among her habitués. She was with me in a moment, in a movement so swift and graceful she scarcely seemed to have had time to cross the expanse of the salon. This was astonishing. But there she was, planted before me, her arms crossed under her provoking bosom, her head bent sideways, a quzzical expression on her rosebud of a mouth, her eyes wide. She flexed her knees in the slightest curtsey. I felt the blood rush to my face. I bowed.

"And who might this be?" The question was apparently addressed to those around her, but she stared straight at me, a slight smile beginning to play on her lips.

The Comte de Lauraguais, ever impeccable in his manners, spoke from over my shoulder: "Prince Charles of Nassau-Siegen. Of the House of Orange. Captain in His Majesty's Dragoons."

Sophie clicked her heels together and saluted. "I didn't know His Majesty made baby dragoons."

I could think of nothing better than to bow again.

Sophie's smile broadened, dimpling her face. "I've played Psyche for three mortal hours on the stage, and now I must encounter Eros in my own salon?"

I had heard of course of Sophie's boldness—she was famous for saying whatever she pleased—but I wasn't quite up to this.

"Just one more enslaved to Psyche," I murmured, "and entirely at your service."

Though somewhat feeble, the remark apparently was not displeasing to Sophie. "Then we are destined to sing duets together?" she asked.

I summoned up my courage and plunged on. "If you know the melody, I shall do my best to find the counterpoint." Not too bad.

"Hah. You'll have to do better than that. Write my libretto. Lead the orchestra."

"Surely Mademoiselle Arnould has servants more qualified than I in those domains. Simply give me a walk-on part."

"One of those cherubs from Act I?" Now she turned to Frascati. "Did you snatch him from the corner of some boudoir decoration? From a Boucher painting, perhaps?"

Frascati now proved himself a friend. "The Prince does indeed look cherubic, my dear Sophie, but he's been a soldier for three years, out fighting in the Low Countries. Dangerously experienced for a cherub."

Sophie's face took on the drollest expression. "*Vive le danger,* then. Cherub, I am at home tomorrow from three to five." She spun on her heel, and in a moment was in the midst of a circle of her admirers.

Frascati and I glanced at one another. He smiled. "I think you have a rendezvous," he said quietly.

"We'll see."

This was stunning, almost too rapid. Though I couldn't quite admit it to myself at the time, I was overwhelmed. Gratified, yes, but also a bit scared. I had been told by women that I was good-looking, but I don't think I was particularly vain. Madame Vigée-Lebrun, who painted my portrait, said I looked like a virgin just leaving the convent. But at eighteen, I wasn't quite a virgin. I had my modest chronicle of conquests, mostly among dancers and bit-players at the Comédie-Italienne—nothing to boast of. All one needed to do was be a bit attentive to the girls who weren't already attached. A fresh face, a uniform, and the priapic enthusiasm of youth did the rest.

The remainder of the evening was mainly a blur. I moved from one knot of people to another, surrounded by a kind of envious respect because of Sophie's interest in me, although subjected to a certain mordant raillery from some of this witty company. Frascati and I were about to withdraw when the valet at the door announced Monsieur de Bougainville. Here, I thought, was someone worth meeting. Thirty-four years old, handsome, tall, and well-built, he looked at once the aristocrat and the commander.

"Watch out." Frascati spoke in my ear. "He's reputed to be Sophie's current favorite."

"Favorite?"

"Her heart's companion. Lauraguais reigns officially, but there is always a sentimental favorite of the moment as well."

"You mean?"

"He's your rival. The one you'll have to supplant."

The idea of entering into competition with Bougainville for Sophie's favors was distressing. "Won't that lead to trouble?"

Frascati shrugged. "Could be. But he's a gentleman. And after all, no one expects perfect fidelity from our dear Sophie. 'Twould be contrary to nature."

I continued to stare at M. de Bougainville, watching as he moved easily through the assembly, acknowledging acquaintances with a graceful inclination of his torso. A man to admire, and to imitate, I thought. Comte Louis-Antoine de Bougainville had distinguished himself in fighting alongside the Marquis de Montcalm for our possessions in Quebec. He had been made prisoner by the English, then wounded in the German campaigns. He was also known for having written a treatise on differential calculus, and was an expert in plotting ocean longitudes. Rumor had it that he would soon undertake an immense ocean voyage to make good our country's claim to the Malvinas Islands. I didn't know then, of course, that I would serve under his command in a far longer voyage, one that would make all the difference in my life. And I often wondered, later on, whether I would have taken Sophie Arnould to bed—no doubt the same bed she had shared with M. de Bougainville—had I known that for two and a half years I would be sharing Captain's mess with him as we traveled around the world.

Not the most propitious footing upon which to embark on being ship-mates.

But of course I did go to bed with Sophie. Our rendezvous the next day was easier and more natural than I had expected. Sophie had made sure we would be alone, and she received me from her ottoman, dressed in a *négligé* that seemed at once to cover and uncover her charms. She beckoned me to a place by her head, on a Turkish cushion set on the floor. When I was seated, my face was level with her eyes, those famous eyes. My mouth was dry; I feared I would have nothing to say. I felt awkward. But Sophie's easy manners and sense of humor quickly banished my fears and turned my stilted flattery into warm and passionate declarations. In the end, it took us only a short time to get where we both wanted to be.

A divine woman. Sophie was not the most beautiful mistress I was to know, but no man would ever think that bed with her was less than paradise. She was artful, rendering lovemaking graceful and easy, sheer pleasure. She was also amusing. She had a witty body, and used it to talk to you in various tones and moods. She could go from the sultry to the comical in a moment, appeal to the deepest sensations of love, then show you none of this was to be taken seriously. The love that we claim to be the source of our pleasures is really their pretext, she once told me. I took momentary umbrage at this—I wanted to be the one, the only, the very principle of pleasure. But she of course was wiser than that. She kept me sufficiently flattered by the praises she lavished on my body—but who knows, this may have been part of her usual script—while also holding me at bay. She didn't want any un-controlled reactions on my part: no duels with Bougainville, no upset-ting of her arrangements with Lauraguais.

Between our bouts of lovemaking, we talked. Sophie was a mine of the latest knowledge about all sorts of things. She listened to the con-versations in her salon. She even read some of the books that her ar-dent admirers left on the table in the foyer. Once I picked up from the elegant inlaid table in her boudoir a volume by M. Rousseau, his *Dis-course on the Origins of Inequality Among Men.*

"You read such things?"

Her face became prim and serious. "M. Rousseau used to come to see me from time to time. Not when there was a crowd—he couldn't stand that—but in the afternoon. I try to keep informed of my friends' writings."

"But this? Not reading for a lady, I should think."

"I haven't the weakness of being a 'lady,' " she replied tartly. "There are, thank God, some advantages to not belonging to that category."

"Still," I persisted. "He's in exile. His last two books were condemned by the Sorbonne and the Parlement of Paris. Burned publicly."

"So? And have the powers that be treated you so well that you have no sympathy for the outcast?"

This was a barb, a reference to those persistent old stories about my illegitimate birth, which had deprived me of my property in the German states. I would have been immensely rich with them. Instead, I was beginning to be ominously in debt.

"No. To be sure. Curses on all their corrupt courts and lawyers. But beware, this man is a lackey and a scribbler of diatribes against society."

Sophie's look became haughty. "Read it and see for yourself."

I never could determine whether in actuality she had read Rousseau's tract. But I did read it myself, a year or so later. And it made a difference. Yes, I was more than a bit narrow-minded back then. But I came from a circle where conventional ideas were respected. Sophie was just the start in a school of wider thoughts and dreams.

So life ran on, trivial and pleasant. The Opera three times a week, followed by visits to Sophie's dressing-room, playing with her lap dogs while she changed out of her costume—and I snatched the moment when she was stripped to the waist to kiss those insolent breasts—then gatherings in her salon, where I now was tacitly acknowledged as the reigning favorite. M. de Bougainville simply disappeared from sight, which was a relief, though the sense of having created enmity from such a man disturbed me. I arose late every morning, then whiled away my time in my uncle's house waiting for the hour when

Sophie was "at home"—though I by no means always found her alone at home. Other men, the habitués and new pretenders to her favor, came to establish themselves, easily or uneasily, amidst the sweet disorder of her boudoir. She couldn't shut her door to them every afternoon. I knew that my protests were useless. She had a life to keep up. Still, I couldn't always fight off the demon of jealousy.

Then in April the Opera House in the Palais-Royal caught fire and burned to the ground. No one was hurt—it was during Holy Week when all performances were suspended—but it created confusion in Sophie's well-regulated life. Then in July her protector, Lauraguais, went to prison, in the fortress at Metz, for having read to the Royal Academy a memoir in which he proclaimed himself a fervent partisan of the inoculation for smallpox—which, thanks to Lady Wortley Montagu, the English had learned from the Circassians—and in the process poured ridicule on the savants of French medicine. At the time I had no opinion on inoculation, though I have lived long enough to see the practice become accepted, but I thought it ridiculous for a man of Lauraguais' rank to be locked up for his medical opinions. Locking up the scribblers—Diderot, d'Alembert—we were used to; it didn't occur to me to question that. Not back then. But you didn't treat a man of the court in that way.

Sophie became haunted with the notion that only she could win Lauraguais' freedom. Even after the Opera reopened, temporarily relocated in the Tuileries, she was constantly scheming. She and I might have lasted longer otherwise. She thought she had found an ally in another of the scribblers, the playwright Sedaine, who was ever engaged—or so he said—in composing petitions to the Minister, Choiseul, for Lauraguais' release. Now, nearly every afternoon I found him in Sophie's boudoir, sheets of foolscap piled ostentatiously on the inlaid table, pen and inkwell next to them—though I had the impression that rather little actual writing was going forward. Their tender interviews about poor Lauraguais left Sophie with dewy eyes and a heaving bosom. I took offense, but she would hear nothing of my complaints.

"Cherub," she would say to me, "your role is to cover my body with your wonderful kisses. Then to show me that cherubs with soft lips can be hard as a rock when you want them."

This would of course provoke a rush of passion, though given her involvement with Sedaine we rarely found the occasion to fall entwined on her ottoman.

It was Sophie in person, one night when the troupe presented *Dardanus* at a command performance in Versailles, who threw herself at the feet of Choiseul and obtained Lauraguais' pardon after six months of prison. A week later he was back in Paris, frenetically in charge of the household again. And then late that winter Sophie became pregnant. Lauraguais' child, she assured us—the result, she said, of her womb leaping for joy at his release. I wasn't sure, but I doubted that I carried any responsibility in the matter. For some time prior, our rendezvous had become quite infrequent.

For I too had moved on. As I spent less time in the rue du Dauphin I began to accompany my uncle, the Comte de Grammont, more frequently in his social rounds in the great houses of the Faubourg Saint-Germain. He thought it time that I form an attachment more worthy of my rank than one with an actress. Not that he wanted yet to marry me; I was too young, and a soldier besides, who might have to undertake a new campaign if the peace did not hold. No, he wanted me to fall under the influence of a woman of good society, married and some years my elder, who could polish my manners and keep me from improper company until I was ready for marriage.

As Prince Charles of Nassau-Siegen, I had my entrées, and any reasonably prepossessing prince in a uniform—even if denied his rightful fortune—is bound to appeal to some of the slightly older married women whose husbands are occupied elsewhere. So it was that two years after my first encounter with Sophie I met the Comtesse Marie-Isabelle de Lesdiguières. The Comte held some minor charge at Court, and Marie-Isabelle was often alone in the high rooms of their house in the rue de Bellechasse. It was here that late one January afternoon, as shadows gathered in the small salon with its discreet gray and white boiseries and its oval ceiling painted with the loves of Venus and Mars, I became her lover.

It had seemed so very difficult to move from being her devoted cavalier to the physical. If Sophie had intimidated me initially by her worldly wit and her horde of admirers, Marie-Isabelle was daunting in her air of impeccable propriety. She was beautiful, charming, alluring; but somehow her stunningly tasteful dresses, flounced and ribboned, her silk stockings and delicate shoes, didn't seem things that could be got beyond. I could not imagine her unclothed; I could not imagine her naked in the manner of Sophie, her arms and her legs opened to me.

And yet, when it happened, it was quite simple. I think in fact she did everything. I had been kissing the back of her hand—previously our only permitted intimacy—when somehow she shifted her position on the sofa, and my lips found themselves on her shoulder, then her neck, then under the gauzy material covering her bosom. That was all it took.

How vividly I can still recall those late afternoons in the rue de Bellechasse. When at last I had unlaced Marie-Isabelle's corset and she allowed me, worshipfully, to pull her light, lacy shift over her head—something I learned to do in one swift, smooth gesture—she would sigh and close her eyes. I didn't close mine. Her elegant body, all white and pink, was stretched before me on the red damask sofa. Her arms and legs were long and slender, finished with fine toes and fingers, their nails delicately buffed and polished to a light sheen. Her neck, too, was elongated, giving her head the refined manner of a painting by one of the Fontainebleau masters. Her eyelashes were two fans of delicate light brown against her pale face, while her ash-blond curls fell in abandon on the sides of her face and her shoulders. Her nostrils were arched; her eyebrows were arched; her fine lips, colored a pale rose, were slightly opened, and moist. Her elegant breasts, slung low on her chest, finished in pink nipples. Below them, the marks of the corset were visible, and the flesh was almost startlingly white, colorless in fact. Her waist was so very narrow I could round it with my two hands. The swell of her hips was modest, and her white thighs were slim and without visible sinew, as if she were a creature so fine she was not supposed to use her legs for locomotion. A kind of final realization of French civilization, Marie-Isabelle: woman nurtured exclusively for the palaces of the aristocracy. As my hand slid between her thighs she stirred and opened her legs. She groaned in pleasure when I gently touched her.

My adored Marie-Isabelle. Wasn't that love at its most alluring, most flattering too? To be known throughout Paris and Versailles as the lover of the Comtesse de Lesdiguières; to be acknowledged everywhere as her special consort, even by the old Comte, whose business at Court left him no time to be a lover to his wife; to have my entrées to her box at the Comédie Italienne, and my more private invitations to her boudoir—wasn't that perfect happiness for a young man? And yet it couldn't last. There were inevitable complications. Besides, I was not destined to a career in the boudoir. I had a name to make.

II

I SHOULD TELL YOU more about that name, since it has to do with this story. Perhaps I should start with what another uncle (if that one is really my uncle) wrote about me later. I give it as a sort of bad joke. Unlike the Comte de Grammont, who nurtured my youth, acting no doubt from a sense of family duty, the Duc de Lévis never truly liked me, and never truly knew me either. Nevertheless, he was a great one for passing judgment.

So: "The Prince of Nassau-Siegen, tall and well-built, had an inexpressive face to which his mind did not give the lie. His bold fearlessness was matched by the mediocrity of his talents. From his reputation, one expected to see a Knight of the Round Table; when he appeared, farewell to romance—his presence brought disenchantment. Nothing striking, nothing brilliant, not even much animation. His greeting was cold, his manners common, his conversation flat." I hasten to point out that his opinion was not held universally—the Prince de Ligne, my friend, has given what I hope is a much more accurate description of me. But unfortunately the venomous Lévis was supported by all those jealous and self-interested members of my family who had always insisted that I was born a bastard, despite the fact that the legitimacy of my birth was established by a formal act of the Parlement of Paris, in its edict of June 3, 1756. That made no difference to them. Alas, it also mattered not at all to the State Council in Vienna, which awarded all my rightful property in Germany to other members of the family. Family stories are always complicated. The root of this story had to do with my grandmother, and the fact that my branch of the family abjured Protestantism to return to the true Church, which made the German branch claim sole right to the name. To declare I was a bastard was just their way of getting the property that should have been mine. But once the accusation was made, I could never quite get rid of its taint.

The real point is that although I can trace my ancestry back directly to Otto, Count of Laurenburg, who founded our dynasty in the tenth century, I was penniless. I had to go for a soldier. My uncle Grammont impressed upon me from childhood that I had to make my own way in the world and that the army offered the only honorable way to make good on the name I bore. I was only fifteen when I joined up. By age eighteen, thanks in large part to my uncle's influence, I became lieutenant in the infantry, then captain in the dragoons. To anticipate on the future, not from vanity—I believe I am beyond that now—but to give the historical record its due: later on, I would become quite famous as a general and make my way through Africa with the Chevalier d'Oraison, where I fought and killed a lion. Then I served the King of Spain. I married a Polish countess and became the faithful officer of His Majesty Stanislaus-Augustus, of heroic memory to all the Polish people. I became a general in the service of Catherine the Great—her favorite general, she once did me the honor of saying—and commanded her fleets, routing the Turks in the Black Sea and the Swedes in the Baltic.

But all that came much later. This story really begins in 1766, when I was twenty-one, and signed on to M. de Bougainville's voyage clear around the globe.

Yes, I left the red damask of Marie-Isabelle's sofa, and Sophie's iris-scented boudoir, too. At the very moment when my life might have been considered the envy of every young man in Paris, I gave it all up—though not entirely of my own choice—to encounter the unknown.

My chief error was returning to Sophie's salon one evening when Frascati again had taken me to the Opera, now in its temporary new quarters in the Tuileries. It was *Aline, Queen of Golconda* we saw—libretto by the detestable Sedaine, music composed by Monsigny. Dreary stuff, I thought, but Sophie was enchanting. The role had her constantly switching from queen to shepherdess, and you could have sworn she was born to be either. By turn imperious and supplicating, regal and innocent, she was infinite variety personified, absolutely irresistible. So how could I refuse when Frascati insisted that we pay a visit to the rue du Dauphin afterwards?

Sophie had the effrontery to appear still dressed in her shepherdess costume, looking as fresh and delicious as some Swiss milkmaid. I could not long resist approaching her.

"Ah, captain cherub is back. You do us honor," she said. If there is such a thing as an ironic curtsey, that is what I was given.

"Gladly would I put off this uniform for the shepherd's rustic garb," I replied.

"To play upon your pipes of Pan, no doubt?" She had her droll manner of resting her head on one side, her eyes sparkling with malice.

I flushed, aware suddenly of how fatuous I must have sounded. Still, I went on. "If that would be pleasing."

"Oh, but one hears your pipe is otherwise employed."

"Never with as much pleasure as when singing to you."

"Just listen to our young Orpheus. Maybe you'd best stick with women who count, or at least count-ess."

I grimaced. The code of honor I observed at the time told me it was not right to drag Marie-Isabelle into this society.

"Mademoiselle Sophie, shepherdesses don't speak in riddles."

"Monsieur le Prince, a pretty transparent riddle. But it's all right, I pardon an occasional lapse with one of those ladies. I'm sure you're suffering deprivation in the midst of depravation."

"What do you know about ladies?"

"Everything."

"How?"

"From their husbands, of course. I repair the damage done by marriages."

You simply could not be offended with Sophie. I laughed aloud. "Well then, what about reparations on the unmarried?"

"Easily managed, if they know how to make honorable amends."

I sent an immense bouquet to Sophie's dressing room the next evening. She loved it. And so I continued night after night, adding other trinkets as well. I was again in her good graces and was at least one of her favorites—I no longer bothered about my rivals.

Here began my brief life in what you might call debauchery. Afternoons were divided between the rue de Bellechasse and the rue du Dauphin. Evenings, I would dine with Marie-Isabelle, then move on to Sophie's salon toward midnight. It was diverting in its very perversity. I can see now that I was creating complexity and contradiction in my life in order to mask its sense of emptiness and worthlessness. I would bring to Sophie gossip picked up from the Court circles gathered around the Comte de Lesdiguières. And I would bring to Marie-Isabelle something of the gaiety and abandon that flowed from Sophie's crowd. Some of my audacities as a lover surprised Marie-Isabelle. They were importations, perhaps too obviously so, from the rue du Dauphin. While Sophie knew about my liaison with Marie-Isabelle and rarely failed to needle me about my weakness for "ladies," Marie-Isabelle was convinced of my utter devotion and fidelity. The situation was too delicate not to be doomed to spectacular failure.

It was tiring, too, even for a twenty-one-year-old with no other battles to fight and a reasonably inexhaustible capacity for lovemaking. I found myself dozing off at dinner in the rue de Bellechasse as the Minister of Foreign Affairs droned on about the vulnerabilities of the English fleet. On my way to the rue du Dauphin, I would find myself walking more and more slowly, actually reluctant to arrive. Most significantly, though, my life was costing me more than my uncle's modest stipend allowed. I was spending a fortune on trinkets for Sophie, and on my tailor to look impeccable in the rue de Bellechasse. I owed the tailor two hundred livres, and I had borrowed another three hundred from Frascati. I began to think of the gambling tables of the Palais-Royal: the salvation—or the ruin—of many a young man before me. But I couldn't put together enough of a purse to make a visit there worth undertaking. And the idea terrified me. I was brave enough when faced with dangers I could see, but to give myself over to chance, to hazard everything on the spin of a wheel—the idea brought sweat to my temples as I dressed for the evening and realized that I would sally forth with only a few coins in my waistcoat pocket.

As it turned out, the dénouement arrived before the debt burden became wholly crushing—while it was still only embarrassing. Fate took the form of someone's perfidy—whose? I never could find out for sure. Not Frascati, certainly—he was too loyal a friend. Perhaps the Prince de Conti, who frequented the rue du Dauphin and encountered the Comte de Lesdiguières at Court. I think he aspired to admission to Sophie's boudoir. Be that as it may, one afternoon I found Marie-Isabelle awaiting me with an expression of haughty disdain, which I at once knew betokened disaster. The valet had no sooner closed the doors to the small salon than she came to the point.

After all these years, I still cringe with shame at that interview. I shan't recount it. Her anger was one thing—I think I could have managed that. But her contempt! The idea of sharing me with an actress fairly choked her. Her words were venomous. I sought to excuse myself by way of my youth, the bad example of the times. I assured her that for her alone did I feel love and adoration, that Mademoiselle Arnould was simply a matter of youthful vanity, piqued by rivalry. These of course were vain defenses! I know now I should simply have denied anything and everything. Although she had reliable and detailed information and would no doubt have disbelieved my denial, nonetheless it would have been the only dignified response. She could have heard me lie, and known me to be lying, but still preferred it to my confused admissions and explanations. When she dismissed me, with orders never to appear in her house again, I bowed to her in silence, and left—clearly the stupidest possible thing to do. And not, I suspect, what either of us wanted. Not that the liaison would have continued indefinitely. But it should have ended more honorably, with a retreat with colors flying afforded to both of us.

It was not in Marie-Isabelle's interest to have public scandal touch our separation any more than our liaison. So surely it was not she, nor the Comte, who informed my uncle of my amorous complications. Perhaps it was again the Prince de Conti, or someone in his circle. But it was only a week following the scene with Marie-Isabelle when I was summoned by Lejeune to my uncle's library.

His distinguished face looked weary as he glanced across his desk at where I had taken a seat on a wooden bench, having passed up a soft bergère as inappropriate to what I sensed would be a solemn interview. Before him lay open a large leatherbound volume, Lord Anson's *Voyages*—one of those books of travellers to far places that he found the most nourishing of reading. Though his brief diplomatic career, now long past, had taken him no farther from Paris than Utrecht and Potsdam, he spent many hours in revery over trips to the ends of the earth.

"Charles," he began, "I must speak of unpleasant things."

"Yes, sir."

"You are old enough to manage your life. I have nothing against careless youth. But when I accepted to be your guardian . . ."

He paused, looking perplexed as to how to continue.

It was up to me to come to his assistance. "I have been thoughtless and indiscreet, sir."

He waved his hand. "Indiscretions are fine if their outcome is fortunate. The indiscretions of lieutenants can result in the rout of the enemy. But to earn the enmity of the Lesdiguières, to be banished from their company . . . and all because you can't manage an affair with an actress . . ."

"I know, sir. I have behaved inconsiderately."

"Worse than that, Charles. Because you see, you're not in a strong position. If you had an income of five thousand livres, it would be different. Indiscretion would be just that—and reparable through further indiscretions. For it'd be you who set the tone. Maybe not the tone I would find honorable, but some of our *roués* are fashionable and are received everywhere, no matter how censured their conduct."

He paused again. I now began to feel truly ashamed.

"I see, sir." I couldn't think of anything more to say.

"Charles, you bear a great name. But even that is contested you. You have no fortune, and you have debts. In addition, you are making a mess of your life. And now that there is peace in Europe, I have no doubt you will continue to bleed my purse—which is not so deep as you might think, my boy—and to live worthlessly."

"Not what I want, sir," I mumbled. "And my gratitude to you . . ."

He waved this off. "The point is not what's done. It's what resolutions you are capable of taking for the future."

"I'll do better, sir. Really. I'll make myself keep away from Mademoiselle Arnould. I'll . . ." But, of course, what I would do was by no means clear.

"But what are you to *do?* I've thought about it. A foreign garrison? But you'd live just as worthlessly there. More liaisons, more debts."

Exile from Paris? Not appealing, unless there were a chance of a military campaign, and nothing of that sort was in the offing. The Choiseul ministry seem dedicated to peace at any cost. And the royal treasury was in parlous condition following seven years of war.

My uncle's eyes now rested on Anson's *Voyages.* He cleared his throat. "I do have an idea. M. de Bougainville, with whom I understand you have some acquaintance"—a quick glance from under his arched eyebrows accompanied this phrase—"has been commissioned to make a voyage. A return to the Malvinas, which he claimed for the Crown two years ago, but which now are to be handed over to Madrid. Don't ask me why. Foolish policy, in my view. Anyway, once that deed is done he's to proceed westward, either through the Strait of Magellan or round Cape Horn, at his choice, and into the Pacific Ocean, there to reconnoitre the various islands marked by previous voyagers, and other lands undiscovered, to inventory their riches, to take possession of the most promising of them for King and Country. In short, it will be a voyage around the world."

At the name of M. de Bougainville, an involuntary smile touched my face. But the rest of my uncle's message returned me to dead seriousness. A voyage around the world. A circumnavigation. Extraordinary. I had experienced combat. I had led men into battle under a hail of fire. But this!

"I've spoken with M. de Bougainville. He's willing to take you on as a volunteer. You'll probably be gone two to three years." My uncle spoke in response to my silence.

Two to three years confined to shipboard. No Marie-Isabelle—but she has gone in any case—no Sophie. None of those delicious afternoons spent between her warm thighs. Total deprivation on that score, in fact. Whatever would I do? The sweet bliss of lovemaking had become a virtual necessity in my life. This was simply not possible.

"So much to think about," I murmured. "So much to give up." And yet when I said that, I flushed. I couldn't content myself forever with bedding women in the boudoirs of Paris and hunting an occasional boar in the Ardennes. No glory there. I needed to conquer a right to the great name I bore. I needed to prove that despite malicious rumors, I was a true Nassau-Siegen. But to lose touch completely with my own world! To give up all its comforts and sociabilities for the hard life of a mariner. Again my mind flashed back to Sophie. I couldn't help it. She was lodged somewhere behind my eyes, her provoking breasts raised toward my lips.

"Think," said my uncle—he seemed to be following my thoughts— "you'll discover lands never trod by European feet before, and peoples unknown to us. Giants, dwarfs. Other societies, mankind in its infancy, the state of nature."

Yes. There was the true allure. It wasn't so much the call of unknown landfalls in the boundless Pacific as it was the promise of new peoples, unimaginable in their looks and ways. To see my own race in the strange mirror of primitive mankind. Mankind who took us back to the dawn of time, before the manners of our civilization had covered over natural instincts. The witty banter of Sophie's salon, Marie-Isabelle's white flesh marked by the corset—there must be something else, something more universally human out beyond the horizon. Just recently, after Sophie's challenge I had finally begun to read M. Rousseau. Something about those first societies in which man emerged from the state of nature whispered compellingly to me. There would be darkness there, I knew, but maybe some unimagined light as well. Some inner illumination. Some chance to find one's own truth.

"I'll go." I blurted it out, as if aware that if I took time for further reflection I'd back away from it.

My uncle smiled. He rose stiffly from his chair and extended his hand to me over the table. "*Nous n'avons qu'un honneur, il est tant de maîtresses!*" he said as he shook my hand.

Nous n'avons qu'un honneur! The old Don Diègue speaking to his son Rodrigue in Corneille's *Le Cid*. Mere literature. But maybe that was right: only one path to honor, and mistresses didn't point the way.

"So it's all arranged. You'll join M. de Bougainville at Nantes come November."

Did I know what I was getting into? Of course not.

III

Two months later, I rode into the courtyard of the Hostellerie de Paris in Nantes. I was greeted cordially enough by M. de Bougainville, though I thought I detected a certain irony in his manner, as if in allusion to our past rivalry for Sophie's attentions. What kind of shipboard bond, I wondered, might come from our having shared the bed of the same woman? Did we have the same memories, the same indelible images imprinted on our erotic imaginings? And what would this mean when the erotic was reduced purely to the imaginary? Would we ever talk about it? Foolish thought. He was now my captain. And I, though a volunteer on the voyage—at my uncle's expense—was under his absolute command. The law of the sea.

The frigate *Boudeuse* had come out of the shipyard two weeks before. She now lay out in the roadstead. M. de Bougainville described with the precision of the mathematician her equipping and provisioning. From his earlier voyage to the Malvinas—those islands the English call Falkland—he was minutely aware of what was needed for the Atlantic crossing. Then the *Boudeuse* would be joined at the Malvinas by the storeship *Etoile,* bringing livestock and other supplies. The two ships would together turn south and westward, toward the tip of the South American continent, to seek passage into the Pacific. It was to be an adventure in uncharted waters, to destinations unknown.

The next afternoon, the longboat took me from the quay, with the nine cases of my necessities I had earlier shipped from Paris, and ten minutes later I was looking up at the high, black sides of the ship, crossed by a broad white stripe at the gun deck where the brass cannon barrels glinted in the pale November sun. The *Boudeuse* appeared a good ship, standing at anchor in the harbor where the Loire spread wide: a hundred and twenty-five feet long, nine hundred sixty tons, carrying twenty-six twelve-pound cannon. Up the ladder to the deck, where M. de Bougainville introduced me to the first officer, M. Duclos-Guyot. A smell of new wood and fresh tar and varnish everywhere. I was taken to my cabin in the taffrail, commodious enough, in truth—M. de Bougainville may have regarded me as a nuisance in his amorous life, and as an untried mariner, but he still had a proper regard for my station in life. We dined that night on board at the Captain's mess, where we were fifteen: besides M. de Bougainville and Duclos-Guyot and myself, the three ensigns, the Chevaliers de Bournand, du Bouchage, and d'Oraison; then the officers of the marines, the Chevaliers de Suzannet and de Kerhué; the merchant officer M. Le Corre; the ship's writer, M. Saint-Germain; the chaplain, Father Lavaisse; and the ship's surgeon, M. La Porte; another volunteer, the apprentice pilot Fesche; and in addition, the astronomer Véron and the naturalist Commerson, who were to sail on the *Etoile* and join us later. M. de Bougainville had furnished himself with two cooks and two maîtres d'hôtel, as well as his valet and three negro servants. All in all, the *Boudeuse* would carry two hundred and ten men, the *Etoile* one hundred and twenty, as well as livestock, provisions, and supplies for trading with the natives of the lands we discovered.

On that first evening in the Captain's mess I had little intimation of the future that lay so close to hand. How to know then that the voyage of the *Boudeuse* would be the farthest reach of my adventures, in a life that has been far from uneventful. And that it would prove the deepest probe, too, into the truth of things. It is curious now to think back to that first gathering on board with the group of men I was to spend so many months with, to become fast friends with some, and to discover only antipathy or indifference for others. Later images efface those first ones: d'Oraison deeply tanned, his black beard and hair all unkempt, sweaty, and muddy, standing in perplexity at the foot of an astonishing cascade of water falling in an uninterrupted plume deep in the island fastness. Bournand, his robust body shivering in his seacoat, at the tiller of the longboat as it roared down a treacherous channel in the Strait of Magellan. Commerson racing down a sun-drenched beach, his belly quivering over his spindly legs, to effect the rescue of his valet Baret, who'd been stripped naked by the delighted islanders. Véron taking his elevations at the very foot of the globe. La Porte facing down a witch doctor as he ministered to a dying savage boy. Poor Bouchage, dead of scurvy, his body consigned to the sea off New Guinea. And M. de Bougainville himself, nodding politely, his face flushed, his upper body rigid as he sat cross-legged on the straw matting and watched a beautiful young woman toss off her clothing and offer herself to him. Companions all. And others, such as Saint-Germain and Father Lavaisse, who simply never counted at all, who somehow drifted to the periphery of my attention.

The next day with the tide we weighed anchor, glided down the river, and reached Saint-Nazaire, where we spent a week loading water and further provisions. We set sail November 15.

While my story is of an immense voyage, this is not a tale of the sea. Don't expect those details of navigation which I know M. de Bougainville has consigned to his journal. Don't expect, either, a nautical yarn. The sea doesn't interest me. It's what lies beyond that captures my imagination.

But I must tell you that two days out, it started to blow with high and variable winds from the west-south-west. We rode out the night under bare spars, with only mizzen trysail to steady us. Sick? Yes, I was sick, but I was young then, and refused to let the turmoil of my stomach stand in my way. An hour after midnight, I was back on the heav-

ing afterdeck in the screaming wind, the waves streaming past as the
Boudeuse rose and rolled, finding her way back into the troughs of the
sea. There was no horizon, the black sky met the black sea without any
line of separation, and the waves rose towering above us without
warning. Sometimes a rent in the clouds gave a glimpse of the pale
half-moon, at once blown away. Duclos-Guyot, wrapped in his seacloak, stood behind the helmsman, his face closed and unreadable in
the spectral illumination of the dark lantern over the compass. I raised
my voice in greeting, but the wind hurled my words away. He did not
seem to hear me. He did not move. I could now see that his gaze was
fixed high in the rigging of the mainmast. It was dizzying to watch as
it pitched forward and back and whipped side to side. I must have
lowered my eyes, for I didn't see what happened next. A sharp crack,
and the sickening sound of splintering wood. The main topmast had
broken off just above the crosstrees, and hung like a detached limb
from the rigging, its end catching in the tops of the waves. At once I
heard the sound of the gong as Duclos-Guyot summoned all hands on
deck to cut away the rigging.

It was a nightmare of motion, though strangely without voice—no
point in trying to talk in this wind—as the men swarmed into the rigging. By now that upper half of the mainmast was dragging in the water, tossed up and down by each passing swell, and the ship was
begining to list seriously to starboard. In great peril to their lives, the
men managed to cut free, and soon the wreckage of the mast swirled
past the afterdeck. I watched it turn and roll in the wake for a moment. But then another sickening crack, and I found myself thrown to
the deck and enmeshed in a web of rigging. Just above me, the
mizzenmast had broken, this time only feet above the deck.

"Lie still!" Duclos-Guyot barked at me. Chest down on the slimy
wet planks, I was nauseated by the heave and shudder of the ship. With
the mizzen staysail gone, she was rolling more now. I had to brace myself with my toes and the palms of my hands to keep from sliding under the mess of rigging. Then two men were at either end of me,
grunting as they worked their knives through the rigging. Another

moment, and one of them grasped my hand and pulled me to a standing position. Still holding his shoulder, I picked my way across the cat's
cradle of lines to the companionway.

I nearly stumbled into M. de Bougainville, who had just emerged
on deck, buttoning his seacoat. His face was furrowed and grim.

"Passengers below," he spoke curtly. "No way to rescue men overboard in this. Not even princes."

I bridled at this. "I'm part of the watch, sir."

"No you're not. Landsmen below. A night for true sailors."

I stared for a moment. Where was the urbanity of the man I had observed in Sophie's salon? But he gave me no time to protest. He
pushed me toward the companionway and moved aft to the helm. The
law of the sea, I told myself, and went below.

M. de Bougainville set our course back to Brest. We would have to
put into the Royal Navy Yard for repairs. And for modifications to the
ship. He decided that we were carrying too much sail for an ocean
crossing. The masts were too tall, and the curve of the ship's sides as
they came up to the level of the deck made the deck too narrow to
stay them securely. The stays needed a broader angle. And the ship was
too stiff for ocean storms. Ballast needed to be removed, so that it
could roll more freely.

So much for the foresight of our mathematician turned sailor, I
thought when I came back on deck at first light. Yet I admit that I was
impressed by his cool appraisal of the situation. Nothing was said
about the exchange between us during the night. He was polite to me,
but nothing more.

We entered the roadstead at Brest on the 21st. Repairs went forward expeditiously, and, with the singlemindedness of youth in a port
town, I found a chambermaid at the Hôtel de Bon-Repos to relieve
my aching nether parts. Wonderful Ninon! The Bon-Repos deserves a
passing benediction. By December 6 we put to sea again, this time for
an uneventful voyage. On the 18th, we sighted Palma. On January 8,
1767, between 26 and 27 degrees of longitude, we passed the Equator, which involved foolish ceremonies, including a dunking for those

few, like myself, who were crossing the line for the first time. The 31st, at eleven o'clock in the morning, after fifty-five days of sailing, we moored in the Río de la Plata before the city of Montevideo, in the company of two frigates flying the flag of Spain.

Little need be said about Montevideo, a rather paltry city with a citadel that didn't look to me as if it could defend much of anything, and a harbor made dangerous by its many sandbanks. It is true that the land surrounding the city is richly fertile. Where it has been cultivated, it brings forth crops in a profusion never seen in France. But the cultivated areas are small, and the rest is the wild pampas, grazed by cattle and horses (which seemed to have thrived in their new habitat) and infested by packs of wild dogs. We took the longboat upriver to Buenos Aires in order to arrange with the governor for the formal transfer of the Malvinas Islands to the Spanish Crown. Not much to report of Buenos Aires either—a low city where the rich live in haciendas with vast gardens right in the middle of the town, so that in perspective it hardly resembles a city at all. Contrary winds prevented our returning downriver under sail, so we decided to go overland, in an expedition across the pampas, driving a herd of forty horses before us—the only way to have a fresh horse to relay the tired one! At night we bivouacked in the open, under tents made of leather hides, our sleep troubled by the screaming of wild cats. When we came to the broad expanse of Santa Lucía River, we set the horses to swim across, and ourselves entered a narrow boat—a canoe really—with a high side facing upstream. The indian boatman—stark naked, which was the most practical way to be under the circumstances—then led two horses into the water, one each side of the canoe, and attached them to it. So we crossed by horsepower, the boatman struggling to keep the beasts' heads above the surface of the churning water.

As for these indians, they struck me as miserable beyond belief, reduced by Spanish rule to poverty and abjection. When they came to town to trade their hides, they would purchase any spirits that might be available, and drink them until they lay insensible by the roadside. Only slightly less miserable were the negro slaves, brought in contraband to the colony by English traders from the Portuguese colony of Saint Sacrament.

Back in Montevideo, we set sail with the Spanish frigates for the Malvinas, which we reached after twenty-three days. Because M. de Bougainville made the original discovery of these islands, he holds them close to his heart, and has written of them with much feeling. I yield to him the privilege of paternal affection. I must say I found them a bleak and desolate place, suited at most for the making of salt mines. We did observe fifty-four species of birds in our stay on the islands, but only one four-footed animal, which looked half-way between a wolf and a fox. We waited at the Malvinas two mortal months for the arrival of the *Etoile,* which was to meet us there with its stock of fresh supplies. Finally, given the dwindling state of our stores, we set sail for Rio de Janeiro—where we found the *Etoile,* newly arrived, waiting for us.

In the immensity of the seas of the new world, our compatriot ships had found each other, like two bits of magnetized iron. Great was our joy.

IV

M. DE LA GIRAUDAIS, captain of the *Etoile,* was soon alongside in his ship's launch and was piped aboard. With him were his ship's surgeon, M. Vivès, the astronomer Véron, and the naturalist Commerson. We gathered in M. de Bougainville's cabin for luncheon. La Giraudais at once explained the missed Falklands rendezvous: the *Etoile*'s ocean passage had been slowed by a persistent and growing leak, which kept half the crew at the pumps. He was forced to put into Montevideo, where he careened the ship to make repairs. A Spanish galleon bound in from the Malvinas reported our plan to make for Rio, so La Giraudais wisely decided that there would be our meeting place.

I can hardly express how weary I was of sea talk. I was discovering that among the many deprivations of shipboard life, next to the absence of women ranked the absence of any news from beyond the confines of the ship's hull. I needed a change of subject, so I pressed La Giraudais for his view of Rio de Janeiro.

"A wicked city," he replied, "with completely depraved manners. Twenty thousand whites and thirty thousand negroes, the latter from the Portuguese colonies in Africa."

"But the contraband slave trade through Saint Sacrament has now been arrested?" I asked.

"Yes," said the captain, "with enormous losses for Rio. There used to be thirty wharfs along the coast from Rio to La Plata for bringing in slaves."

"Disgusting," Commerson interrupted abruptly.

"Disgusting, yes," said La Giraudais. "But if you have to depend on the indians alone for labor, what can you accomplish?"

"Freeborn men. By what right are they made to wear chains?" Commerson snorted.

"The whole society here is an example of unequalled debauchery," La Giraudais continued. "Look at the the women. They are inside all day, in dark shuttered rooms, visited only by sinister priests and monks. Then, come the night, they wrap themselves in cloaks, pull great hats low over their forehead, and wander through the streets picking up whatever men they choose. Hypocrites and prostitutes."

"Scarcely credible?" I suggested. The information created an inward thrill, suggesting possible future adventures. Could it really be so easy?

Commerson broke in again. "Prince, our captain doesn't exaggerate. Never have we seen a city so entirely given over to the lascivious. We went to the opera the other night. There were priests along with mulattos on the stage, speaking lines of the most unimaginable obscenity. A curious and depraved world."

I gazed over at the man who had spoken so emphatically. Philibert Commerson was in his early forties, though his bald head, fringed with mussed gray hair, and the potbelly hanging from his waistcoat over his spindly legs, made him look older. He possessed a high forehead and piercing eyes, but a mouth somehow incongruously delicate and tender. A pair of spectacles dangled from a black ribbon round his neck, when they weren't perched on his nose. Not altogether an appealing figure; more a troubling one. But I had been told he commanded a great reputation among savants and that he had studied medicine at Montpellier, and then learned botany from the great Linnaeus himself. His brilliant correspondence with M. de Voltaire had led to the offer of a private secretaryship, which he had declined. Three years before our voyage, he had been appointed botanist and naturalist to the King, freeing him to take his passion for plant collections to the very ends of the earth, which he did in style, voyaging with his private valet, one Jean Baret. My instinctive antipathy to pedants struggled with a sense that he might be a considerable figure, someone who could teach me things.

"They send back to Lisbon at least 150 million piastres in gold and diamonds every year," La Giraudais went on with his usual didactic precision. "And that's not counting the trade in sugar, tobacco, cotton, and leather. Incredible with these indians, but they've created a foolproof system to make sure that every ounce of gold brought up from the mines is accounted for. And that the crown gets almost all of it."

"You should see the gold ingots stacked in the Praybuna," added Véron, whose spectacles and fresh round face gave him the air of an eager schoolboy, "each one stamped with a number and with the royal arms. You can't go in or out without being subjected to the most humiliating body search.

"With the diamonds, the precautions are even more extraordinary. Sealed in three nested strongboxes, shipped to Lisbon, and opened only in the presence of the King himself. Any contraband in diamonds is punishable by death."

"And yet," Vivès interjected, "there is a contraband. We've seen it."

"Inevitable, with eight hundred slaves working the mines, and all the foremen and others."

"Colonies held only for the ruthless exploitation of riches," said Commerson. "No thought for the well-being of the people whose land it once was. No attempt to establish a decent polity. Sheer greed."

"And intrigue everywhere," La Giraudais added. "Why do you think we have been so well received by the Viceroy? Not our merits alone, but his desire to put the Spanish in their place. There are skirmishes going on in the Río de la Plata. Watch out—they'll try to drag us into it."

"I do not see," spoke M. de Bougainville, "how a country so consti-
tuted, established on the bases of greed and pleasure, can ever become
a place of civilization."

"Tell me," I asked, "what they say of those notorious Jesuit plantations in Paraguay?"

"Most extraordinary," said La Giraudais. "The Jesuit Fathers are said
to have absolute authority over the indians, whom they have converted into the most docile Christians. They whip them for the most
minor infraction. They teach them to write their own language in European characters—but never teach them Spanish, which might provoke independence of mind. They live in well-ordered colonies and
practice all the arts. Especially music. Their singing is said to be beautiful."

Commerson was becoming apoplectic. "Imagine giving the rule of
innocents to the Jesuits! To those blackguards who respect neither law
nor king!"

Silence ensued. Though none of us, I believe, felt much sympathy
for the hypocrites of the Society of Jesus, it was unsuitable to display
hostility even to such a controversial religious order at M. de
Bougainville's table. Not that he was a hypocrite, or a prude—there
had been Sophie, and rumor imputed him an Iroquois mistress in
Canada—but as commander of a royal expedition and captain of the
ship, he was obliged to maintain a certain official order, a simulacrum
of the world left behind. He met Commerson's outburst in the manner I was to witness so often during our voyage: where you awaited
the response of the man, you got only the mask of authority, silence,
and an impassible countenance. No, I didn't warm to M. de Bougainville. But I had to admire him.

Yet, the question of the Jesuits in Paraguay would not leave us
alone. It became the theme of our stay on these shores. And a troubling introduction to questions that still worry me today. I have seen
revolution, wars of national independence, empire. Still I don't know
what to think. It was a conundrum. On board the *Boudeuse,* I found
myself worrying for the first time in my life about society, civilization,

the meaning of progress, the nature of governments. New problems to me. I hadn't yet thought much about the ways of ruling mankind. I couldn't figure out whether the Jesuits had carried the mission of civilization to its zenith—and were paying the price to a ruthless politics that had no use for justice and compassion in the new world—or whether they had instead enslaved the indians to the dark prejudices of their black-robed order.

The impending catastrophe fell on the Jesuit missions a few months later, when we had gone to winter in the Río de la Plata and there found ourselves in the midst of this grim political struggle. The Spanish Crown had long been preparing an overpowering military strike at the plantations. It was carried out rapidly, ruthlessly, to the utter extinction of these strange and perplexing communities. It must have been while we were en route from Rio to Montevideo that the Viceroy Cevallos was recalled to Madrid, and the Marquess of Bucarelli dispatched in his place, with secret orders to expel the Jesuits from Paraguay and to close all their plantations, which the Spanish believed to harbor secret accumulations of gold. By the time we reached Montevideo, the city was in an uproar over the events.

I found myself discussing the subject once again with Don Joachim de Viana, the Governor of Montevideo, when we went to dine in his palace the night following our arrival. As we sipped his quite detestable Spanish brandy, he recounted his trek into Paraguay, where he'd visited four of the plantations. There were thirty-seven in all, grouping perhaps three hundred thousand indians in what some have judged to be the most peaceful and prosperous communities of the new world, or perhaps of any world.

"From the very beginning of their mission into this wilderness," Don Joachim asserted, "the Jesuits stipulated that they alone would hold temporal as well as spiritual power over the indians. The idea was to protect them from the corruption of European ways. I was told that when the indians wish to make a representation of the King of Spain, they figure him in the traits of Saint Ignatius Loyola! Imagine!"

"Quite extraordinary," I assented. Though really, the choice between the King and the Saint struck me as trivial. "But how did this happen? How does the Society of Jesus come to be an arm of empire? I mean to say, rule of the priests? Is that right?"

Don Joachim paused, his heavy-lidded eyes narrowed. I sensed he needed some reassurance that I was not a partisan in this conflict.

"Speak freely, I pray you. My mind is open."

He scrutinized me for a moment. Then he went on. He was evidently choosing his words carefully.

"Each community is ruled by two Jesuit Fathers. All the indians have been converted to the Christian faith. They worship morning and evening in a magnificent church at the center of the community, where the dwellings, all identical, are laid out in neat rows. Communal workshops—one for the men, one for the women—are the center of thriving industries, which produce everything needed for the community as well as stockpiled items, especially the *maté* tea leaves, to be used in trade."

"Wait. You are telling me that here we have a magical government founded only on spiritual values and sweet persuasion, without private property, where each works for all, and all provide for each."

"Yes, and where children and the aged find themselves well provided for by the work of those in the force of their age," added Don Joachim.

"Utopia, then? And created by the Jesuits!"

"Let me continue," said Don Joachim, with a touch of impatience. "The days pass in industrious pursuits, opened and closed by prayer and religious theatrical performances—something like the 'mysteries' I am told were performed, in times long past, on the steps of your cathedrals back in France—and especially music, for the Jesuits have most astonishingly taught the indians to become fine musicians on European instruments. Peace reigns in these communities, and the indians lead exemplary lives, equally far from the savagery of their native conditions and from the corruptions of European civilization."

"You almost convince me. At least, it sounds far better than the sheer exploitation we witnessed in Rio." Yet still, I wondered: the Jesuits?

The trace of a sardonic smile played on Don Joachim's lips. "And yet," he said quietly, "the indians are deeply unhappy, devoured by melancholy, victims of that boredom that we so rightly describe as mortal."

Later I was to see some of these indians, when in September they began to arrive in Montevideo. Long files passed quietly into the Plaza Mayor. I scrutinized their faces. They looked intelligent to me, but sad. Their expressions seemed empty, drained, as if broken under the weight of their yoke.

"Consider," Don Joachim continued, "that the Jesuits conceive of the indians as overgrown children, whose intelligence never can rise to an adult level, who need to lead an existence constantly cloistered, to be made to submit to a discipline which daily includes the lash—as if they were so many school boys and girls—and whose instruction never includes the Spanish language, so that they can never learn about worlds beyond the seas and about the progress of civilization."

When after dinner we strolled back in the moist, warm night air, past the shuttered haciendas to quayside, I tried to puzzle it out. A people without history, maintained in an ignorance that was the condition of their felicity, and languishing—like all those forced into the cloister, whether in the old or the new world—in an unnatural state. Was that it?

I have no wish to be the apologist for this or any other religious order, for men who would place a vain chimera at the center of our lives on earth and who work to thwart all the natural inclinations of mankind. Yet, the Jesuits had tried something, something with an ideal to it. Something beyond mere exploitation. Of course, it was based on the wrong ideal. Yet, certainly I condemn and deplore the rapaciousness of the Spanish crown, which sees in its colonies only a source of riches to be wrung from the soil and the natives to the last piastre. Greed, lust for gold—though they in fact found none of the fabled metal when they marched into the communities—and for the fertile land of the plantations: this more than fear of theocracy was what motivated the Spaniards.

As I reached my cabin in the *Boudeuse* I found myself resolving that our voyage should prove a mission of civilization, free from base motives, much rather a means of spreading enlightenment and humanity across the globe. In hindsight, I am caught between admiration for my youthful ideals—they were the right ones—and pathos at what the civilizing mission has led to. The rapacity of the Spanish and Portuguese in America stood as an example to us French of how not to rule, and how not to treat those primitive peoples whose right to their own untroubled lives was now entirely destroyed. We must do better. We represented the most advanced civilization in the world, the center of art, literature, thought. And yet, and yet. What I didn't yet understand—I don't think any of us on the *Boudeuse* did at that time—was that our very voyage was part of a general death-knell. Yes, it was part of a broadening of knowledge, an awakening to the wide world, the discovery of kinds of people and their ways of living that changed our understanding of the human family. But that brought death in its wake. As if the prow of the *Boudeuse* cutting the ocean waves were severing worlds, bringing one knowledge and power, the other decay and collapse.

All the while Montevideo could talk of nothing but the fate of the Jesuits and their communities, we frittered away our time on the Río de la Plata. On the night of August 18, during high winds, a Spanish merchantman broke anchor and ran amok, crashing into the *Etoile* and breaking its bowsprit. As a result, M. de Bougainville was obliged to travel upriver once again with the *Etoile* to make repairs.

"May I come with you, sir?" I had been looking for an opportunity to show him I wasn't just a supernumerary, and I approached him immediately upon hearing the news.

M. de Bougainville's handsome face showed a moment's surprise. But this was quickly followed by something close to contempt. Dismissal, at least.

"No, we need a capable navigator. Waters full of shallows and sand-banks. Bournand, you'll go with me and La Giraudais."

I had begun to think that he had chosen to deny our former erotic rivalry by treating me as a child, to be tolerated on board but not trusted with anything important.

So I stayed behind. If I was to be treated as a passenger, I decided, I might as well behave like one. I organized a shore party with the Chevalier d'Oraison, and Suzannet—one of our marine officers—re-cruited a guide named Ernesto on the quayside, hired twenty-five horses, and set forth to visit the interior. Two days out, we hunted and killed a jaguar, a fierce and treacherous beast. We visited one of the fa-mous diamond mines, descending deep into the vast pit, where we observed the miserable indians, entirely naked, digging the tunnels which they then crawled through in search of the precious stones. We came up from the mines to find our horses had been stolen by brig-ands, and had to bargain for new ones to make our way back to Mon-tevideo. Despite our mishaps, this expedition served to cement my friendship with d'Oraison, who was to become my loyal companion-in-arms and confidant for many years to come.

He was six years older than I, and while his face gave him a some-what piratical look—a welt from a cutlass wound received while fighting in the disastrous battle of Lagos on board the *Téméraire* cut a diagonal line from his scalp to his left eyebrow, and his face was dark and furred with a beard he could never keep clean-shaven—he was in fact the gentlest of men. I have often thought he could have served in holy orders rather than in His Majesty's navy. His voice held the rich, lilting music of Provence—he had been born in Aix—but was muted with a certain gravity. There was a deep peacefulness to the man, and something of a contempt for the riches and pleasures of this world. In all my adventures with him, I never knew him to suffer from depriva-tion of the pleasures of the flesh—while I would be quite going out of my mind. I will not mention the bordellos of Montevideo, which are below the dignity of this account, except to say that d'Oraison accom-panied Bouchage and myself only out of a sense of fraternity, and would usually have preferred to spend the evening at a game of tric-trac.

The *Etoile* restored to prime condition, and both ships entirely re-caulked, we dropped down the river and spent several days embarking all the provisions our ships would hold, cutting hay for our livestock, making repairs to the rigging. A lighter from Buenos Aires brought us flour; we took on board sixty barrels, which we managed to store somehow in our crowded hold. We calculated that we now had sup-plies to last for ten months, though it is true that most of the liquid supplies were in the form of eau-de-vie, and we would need to find water along the way. Our crews were now in excellent health. During our stay in the Río de la Plata, M. de Bougainville had insisted that a third of the crew, in rotation, always be camped on the shore. This, and a plentiful supply of fresh meat, had eradicated all the traces of scurvy that La Porte had detected upon our arrival. It is true that we lost a dozen men, deserters, but since we had taken on some extra sailors in the Malvinas, our crews were at full strength.

V

A YEAR had now passed since we first left Nantes. And on November 14, as the sky was just beginning to brighten in anticipation of sunrise, we weighed anchor and set sail for Cape Horn. We fought heavy seas and foul weather, which destroyed most of the livestock carried in the two ships, leaving us with little hope for their future replenishment. After twenty days of sailing, through dense fog and rain we sighted the Cape of the Virgins, which we knew to be the entry to the Strait of Magellan, since M. de Bougainville had reconnoitred here on his earlier voyage to the Malvinas in the *Aigle*. (I should add that he and Véron constantly found the maps and logs with which we were furnished by the few intrepid men to make this voyage before us to be in need of considerable correction as to latitudes and longitudes.) Now began the most dangerous and arduous part of our whole voyage: fifty-two days picking our way through this perilous passage, which the Duke of Marlborough has so rightly named the Strait of Desolation.

Horror seizes the soul in this most forsaken part of the globe. Although we were now in midsummer, and the sun was above the horizon a full eighteen hours each day, the temperature rarely rose more than a few degrees above the freezing point. Rain, rain without cease, then violent winds, followed by snow and hail. Waterspouts swept down the Strait. Reefs lay beneath it. I salute Bougainville the navigator. Getting us through those waters took great skill and iron nerves. For much of the way, he sent the longboat and the launch ahead of the two ships in order to seek out the most favorable passages and possible anchorages. It was painstaking business. The strain was unremitting, and it wore at all of us. We were at every moment of that dire time in constant danger of losing our ships, even while they lay at anchor, and in danger of becoming castaways on a land where life surely could hold no meaning. Even now, in the quiet evening of my life, I cannot bring my thoughts back to those days and nights in the Strait without a shudder.

It was December 2 when we sighted the Cape of the Virgins, but the winds kept us from beginning our passage into Possession Bay— the first of those many treacherous bays we had to creep around in our passage through the Strait—until the 7th. We spent the days before that tacking off shore, waiting for the wind to take us westward. Finally it sprang up the afternoon of the 7th, but as we entered the Strait another obstacle hit us: even with all sails set and a fair wind from the north-north-west, we could make no progress against the tide, which was rampaging out of the Strait. It must have been running at seven knots. The ships began to slip backwards. Nothing for it but to enter Possession Bay and seek an anchorage.

The night of the 7th was clear, but very cold. The Strait was bringing everyone's worst temper out in the open. I felt exhausted from the bickerings of the Captain's mess. Saint-Germain, our official ship's writer, in particular was getting on my nerves—a more miserable pedant I have never known, totally unsuited for good company. Our chaplain, Lavaisse, was also a narrow-minded bore, but scarcely to be reckoned part of the problem, since he was constantly sick and kept to his cabin. M. de Bougainville himself had taken to retiring to his cabin directly after dinner, offering little opportunity to move beyond the very formal basis of our acquaintance. It's a measure of my state of mind that by now I could hardly abide any of my companions—I except of course d'Oraison, whose steady good spirits rarely failed to buoy mine. My only consolation came from Commerson's reports that the Captain's mess on the *Etoile* was much worse—not a gentleman among them—whereas in all candor I cannot say that Bournand, Bouchage, and La Porte were not formed in polite society. And Suzannet and de Kerhué, our marine officers, were good fellows. It's just that our arrested progress made us all rub each other's nerves raw. I had myself by this point become overly sensitive, taut like a cord of the rigging. As for Commerson, he would have requested transfer to the *Boudeuse,* which the Captain surely would have granted, but for the fact that he had a reason, as we discovered later, to prefer the less intelligent and penetrating observers of the command of the *Etoile.* He could put up with their rustic manners in order to preserve his secret pleasures.

On deck, it was a kind of deep twilight. The sun had not quite set; it was hanging over the horizon, striped with low clouds. To the south, I could make out the shrouded forms of Tierra del Fuego, land of precipitous cliffs, ice, and mists. Before us, the roiled waters of the Strait, black and uninviting. My eyes could not long dwell on so disheartening a sight. I turned to look northward. Lights. At that moment, I became aware that there were points of light dotting the shore—about a dozen of them. They flared and glittered in the deep shadow. Campfires. The Patagonians? My heart leaped.

I realized instantly that this was what I had come for, this was why I had decided to endure the thousand discomforts and perils of the voyage. I longed to encounter man in the savage state, pure unaccommodated man, man as he was before civilization, in his original nakedness. I discount the indians of South America, long since enslaved and corrupted by the Spanish and Portuguese conquerors, a fallen and bastard race. These lights on shore promised the real thing.

Don Pernetty, chaplain of the *Aigle,* which had partially explored these regions some four years back, left a memoir of his voyage in which he claimed that earlier voyagers spoke truth when they recounted that the Patagonians were giants. It was La Porte who reminded me of this. He had emerged from the companionway and was at my elbow.

"We'll see tomorrow," I answered.

"But what do you think? Can it be so?"

"I am much inclined to disbelieve it. Man, I think, must be everywhere the same. And no different from us except as youth is different from age."

"So you say. But Don Pernetty argues that the polar latitudes, where the atmosphere is thinner than at the equator, and the elements more rude, must necessarily breed a race of giants. Just as they say there are pygmies in some of the hotter climes."

I pondered. "You are the one schooled in anatomy and physiology. Do you think it really works that way?"

" 'Tis certain that the physical milieu in which the different races live determines their physical characteristics—just as those who live in the hottest climates have dark skins, and those who live where the sun's rays are more temperate have light skins. And as you move toward the extreme north of Europe, they become nearly white: bleached, you might say."

"Still, giants?"

"In truth, I must agree with you. And yet, I cannot but wish for prodigious things."

"The stuff of travellers' tales," I mused. "But surely this age in which reason has chased the shadows of superstition must bring another kind of report from the ends of the earth."

La Porte smiled. "Yes, and you who are young shall bring those reports. As you grow older you find yourself wishing for something new, something unheard of, something beyond all that we have measured and classified."

"Dreamer!" I spoke gently, with a smile.

"Of course," he said. "Under the mask of the doctor you find the dreamer. Maybe tedium with flesh and bones."

I had liked La Porte from the beginning. He exuded competence while never ceasing to be modest. He came from humble origins in Brest, I knew, but had managed to gain not only a medical degree, but as well a deep knowledge of medical science that had given him, while still young, an enviable reputation in the Navy. Now I found in him a thinker whose thoughts ran along the same course as mine.

We lapsed into silence, our eyes still fixed on those campfires. Then we shook hands and went below, strangely excited—I know I was, at least—by the thought that tomorrow we might meet the Patagonians.

M. de Bougainville had us weigh anchor early in the morning, and by noon, with a south wind and a favoring tide, we had made it out of Possession Bay, round the point, and into Boucault Bay. There, both wind and tide failing us, we anchored at three in the afternoon. M. de Bougainville, no less eager than myself, at once lowered the launches of the *Boudeuse* and the *Etoile*. I claimed a place in our launch, along with the marines, their rifles at the ready in case of a hostile reception. I loaded and primed my pistols. M. de Bougainville also ordered two other boats made ready by the ships, with crews in them, to come to our aid if needed. And so we set out.

The bow of the launch scraped onto the gravelly gray sand. From my place in the bow I leaped ashore, and as I held the launch with my left hand while the others prepared to come ashore, at once I saw them. There were six of them, on horses at the gallop, bursting from behind a line of boulders that edged the beach, and crying out something that sounded like *chaoua*. In a moment they were upon us, and slipping from their horses they held out their hands to touch ours, crying *chaoua, chaoua,* apparently in the greatest joy. Giants they were not—La Porte and I later estimated that the tallest among them must have been five foot eight to five foot ten inches. But their physique was massive, with broad shoulders and with stout arms and legs, and they had large, flat faces. Their color was a kind of bronze, and some of them had red paint marks on their faces. Their teeth were sparkling white, and they appeared to be in robust good health. These men—I saw no women—all wore a simple leather loincloth, and a large coat made of either guanaco or skunk skin, belted around the waist and hanging nearly to the ankles, but the upper part folded to the waist, so that their chests were bare despite the rigor of the climate (our thermometer never climbed out of the thirties during this time). They wore leather slippers, and carried leather cords tipped with two large stones, which they used, like the indians in the Río de la Plata, to lasso animals. In our conversations at Captain's mess that night, we decided they must be nomads, like the Tartars, roaming the vast desert spaces of the tip of the continent.

Now more of them emerged from behind the boulders, and again there was the cry of *chaoua*. Their horses, small and nimble, had saddles of wood and leather, and these newcomers were followed by three small and wretched-looking dogs. We were now surrounded by about thirty of them. They were noisy and friendly, apparently joyful and without fear. They didn't seem at all surprised to see us. One of them pointed to the rifles carried by our marines, and made a kind of *boum, boum* sound with his mouth. I noticed then that some of them had in their belts small iron knives, so clearly we were not the first Europeans they had seen. A pity. M. de Bougainville conjectured that they must have obtained the knives, and their knowledge of firearms, from Commodore Byron, who had passed through these Straits three years before us. Their language, like their manner, seemed pleasant. Nothing suggested that these were the fierce savages we had been led to expect.

M. de Bougainville now ordered the sailors to get from the launches some bread and cakes that we had brought with us. We each took a piece and offered it to one of the Chaouans, as we came to call them. They ate avidly. Then Bournand fetched our bag of trinkets— the hold of the *Boudeuse* was full of these—and we gave them glass beads and tiny mirrors, which seemed to please them very much. In return, they tossed guanaco skins at our feet. Bournand, who despite his rank sometimes had no more sense than a child, then reached under the thwarts of our launch and brought forth a bottle of eau-de-vie, which he offered to the nearest native. He put it to his lips, drank—fortunately only a mouthful—and then struck his throat and emitted a long strangled moan. The bottle passed from hand to hand, and each drink was accompanied by the same gesture and sound. I must say that I cannot approve giving strong spirits to those whose thirst is ordinarily satisfied by water alone. I remembered the drunken indians of Spanish America, abject victims of conquest.

Commerson had already strayed from the group on the beach. His valet, Baret, was with him, carrying his specimen basket as he pulled up the small plants that grew along the margin of the beach. I moved to help him, and three of the Patagonians at once came to help us. But one of them had a suppurating left eye. He kept pointing from his eye to Commerson's specimens, with a quizzical expression.

Commerson rose from his knees, his face grave.

"I think he's looking for a plant to apply to that eye," I suggested.

"Exactly. Clearly they know about herbs and simples. But nothing I've got here would be of any help."

"Should you give something a try? Might make him feel better, at least."

"I don't want to deceive him."

Our uncertainty was cut short by the sound of the ship's whistle. M. de Bougainville was calling us back to the launches. The Patagonians had all frozen in their tracks. When they realized that we were reembarking and were about to leave them, they appeared downcast. They gestured to the woods, then made little running steps down to the water's edge as if to indicate that more of them would be coming from their camp to meet us. We shook our heads. Commerson pointed to the declining sun, then swept his hand in an arc back to the eastern horizon, pointed to the launches, and mimicked stepping ashore to indicate that we would be back the next day. Whether they understood, I can't say. We piled into the two launches and pushed off. But now several of them were in the water, alongside, and reaching into the launches. One of them grabbed Commerson's little sickle, but returned it when a sailor shouted at him. We now saw more Patagonians come from up beyond the boulders, and gallop to the shore.

Our sailors now had their oars out, and with a concerted thrust we pulled away. The last Patagonians let go. Free of the shore, from thirty feet out we all cried, at the top of our lungs, *chaoua, chaoua!*

As it turned out, we weren't able to make good on our promise to return the next day. At four-thirty the next morning, the wind having turned to the northwest, M. de Bougainville had us weigh anchor and begin again our painful progress westward. After another arduous week, through hail and snow, we reached Cape Forward, southernmost tip of the continent. We sent the launch ashore to plant the flag of France, and for the first time in the history of the world the rocks and caverns of this place where a continent ends, or begins, echoed to the cry of *Vive le roi!* Five days later, we moored at Observation Islet, in a calm and protected bay, to allow Véron to take bearings and for the *Etoile* to ferret out the source of the leak that was continuing to make it take on water. While we were there, I went ashore every day with Commerson to search for specimens. Despite my antipathy for his sort, we were becoming friends. This astonishing man never ceased to amaze me. In appearance a Parisian voluptuary with a protruding belly and weak legs, delicate and much in love with comforts, unhappy unless he dined off delicacies every evening, once ashore he proved an indefatigable athlete. Baret, his valet, had been used to accompany him during his "herborizing," as he called it. But Baret, a wisp of a boy—so we thought at the time—was quickly tired out by Commerson's fast pace. So I came to be the naturalist's chosen companion.

While the weather continued very cold, the midday sun was hot enough to melt the snow that covered the rock cliffs and the sheer peaks, and in the crevices sprouted hardy little plants with bright blue and white flowers, something like mountain lilies, as well as several varieties of creepers and mosses. Up, up we went, Commerson leading the way, his sickle and trowel slung from his belt, his collecting bag slung from his shoulder and bouncing at his side. I had discarded my seacloak after the first of our expeditions, and wore instead a short peajacket. Even so, I was soon covered in sweat, which was disagreeable, since the cold wind then iced it at my wrists and neck. I carried a basket for the most delicate specimens, those he didn't want to go in the bag.

"At least a dozen new varieties today alone," he exclaimed as I puffed up to where he had come to rest, his back against a boulder.

"Quite amazing, in such a godforsaken place. At first glance, you wouldn't think anything at all could grow on these slopes."

"The wonders of creation, my lad. Something living that can adapt itself to any climate, any terrain."

"To what purpose, you have to wonder."

"If I were a believer, I would say it is all part of God's design. The infinite bounty of creation."

"But since you're not?"

"Nature. Nature at her work everywhere. Life struggling to manifest itself in all forms. Seed taking root wherever it can. The great cycle of birth, copulation, and death."

"Not much copulation on this voyage, so far as I can see."

He looked grave a moment. "Well, we haven't met any of the Patagonian women yet . . ."

"Not too likely that we will be tempted even if we do."

"Not even as an experiment?"

"What is your medical phrase? 'Let us make the experiment on an ignoble soul?' "

"Correct. *Facimus experimentum in anima vili.* But you'd be part of the experiment too."

"Exactly. I think better of myself, even in a state of deprivation."

I sat beside him. Shoulder to shoulder against the rock, we gazed down into Observation Bay. The ships looked like toys in a carp basin, lying neatly at anchor, fore and aft. The *Etoile*'s longboat was under its bow as the carpenters removed planking in order to work on the leak. Just two frail ships in the midst of a barren landscape of snow-covered peaks and rock cliffs, the sun sweeping their decks, the water dark and crystalline. The ends of the earth.

"Incredible to be here, isn't it?" It was I who spoke, though it could have been either of us.

"Yes."

"What makes us do it?"

"It's as if . . . It's our version of those plants pushing up from the snow in every crevice. The will to push out. To strive on. To carry our life force everywhere."

"And the Chaouans. With the vast tracts of uninhabited wilderness in this continent, why would anyone come to live here?"

Commerson shrugged. "Who can tell? Driven here by war, by famine, by natural cataclysm. And then once here, adapting to it. No motivation to return. No memory of warmer climates. Or maybe, just a memory of fear and horror."

I thought for a moment. "Probably. Still, you wonder. How did they get here? Walked? Shipwrecked in their canoes? Cast away by their enemies? Or somehow their seed blown here, like those plants?"

"Do you suppose," Commerson ruminated, tapping his spectacles on one kneecap, "that all of mankind began in the same place and then spread out over the globe, adapting to different climates and terrains as they went?"

"Began how? From Adam and Eve, as the Oratorian abbé who was my tutor taught me?"

"Poppycock. Tales for infants. We cannot know those beginnings, but we can be sure they were natural."

I gazed out on the Strait. In the sparkling weather, you could see clearly the distant crags and snow-topped peaks of Tierra del Fuego on the other side. "Do you suppose there are people even there?"

"By all the accounts we have, yes. But we'll see."

VI

I found out a few days later. Time weighed heavily on us in that anchorage. Crews were ashore every day, cutting wood and filling the empty water casks. I tried hunting, but there was no game of any kind. Fishing was no better. Even Commerson admitted there were no more plants to be found. Then for the first time M. de Bougainville singled me out—I don't know why. I was chosen, along with d'Orai-son and Bournand, to undertake a voyage in the longboat, to seek out anchorages on the southern side of the Strait, so that we could be assured of our stopping places once the wind permitted us to move forward again. We set out on December 27, at four in the morning, crossing quickly to the coast of Tierra del Fuego, which we moved along in search of safe harbors. In a deep bay, we came upon a school of whales, awesome monsters of the deep that I had never seen before, spouting in the air and diving beneath our boat. M. de Bougainville surmised that this bay might in fact be a channel leading through Tierra del Fuego into the southern ocean. But we didn't have time to follow it. Now on the shore off our port bow, Bournand spied a campfire. Then the light was eclipsed. Then again it was there. Then out again. A signal, evidently. Now we saw them: a group of some forty natives gathered on a spit at the other end of the bay. M. de Bougainville put over the helm and steered directly for them.

They greeted us with shouts of *pecherais!,* as the Patagonians had cried to us *chaoua!* So this people became for us the Pecherais, as those on the north shore were the Chaouans. If we thought the Chaouans were bereft of most of the comforts of existence, how blessed they appeared compared with the Pecherais. These people were short, ugly, and skinny, and they exuded what to our nostrils was an indescribably foul odor. Their teeth were brown and decayed. They were virtually naked, wearing only wolfskins much too small to cover them. The women had loincloths to cover their natural parts, but the men did not seem to bother—their coverings hung every which way, disclosing their genitals in a manner I had assumed even the most primitive avoided. Pulled up on the beach were two of their little canoes, made of bark crudely stitched together with reeds, with much moss stuffed in the open seams. In the midst of each canoe was a pile of sand with a banked fire, which we supposed they kept going at all times to parry the difficulty of lighting a new fire in this wretched climate.

As they stood in a semicircle around us they appeared gentle souls, though so miserable-looking, so weak and unprepossessing, that none of us seemed able to react with the enthusiasm that animated us with the Chaouans. Here, then, was man in the exact state of nature, barely emerged into society at all. What would M. Rousseau think of them? We later discovered that they live pell-mell—men, women, and children—in wigwams, around a central fire, ruled by superstition. They are not numerous. Perhaps their weakness checks their reproduction. In any event, they must lose many children to the ferocious elements they live amidst.

Evening was upon us, and M. de Bougainville evidently didn't want to spend the night among strange people whose welcome, though apparently warm enough, couldn't be relied on. On his murmured order, we executed a prompt departure in the longboat and sailed to an inlet in the opposite side of the bay, there to bivouac for the night, and

then to return to the ships the next morning. But we were to see some
of the Pecherais again a couple of weeks later, during our enforced
three-week stay in Port Gallant, where we rode out the worst weather
ever seen—even by that old sea-dog Duclos-Guyot. Even M. de
Bougainville was not proof against the depression that worked into all
our souls as the year turned, and we began 1768 immobilized at the
foot of the globe. The morning of January 6, he read to us at breakfast
from the Psalmist: "*nix, grando, glacies, spiritus procellarum*": "Snow,
hail, ice, winds that arouse the tempests." Every day, we made ready
the longboat in the hope of exploring farther the route to follow with
the ships, but always the wind and the weather cancelled our plans.
In the early afternoon on the 6th, the wind had appeared to veer to
the southwest, and M. de Bougainville ordered the stern lines brought
in, in preparation for departure. No sooner had we done so than the
wind whipped back to north-north-west, bringing with it violent
squalls, and there was nothing for it but to re-moor.

Then it was that d'Oraison and I, standing idly at the rail, saw four
canoes appear round the point of Cape Gallant. They rested there for
some time. Then three headed for the shore at the head of the bay,
while the fourth came on directly toward the *Boudeuse*. Fifty yards
from us, it paused. The paddlers—we could see they were a woman as
well as a man, her scrawny arms and shrivelled breasts tensed as she
pulled against the current—then paused again. They waited, drifting,
for another half hour, the current bearing them out into the Strait
again. We took turns watching the canoe through La Porte's spyglass,
the best we had on board. There were also two children in it. Then it
came on again. We made beckoning motions. Soon it was alongside,
and the man clambered up the rope ladder we lowered to him. We
surrounded him at a respectful distance so as not to frighten him.
Now two of the canoes that had made for the shore turned back, and
were soon alongside. The men and children came aboard, while the
women remained to secure the canoes. M. de Bougainville sent below
for some food, the leftovers from our midday meal. Bread, salt meat,
pork rind—they swallowed gluttonously everything we offered them.

They spoke little. They wandered around on deck, without even signs of curiosity for what must have been a marvel of construction to them. But to be curious about what man has wrought, no doubt you have to be somewhat more advanced in the ways of civilization than these miserable peoples.

We had trouble getting these unappetizing guests to leave the ship. Finally, we had to carry some salt meat and bread down into their canoes, which persuaded them to follow. But they hung around the bay for the next three days. It snowed during the nights. At one point, we had four inches on the deck—remember that we were at the height of summer!—and we generally kept below. The afternoon of the 9th, the sun came out, and a Pecherais canoe again came to meet us. They had clearly arrayed themselves in their finest for the visit—that is, they had covered their bodies with red and white spots. M. de Bougainville wisely decided we had had enough of the Pecherais on board, and ordered the launches manned to go ashore. When they perceived us to head for the shore, the Pecherais followed, and we had quite a jolly reunion on the beach. Just up from the beach was their encampment—it looked too temporary to be a village. The women, some twenty of them, all retired into one wigwam. When Commerson and I attempted to follow them inside, the smiling and welcoming cries stopped. A small wiry man, all covered with his colored spots, stood before the entrance where the leather skins parted, and drew from his side a kind of whalebone knife or harpoon head, which he held pointed at us. We did not insist.

But we were welcome in three other tents, among the men and the boys. Bournand and d'Oraison were already opening one of our sacks of beads and little mirrors. The latter had the most extraordinary success among the natives. At first, they seemed simply to find them pretty. Then d'Oraison, taking one of them by the hand—I could see his nose wrinkling as he did so—held the mirror up to the man's face. How to describe what happened then? A look of puzzlement. Startled, the man lowered the mirror. Then raised it again. Then, some dawn of recognition. He chortled, turned on his heel, whirled, began a dance.

All the Pecherais crowded around the sack, wanting mirrors, and we soon exhausted our supply. By now the mirrors seemed to have created a festival atmosphere. The men and children all began to dance, some singing in a kind of three-note chant as they whirled and stamped. The scene was both awesome and grotesque, as these sad and deprived little men flamed forth with lugubrious joy.

Alas, the joy was destined to be short-lived, and through our own inattention. In the bag were some cut-glass beads which they had taken by the handful. One of the boys—he must have been around twelve years old, and had a particularly appealing look, and Suzannet had placed his own watch cap on the boy's head, which gave him a raffish air—suddenly began to spit blood and to writhe in convulsions. It quickly became clear to us that he had swallowed the beads, no doubt even chewed them, thinking they were some sort of magic herbs. His lips and gums seemed to be all cut up. Blood poured from the corners of his mouth. Now he was rolling on the ground, groaning between clenched teeth.

In a moment, one of the men stepped from the shadows behind the fire in the middle of the wigwam. He grabbed the watch cap off the boy's head and threw it scornfully at Suzannet's feet. Then he stretched the boy full length on the ground, and knelt between his legs. He cupped his hands on the boy's belly, as if grasping the pain in his hands. Then he opened his hands suddenly, blowing over them as if to blow away the pain, like a bad spirit. Now an old woman joined him, kneeling by the boy, her mouth to his ear, screaming at the top of her lungs—what, I could not distinguish. The boy appeared to be suffering as much from these ministrations as from the source of his pain. Then the sorcerer interrupted his efforts and left the wigwam. He was back two minutes later in full regalia, his hair powdered white, wearing a headdress with two long white feathers, a bit like the cap of Mercury.

In his absence, I spoke in an undertone to d'Oraison, who left with three sailors to apprise the Captain of what had happened. The rest of us waited anxiously. I stroked the handle of the pistol under my belt, but I didn't want to make the provocative gesture of pulling it out and priming it. Yet, I felt—and I think the others did as well—that we didn't have the right to leave, since we were the cause of this catastrophe. Now a second sorcerer had appeared. Together they knelt over the prostrate boy. Shadows from their feathered headdresses cast by the fire in the center of the wigwam swayed across the boy and the patch of clear beaten earth where he lay as his tribe stood in a semicircle around him. His pain appeared to be getting more intense. A man and a woman, no doubt his father and mother, now came to kneel next him, holding his head, their faces bathed in tears. All the Pecherais appeared deeply moved by this tragic spectacle. So were we. And such is the power of human sympathy that we were not enemies but brothers in misfortune.

The boy's father now was sucking the blood from his son's mouth and spitting it on the ground. I felt a hand on my elbow. The surgeon La Porte was next to me, and with him a sailor carrying a jug in one hand, a teapot in the other.

"Will they let me do anything?" asked La Porte.

"Let's try." I took my place between La Porte and the sailor bearing the goat's milk and the camomile tea and escorted them forward to stand at the foot of the patient.

One of the sorcerers swung toward us, his face distorted with anger, a hiss on his lips.

"Steady," I whispered to La Porte.

The two sorcerers paused for an undertone consultation. One returned to holding the boy's belly; the other rose to confront us. He stamped his foot. Arms flung wide, he hissed. Then he gestured toward the entrance to the hut. His meaning was clear. Begone.

La Porte stepped forward. He was face to face with the sorcerer, nearly touching him, overtopping him by a few inches. He turned slowly, with a gravity I admired even as I realized my heart was racing, and took the milk jug from the sailor. He put it to his lips, in a pantomime of drinking. Then he smiled, and with his other hand patted his stomach in satisfaction. Then he held forth the jug.

I thought the sorcerer was going to dash it on the ground, and himself explode from rage. But then a strange thing happened. The boy's father appeared, somehow slipping himself between the sorcerer and La Porte. With an expression of appeal to the sorcerer—an expression that anyone could read—he reached out and took the jug. He peered into it, then looked questioningly at La Porte. La Porte hesitated, then pointed to the bare nipple of the boy's mother, with a gesture showing liquid pouring forth. Milk. The father appeared to understand. He returned to his place by his son's head. Together, he and the boy's mother began feeding the milk.

Confusion ensued. As the parents were giving the milk, one of the sorcerers began a dance that seemed to be hostilely aimed at La Porte, as if to conjure away the evil influence that he brought. The other, however, seemed to adopt a different strategy. Sidling up to La Porte, he opened the leather sack he had slung from his shoulder, displaying inside a bowl of white powder and some talcum rocks. It was as if he had decided to share the secrets of the trade with another practitioner. The sack was quickly closed again, however, and then this sorcerer simply sat on the ground, his arms folded.

The boy started to vomit. Blood and vomit dripped continuously from his mouth. La Porte took the teapot, and the soothing camomile was administered in place of the milk. The boy appeared less racked by pain. Still, the continuing presence of blood in the vomit made me fear that some of the glass had reached his stomach.

Now d'Oraison spoke in my ear. "We're now about the middle of the evening watch. What do you think?"

There was nothing more we could do. The milk jug and the teapot exhausted our skills as sorcerers. "I think we should leave, quietly and with all the dignity we can muster."

D'Oraison signalled to our men, who stepped one by one out the opening of the wigwam. Then I made a low bow to the natives, imitated by La Porte, and gestured to jug and teapot to show that we gave these to them. We slowly withdrew. No one tried to prevent us. The launch was at the ready. We vaulted in, and at once we were under way.

* * *

It was a gloomy evening. Commerson and Véron, who had come over from the *Etoile,* agreed with La Porte that the boy was probably condemned.

"And so," said I, "we will have come into their world only as evildoing creatures, destroying their young."

"And when you consider how few they are in that miserable tribe, a young male taken from them must be a catastrophe," La Porte added.

"Especially," Véron spoke, "when you think how few survive childhood to arrive at puberty. The mortality among infants must be frightful."

"What can we do?" I asked. "Must we be simply a malevolent force among these innocents?"

"Peace, lad." Commerson reached his bearpaw of a hand round my shoulder. "Let be. 'Twas an accident, of a sort we must strive to prevent in the future. But there are bound to be others. We can't bring our shipload of civilization to the primitives without there being some kind of fatal impact from time to time."

"But then maybe we should simply stay home? And leave them in peace, for their manners and customs to progress as nature and their intelligence wills it?"

"To be sure, 'twould be better for them. But it cannot be. If not these Frenchmen, it would be the English or the Spanish or the Portuguese."

"At least," said La Porte, "we must be true to our country and our century, and do the least harm possible."

At this moment, even though the cabin windows were shut tight, we heard a monstrous howl of pain borne on the offshore breeze. It rose to a tremulous pitch, it dipped, it rose again. We sat in silence, all aware of what it must mean. The howling continued for a quarter of an hour, then silence. We shook hands. I went to my cabin with a heavy heart, while Commerson and Véron prepared to bunk down, as they often did, on the settees of the dining room.

I found them on deck at dawn, Commerson with spyglass to eye. The Pecherais were breaking camp, and loading into their canoes. The weather had turned to storm again, with freezing rain falling and an onshore wind that was making breakers along the beach where the canoes were pulled up. They launched the canoes despite the breakers, spray flying over them.

M. de Bougainville was beside us. "*Satis est gentem effugisse nefandam,*" he uttered. " 'Tis enough to have escaped the accursed brood! As Aeneas says in fleeing the Cyclops."

Our Captain's penchant for quoting Virgil was by now well known to us.

"No doubt they consider that we have brought a curse to these shores, so they must leave them," said Commerson.

"How sad that we must be that accursed brood," I added.

The Pecherais were having trouble making progress against the wind and seas. A few minutes later, the wind subsided, and they raised the leather scraps of sails they used. Sure enough, when the wind returned it was now blowing offshore, and the canoes scudded toward the point at the foot of the bay. But just as they were about to round it, the sky blackened and a violent squall blew off the cliffs. I saw the canoes plunging and bucking downwind. One of the sails was blown clear away. The eleven canoes had left the beach together. Now they were scattered across the Strait, and lost in the rain and the darkness.

VII

I WOULD WEARY my reader—worse, I would blight my reader's very soul—were I to tell in detail of the rest of our time in that Strait. Even when, in the longboat, we explored a more forested area farther to the west, where Commerson and I found new specimens, and we came on a grove where the English had cut wood for their vessels—we found a tree engraved "*Chatham. March 1766*"—we could not shake the melancholy that insinuated itself into our very bones. Men of the most debonair character must lose their good spirits in this frightful climate, which even animals seem to flee, and which is inhabited only by the most miserable of human creatures, whom our visit had rendered more miserable still. Commerson gave me a brief moment of delight when he named a kind of heliotrope for me: the *Nassauvia suaveolanus.* And Bournand, Bouchage, d'Oraison, and I all had the honor, if such it is, of having islands in those godforsaken Straits named after us. Immortality takes strange forms.

On January 24, the weather finally improved. We added ballast to the *Boudeuse,* since she had been sideslipping more than the *Etoile* in the currents of the Strait. On the 25th, the wind sprang up from the east. We weighed anchor and stood out of Gallant Bay, where we had been confined for three weeks. The wind continuing fair, the Captain ordered all sails set for the first time since we had entered the Strait. We held to the middle of the channel, equidistant from the two shores, and we fairly roared westward. As night came on, M. de Bougainville decided to profit from the fair wind by reefing and continuing to sail at night with shortened sail. After we had taken in the topsails and reefed the mains, a dense fog descended, then rain, and the wind increased in force. We were obliged to reship our launches. Soon night, rain, and fog prevented us from seeing either shore, and we were nowhere near an anchorage. M. de Bougainville ordered us hove-to to starboard, and he doubled the watch. I spent the next four hours at the rail with the men, peering anxiously into the darkness, fearing at every moment to hear the crunch of our hull against a rock, or to see a headland looming out of nowhere.

At three-thirty past midnight, a brightening band streaked the sky in the east. Soon we could see that we still were in mid-channel. All sails were set again. The wind backed to the east. We were under way. In the late afternoon, a wide vista opened before us. The South Pacific! Thirty-six hours of a good breeze had carried us through the Strait, where we had picked our way for the fifty days preceding. M. de Bougainville, though with his usual modesty, said that night that he thought so rapid a passage through nearly half the Strait was unprecedented in navigation.

A cold sun was shining; the waves churned from our bow. Land was falling away to starboard and to larboard. We were in the Pacific. The immensity of sea opened before us.

M. de Bougainville planned to work northward to the Juan Fernández Islands, whose location seemed pretty well fixed on all our charts—they all were more or less in agreement, at least—and there take our own observations, in order to establish a fixed bearing before we began our crossing of that vast ocean, so poorly mapped that its very extent and shape remained conjectural. But a few days after clearing the Strait of Magellan, advancing slowly under variable winds from the west and southwest, we picked up steady winds from the south and south-south-east sooner than the Captain had expected. His decision was not long in coming, and as usual it was firm and final. He decided to give up the stop at Juan Fernández, and profit from the winds in order to head due west, toward an unknown horizon.

M. de Bougainville and La Giraudais now established the system they were to follow for the months to come. The idea was to sweep as much of the ocean as two ships could. Every morning, the *Etoile* fell away to the south, till she was just barely visible on the horizon. Then as evening came on the two ships converged, to spend the night a mile or so distant, in case one needed succor from the other. But we moved forward without much incident, though our following wind did not always continue, and we encountered more stormy weather than we had been led to expect in this Pacific Ocean. On January 30, we lost a man overboard in high winds and seas. Though we hove to and cast out ropes with corks, the seas were too wild to get a boat lowered, and we were forced to admit defeat. In February, several of the men complained of sore throats, which La Porte attributed to the weather undergone in the Strait. He put them on red sourballs and a pint of vinegar a day, and soon they were better. Only four men showed signs of scurvy. Fortunately, soon after we made a magnificent catch of bonito, and the fresh fish restored them wonderfully.

I now whiled away my evenings in reading. I have never been what is called an avid reader—I would rather see things for myself than read about them. But Commerson had lent me one of the books from the library he had brought with him, M. Rousseau's novel *Julie,* which had created such a furor in Paris a few years back. Though I had always considered it a book for women, I confess I was enchanted. I lived with those two young lovers in the Alps as we ploughed through the uncharted Pacific. Here was the very voice of passion, I said to myself. Here is what love could mean. Even when suppressed by the sage M. de Wolmar, the longing of Julie and Saint-Preux for each other was an unquenchable flame. I was tortured with memories of Sophie and Marie-Isabelle, yet under all that lay the desire for something else, an all-devouring passion, a love I could trust, and live for. I left off my readings much too late at night, haggard with imagined love.

On February 2 1 , one of the men caught a great tuna fish, and as our cooks were gutting it they found in its stomach, still undigested, five little fish of a type that Commerson claimed are found only in coastal waters. And in fact, at six o'clock the next morning the lookout sighted four islets to the south-south-east and another to the west. We made sail for this last, which lay in our path. The four spyglasses we had aboard were soon all in use as we pressed along the rail.

As we came nearer I could perceive an uninterrupted stretch of white sand, and behind that a line of deep green brush, over which towered palm trees, laden with coconuts. Flowers that I couldn't name were everywhere, splashes of lush pink and orange and deep purple. Hundreds of birds strutted the sand and wheeled over the water, no doubt indicating good fishing. Our hearts longed for a stop on shore. Unfortunately, offshore, for the whole length of the coast, the sea was breaking over an underwater reef, and there was no channel that we could discover, no way in through the reef, no possible anchorage. We were falling off, to continue our journey, when the lookout cried out that he saw men on the shore.

M. de Bougainville at once ordered the ships brought up into the wind. When La Porte and I joined him by the helm, he asked whether we thought so small an island could possibly be inhabited, whether the men we saw weren't more likely Europeans stranded from a shipwreck.

"Now there are fifteen or twenty of them." La Porte had steadied his magnificent spyglass on the rail. "And naked. And they look as if they have spears, or pikes."

M. de Bougainville and I trained our spyglasses on the shore. There they were. They looked tall and well-built, and of a bronzed color. One, two, now all of them were making chopping motions in the air with their spears. I couldn't really make out their faces. But their bodily motions looked distinctly unfriendly.

"I can see their huts," said La Porte.

Yes, carved into the brush, under the palms I could now make out an uneven row of huts, apparently thatched with dried palm leaves.

"Can you imagine, sir, how such a place came to be inhabited?" asked M. de Bougainville. "How can they have got there? Are they in touch with islanders from other places?"

La Porte thought a moment. "Borne by the sea, I supposed, as plant seeds are borne on the wind. Scattered from islet to islet."

"But this one can't be more than three miles in diameter, at most. How can a people thrive in such a place?"

"It's so small you'd think it would quickly get overpopulated."

"Yes, I wonder how they manage to keep their population to a manageable size."

"Do you think they've discovered some natural means to limit their fertility?" I asked.

La Porte shrugged. "Some primitives are supposed to make systematic use of infanticide."

As we were mulling over this lugubrious idea, M. de Bougainville, ever attentive to correcting his charts, went to the mate of the watch to order more soundings. Just a mile from the breakers over the reef, we found that two hundred fathoms of sounding line didn't reach bottom. This tiny island was a speck of land rising from deep in the sea.

M. de Bougainville named the island Spear Island. Then he ordered that we proceed under reduced sail, fearing to come unexpectedly on some low spit of land. The morning of the 23rd, the lookout indeed sighted another long, low island, covered with trees, and again bordered by breakers along a reef. In the lagoon between the reef and the islands, we saw natives in their canoes, some of them with sails. And later in the day we sighted some of them gathered at the end of the island, once again with spears in hand. Again, we had to give up any idea of landing—even our launches could not have safely made the trip over the breakers. The Captain named this land Harp Isle, for its shape, and we continued on our way, wondering at a people living on such a low, exposed land, which a tempest could easily cover with water.

Next we came upon a whole group of low islands, once again inaccessible because of their barrier reefs, which we called Danger Archipelago, since we had to pick our way through them with extreme caution. We were now in the region where the Dutch Admiral Roggevin, basing his views on what was written in the journal of the Portuguese Quiros, claimed in 1722 to have learned that there was a vast continent to our south. And many men of learning have long held the theory that there must be a *Magna Terra Australis* stretching across the foot of the globe, to balance the land masses at the top. We fell away to the south, to be clear of Danger Archipelago, but never saw any sign of a continent. To be sure, so many islands appeared to announce a mainland, but there was simply none to be found. Theories are fine, but facts are better.

The weather continued to be warm, but with frequent rainfall. The humidity brought with it another outbreak of scurvy, more dangerous this time. M. de Bougainville made the men drink a pint of lemonade each day, made from the powdered fruit we had brought with us. Every night we lit the fire under the still that produced desalinated water; this made us a barrel every night, which we used for our cooking. Still, I understood that the Captain was worried about our water supplies.

On April 2, we sighted what appeared to be an isolated mountain. As we approached we picked up the sight of another, larger island to the west-north-west. Since we were by now beginning to feel an urgent need to take on wood and water and fresh fruits or vegetables, we made a run for the island. During the night of the 3rd to the 4th, as we were tacking northward, we began to pick up the sight of fires along the shore. As the night deepened we saw more and more fires, dozens of them. Land, and inhabited! Shortly after dawn, I was back on deck—almost all of us were. Suddenly a canoe shot from the shore. A moment later, it was followed by a whole fleet of slim, fast canoes with outriggers to balance them.

The lead canoe came on, directly toward us. It was paddled by a dozen men, naked to their loincloths. Approaching the *Boudeuse,* they laid down their paddles and picked up branches of banana trees, which they waved gently in the air. Evidently it was their version of the olive branch, a sign of peace. The Captain ordered our flag, white with its blue fleur-de-lys, carried to the bow chains in sign of friendship, and we all doffed our hats and caps and waved them in the air. Soon the canoe was alongside, and the rower in the bow, remarkable for his great head of hair parted in rows, held high a piglet and a large bunch of bananas. We cheered and waved, and threw him a line. Soon the bananas, and what was left of the piglet, were on board. We attached a bundle of bonnets and scarves to the line, and lowered it into the canoe, where it was eagerly unpacked.

Now the *Boudeuse* and the *Etoile* were surrounded by more than a hundred outrigger canoes of different sizes. They were laden with coconuts, bananas, and breadfruit—just the kinds of things we needed to restore our health. Our trading system seemed to get established easily and without friction. One party would hold up its proposed item; the other, what it would give in exchange. There would be the shaking or nodding of heads, then a basket on a rope would transport the goods. They seemed indifferent as to whether their item or ours was passed over first, which gave me a good opinion of them from the outset. And the men—they were all men, and seemed handsome and well-built compared with all the other native peoples we had encountered thus far—appeared to be completely unarmed. The canoes stayed with us for the rest of the day. When darkness fell and we set our course seaward, in order to spend the night in safety, they headed back to land. But that night the whole coast was dotted with fires, so close to one another that it appeared an irregular string of beads flung on the shore and the slopes behind.

The morning of April 5 we began tacking back to the coast, in search of a safe anchorage. The island before us offered a sight that lifted our hearts in joy. No arid sand-spit here, no forbidding crags, but the voluptuous shape of hills, rising high, yet covered in luxuriant vegetation to their very crowns. Some of the mountains looked like pyramids, gracefully shaped and then draped in verdure. The lowlands were covered with prairies and groves of trees. Along the coast, just back from the beach, there appeared to be plantations of bananas, coconut palms, and other fruit trees, and within the groves I began to pick out some of the natives' huts. As we moved along the coast we came upon the most spectacular waterfall I ever have seen, descending in a spume from high on a mountainside. A small village was nestled at its feet. One could almost hear the whole crew of the *Boudeuse* sigh aloud, in longing and desire. But the soundings were not good. M. de Bougainville sent out two launches with the lead-lines, but they found a rock bottom that wouldn't hold an anchor. Nor was there any shelter from the wind. We had to continue on, up the coast.

The canoes were back that morning, and our trade with the natives continued. They passed us some fish hooks, most ingeniously fashioned from shell and mother-of-pearl. In exchange, we offered nails and earrings. Once again, the trade proceeded with the utmost aimiability, without any signs of dissatisfaction on the natives' part. I was coming to be much impressed by this island people, who seemed intelligent and docile. And they were distinctly handsome, of a lighter color than any primitives thus far encountered, with pleasing features. So far, all we had seen were the males. But toward sunset, La Porte called me to his post at the rail, and offered me a view through his telescope. In one of the canoes idling at the fringe of the trading area, seated in the middle, there was someone distinctly female—a fact easily discerned, since she was naked to the waist. I steadied the telescope against the rail, but my target was itself rising and falling on the swells, so I couldn't make anything out with much exactitude. But she appeared pretty indeed, with long black hair falling on her shoulders, and a flower apparently fixed in it.

"What do you think?" La Porte asked.

"Hmm."

"Go on—a judgment from an expert."

I knew better than to be annoyed by La Porte's needling. "Aren't you the anatomist?" I replied.

"Ah, but you are the epidermist, Prince."

"Looks promising, I must say." The sight of two high-mounted breasts had defined itself in the telescope. "Let's get ashore."

But the tropical nightfall was gathering swiftly. M. de Bougainville ordered the helm put about, to stand off shore where we would spend the night tacking back and forth. At his mess that night, d'Oraison and I expressed our anxiety that once again the coral reefs surrounding these islands might prevent our landing. But M. de Bougainville announced his determination to find a way ashore, since our need to find fresh water was imperative, likewise the need to put our scurvied men on a steady diet of fruit and vegetables. At dawn, he had the longboat lowered, with instructions to explore further up the coast. The boat was back at noon, and Bournand announced that he had found a break in the reef two cable-lengths wide, with a depth of thirty to thirty-five fathoms, leading into a roadstead where the depths went from thirty-five to nine fathoms. The bottom was sandy, and more than one stream appeared to flow into the bay, promising fresh water. It just might do.

M. de Bougainville decided at once that it was worth the risk.

And so, on April 6 of the year 1768, the *Boudeuse* slipped through the passage in the reef, at once doused all canvas but the mizzen mainsail and jib, and came up into the wind. From the bow chains the sailor called his soundings every minute. He was getting thirty-four fathoms when M. de Bougainville ordered the anchor let go. With a mighty splash it went down into the clear water. As we were letting out scope, the *Etoile* passed to windward of us, to anchor in shallower water a cable's length away.

By now the two ships were surrounded by canoes, some so close that we had to wave them off as we took up scope on the anchor line. As soon as the *Boudeuse* came up to the pull of the anchor, the canoes were at her sides. Cries of *tayo, tayo!* came from all quarters. And now there were canoes carrying not only men but women. As they came alongside, the oarsmen put down their paddles and turned to the women and lifted off the simple wraps that they wore, so that now the boat was surrounded by a dozen naked young women, their bodies golden in the afternoon sunshine. Everyone on deck, from our Captain to the simplest seaman, stood enraptured. This was surely the island of enchantment.

Then there came a cheer from the afterdeck, where the sailors were manning the capstan for the stern anchor. One of the young women had somehow been lifted by her companions to the gunports just above the men at the capstan, where she let fall her wrap, exposing herself completely naked, like Venus for the Judgment of Paris. Indeed, as she stood on tiptoe clinging to the opening of the gunport, her raised arms lifting her small round breasts, her lush black hair ornamented by a single white flower, her body smooth and golden, she had for us the divine appearance of a goddess.

Never had the capstan turned with such speed. The stern anchor was out, its scope taken up. All sails were furled in ten minutes' time. The *Boudeuse* was at rest.

VIII

O tahitie. So the natives called it in their harmonious tongue, and so did we. Only later did we learn that the *O* serves as an article and that we should call it *Tahiti.* There was much that we would learn later on from Ahutoru, the young Tahitian who at the last minute decided to ship out with us for the voyage back to France.

Back on that unforgettable afternoon of April 6, the ship was in an uproar. Figure in your mind's eye some three hundred and thirty Frenchmen who had been at sea for six months, who had not seen a presentable woman since our departure from Montevideo, and who all at once were surrounded by voluptuous nymphs risen from the sea.

And the oarsmen who had brought these nymphs alongside the ship were now engaged in a pantomime whose meaning was quite transparent: they were showing us how we were to make acquaintance with the women. They were simply putting on a dumb show of love-making. To be sure, the women who were being offered in this fashion looked a bit abashed. A dozen of them were standing naked in their canoes, their arms at their sides, shy smiles on their faces. *Tayo, tayo!*

called their male companions, a word we understood, correctly as it turned out, to mean *friend*.

Meanwhile, the nymph who had come on board by the gunports now stood on the afterdeck, stark naked, surrounded by a circle of admirers. With M. de Bougainville present, no one dared reach out to touch her. But Bournand looked as though his eyes would fall out from gazing. Bouchage was already perspiring. My own mouth went dry; suddenly I found I was wholly aroused. Couldn't be helped.

Even now, in the twilight of my life, after adventures that have given me a place in the beds of some of the great ladies of Versailles, and on the soft couches of Saint Petersburg, my pulse beats faster as I recall that young Tahitian woman on our afterdeck. I couldn't tell her age: young certainly—we learned that lovemaking in Tahiti begins as soon as nature decrees it ready to begin—and her body was firm and inviting. Tahitian women have strong, solid bodies, running in a clear, firm line from shoulder to toe. Their waists may appear broad by our French standards, but they happily have not suffered the artificial con-straint of the corset and don't bear its marks. The breasts are lifted high and thrust apart; the nipples are dark brown and pointed. This young woman's skin was nearly as white as a European's, though with a more golden hue. The face, framed by her black hair and adorned with a garland of sweet-smelling gardenias, was maybe a bit flatter than our own but pleasing to behold, and when she smiled shyly at us her teeth showed perfectly white, and her black eyes sparkled most invitingly.

But our ensorceled inspection could not continue forever. M. de Bougainville broke the spell and spoke a command to Duclos-Guyot, who in a moment was barking orders to the ensigns, who then went forward to order boats and water casks made ready, and a dozen de-tails attended to so that the *Boudeuse,* so long at sea, could be made shipshape. Every man on board knew that we would not be allowed ashore until our captain was satisfied that the ship was secure and in good order.

The nymph retired over the stern whence she came. And when they saw our boats lowered and making ready for landing, the canoes headed back for shore. So far as I know, no one noticed that one of the crew—it was M. de Bougainville's own cook—had slipped into one of the canoes, evidently lying flat within it. Thus he was the first of us to make it to shore, illicitly. Had he been one of the seamen, his offense would surely have been punished by a flogging. As it turned out, M. de Bougainville considered that he was sufficiently reprimanded by what happened to him on shore.

He was there only an hour, and when he was brought back to the ship, his red face was dripping with sweat, his clothes dishevelled, and his hair mussed, and he wore a most woebegone expression. Though normally he was a rather voluble man, we had trouble making him give a coherent account of what had happened. It turned out it was simply this: As soon as he set foot on shore, he was surrounded by a group of natives—men and women—who at once, without any ceremony, began stripping off his clothes. Off came his white jacket and shirt, his shoes and trousers. The further the stripping went, the more he resisted. But the natives would stop at nothing. Off with his undershirt and his underdrawers. They were not satisfied until he stood entirely naked amidst them. Then began a minute examination of his body—which I gladly spare you, since I have never seen nor hope to see it—and especially of his private parts, which they turned over and around and studied with the greatest glee. They turned out the pockets of his jacket, examined everything there, replaced all the objects, handed back his clothes—and then offered him a naked girl, with all encouragement to make use of those parts of his they had so carefully appraised. It was as if they had to make sure that the visitor was equipped in the same way they were, and could perform in the same way. But our bashful cook was by now in no state to fulfill their expectations. After a while, perceiving him to be useless to the task at hand, they led him back to the boat. Dressing himself as best he could, he tumbled in, and they paddled him back to the *Boudeuse.* So our master of French cuisine met defeat at the hands of natural desire. I realized later that there was something of a lesson in all this.

It was mid-afternoon when we dropped into the launch. Before us stretched the most magnificent beach I have ever seen, fringed with coconut palms and breadfruit trees, behind which rose verdant meadows, and then mountains, climbing in unimaginable forms, straight up to end in high rounded cones, yet covered to the top in rich vegetation. Never had my eyes taken in so grateful a sight. And as our boat drew closer to the shore, the breeze brought us wafts of perfumed air, rich with the scent of orchids, of hibiscus, of gardenias, and of that flower Commerson named for our Captain: the *bougainvillea*. Along the shore a crowd of natives was gathering for our arrival. It was evident that this was to be an occasion. I glanced back at M. de Bougainville, seated in the stern sheets. I must say that I was pleased that the arrival of the old world on the shores of this unknown island was represented by so fine a figure. He had dressed himself in his best blue surcoat with silver epaulettes, over his frogged waistcoat and nankeen breeches and white stockings. As a sole concession to the heat, he had left behind his wig, which indeed I had not seen him wear since Buenos Aires. With his short-cropped black hair graying at the temples, he looked no less a perfect exemplification of command, and a perfect representation of our mission of peaceful embassy.

Next to me, d'Oraison was bathed in sweat under his serge jacket, and behind us the marines, Suzannet and de Kerhué, looked roasted in their blue and scarlet uniforms. I was hot and sweaty myself. I had dressed in the lightest garments I owned, with waistcoat and jacket of linen, but even that was too much. One longed to be naked in this climate. The oars dipped and glinted as they rose to the surface of the clear water. Now from behind the stern of the *Etoile* came her launch, M. de La Giraudais seated in the stern, Commerson and Véron on the thwart before him. *Etoile*. Nantes. One could just read the name and home port inscribed on the ship's stern from here. From the mouth of the Loire, where that river that runs through the heartland of France widens into an estuary before pouring itself into the Atlantic Ocean, to this island, lying somewhere between the Equator and the Tropic of Capricorn, at some point of longitude that must place it somewhere in the middle of that vaster western ocean. From our homeland, graced by its arts and civilization; its polished manners and its renowned savants; its corruptions and its addiction to luxury, property, and social rank; to this world unknown, where nature and art seemed destined to have formed some other kind of alliance.

My solemn thoughts owed something to the gathering visible on the shore, where well over a hundred natives had now collected. It wasn't simply a ragged crowd, as with the Chaouans and the Pecherais. There was some sort of order here, a people massed according to some principle. I could detect that a kind of hollow space had been left for us in the midst of the group. Another five minutes, and I could see bottom, with the flashing of brightly colored fish scattering from our bows. Five more minutes, and the oarsmen rested, to let us glide onto the fine white sand. D'Oraison and I glanced at one another. "Go ahead," he murmured. So I stepped first onto the Tahitian strand.

D'Oraison followed me, then the two marine officers, their muskets held at present arms, then the oarsmen, then Bournand and La Porte. We fell into a double file, so that when M. de Bougainville stepped ashore he walked between us toward the massed crowd of natives.

There was a moment of silence. I remember I could hear a bird call—of a kind strange to me—coming from the palms behind the beach. The sun was intensely hot, but a breeze from offshore fluttered our clothing and cooled the back of my neck. Then came the cries: *tayo, tayo!* The crowd surged forward toward us. The men, tall, well-built, clad in that gracefully draped cloth that we came to know as the *pareu,* knotted at the waist and falling to mid-thigh, held up their hands clasped together. Many of them held branches of banana leaves, evidently in sign of peace. The women nearest us let fall the wrap that covered their shoulders, to stand bare-breasted. A sign of respect and greeting, we later learned, as if in the manner that European men doff their hats. Now the men one after another threw their banana branches at our feet, so the ground between us and our hosts was strewn with green fronds.

How to recount what followed. From the head of the hollow square a middle-aged man, robust, broad-shouldered, wide of girth but graceful, clad in a deep red pareu, advanced toward us, his hands extended, open palms forward. Yet, at the same time the crowd pressed in from the two sides, the boldest reaching out to touch us. I felt hands reaching under my jacket, and quickly grasped the butt of my pistol, thrust into the sash around my waist. Other hands reached under my waistcoat; one even followed the contours of my genitals. It was as if they wanted to make sure, as with our cook, that under our clothes we were the same as they. On one hand, confusion reigned as we strived to maintain our decency. On the other hand, a solemn greeting was being exchanged between the chieftain and M. de Bougainville, who bowed low and introduced himself.

"*Tayo.* Louis-Antoine de Bougainville, sent by His Majesty the King of France on a mission of peace. *Tayo.*"

"*Tayo. Ereti.*"

The women struck their bare breasts with the flat of their hands. "*Tayo, tayo!*" they cried.

The faces around us were illuminated with joy. Suddenly an atmosphere of festival surrounded us. Of danger there appeared not to be a trace. A glance at our men showed that the momentary tension had passed. The marines lowered their muskets to parade rest. La Porte stripped off his heavy jacket and let two natives carry it off. Now the launch from the *Etoile* was landing, and a group rushed to greet it. I saw Commerson spring ashore, his specimen bag flying at his side.

Ereti—for such apparently was the chieftain's name—now grasped M. de Bougainville by the hands and began to lead him up the gentle slope of the beach. I followed, one hand on the pistol butt—I now wished I had left it on board ship—and the other grasping the hands stretched out to me, all the while feeling a quickening in my groin as soft hands ran over my trousers. M. de Bougainville must have had much the same thought, for now he turned to Suzannet and de Kerhué, and I saw them hand their muskets over to the oarsmen, to keep in the longboat. Up the beach and through the stand of palms we were led, till we came to a large open house, some twenty-four by twenty feet, open at the sides and with a mansarded roof thatched in coconut palms descending low, so that when one entered under its eaves the roof was high above one, and the shade grateful. There was no furniture, simply mats piled on the ground, and some idols—things woven in wicker, with bird feathers sticking from them—hanging from the rafters, along with red and yellow tassels made from braided cords, and one idol carved in wood, five feet tall, leaning against one of the trunks supporting the roof. He was clearly a male divinity—not very pleasant-looking, I thought, but aggressive, mean. Across from him, standing at the far corner of the house, was the goddess, with round belly and sharply pointed breasts, taller than the male god, reaching above the lower edge of the roof.

The crowd had followed us but did not enter the house. Still, we were surrounded by a dozen men and women, tugging at our clothing and our shoes. We glanced at M. de Bougainville. When we saw him unbend to remove his coat and his shoes, we gratefully did the same. In stocking feet and waistcoats, then, we stood in the middle of the house, as mats were spread for us. Then Ereti came forward, his hand holding that of a venerable old man—perhaps his father? The old man's head was crowned with a white mane and he had a long, thin white beard, yet his body was astonishing in its muscular youth. No flabby muscles, no protruding belly, scarcely a wrinkle to be seen. This, I thought, is the dignity of old age in a happy natural state. Yet, the old man did not greet us. Of all the natives, he alone seemed disinterested in us. Far from sharing the joy of Ereti and the others, his brow appeared furrowed, his countenance thoughtful, even anxious. After gazing at us for a moment, he withdrew. Did he resent this intrusion into the society in which he had lived many contented and respected decades? Did he—alone of his Tahitian people—sense that something historic and irreparable had occurred? That from now on, these blessed isles would no longer be able to maintain their happy isolation from the world? O respectable patriarch, I murmured to myself, may your fears never be realized! We come in peace.

Now mats were spread outside the house, and Ereti invited us to
sit. The women had disappeared. Young men then came with wooden
bowls full of fruit—mangoes, they were, and bananas and plantains—
and then flat wooden platters with grilled fish, of what kind I do not
know. But when we followed Ereti's example and took up pieces of
the fish with our hands, the meat fell away easily from the backbone,
and it was delicious. Pitchers of water were passed, along with
coconut-shell cups for drinking. Then came mounds of roasted breadfruit, thick and pasty, followed by juicy roast pork. Then we were
served a thick sweet paste called *mahi,* which our hosts deftly dipped
up with a swirling finger and which we got stuck all over our hands.
But vases of water were passed to rinse our hands in. As the feast continued, Ereti spoke to his serving men. One of them disappeared, and
returned carrying pieces of woven cloth—apparently of some veg-
etable matter—and another then fetched two magnificent collars
made of wicker and ornamented with black feathers and sharks'
teeth. I thought they looked a bit like those ruffled collars worn by
our ancestors in the time of François Ier. Ereti himself placed one
round the neck of M. de Bougainville, and the other went to d'Oraison; the rest of us received presents of the cloth, amazingly supple
and finely worked. We expressed by smiles and signs our gratitude.
D'Oraison had furnished himself with one of our bags of trinkets, and
distributed some earrings and fake pearls, which were gravely accepted.

So the feast went forward. When, late in the afternoon, M. de
Bougainville rose from his mat and indicated that he must take his
leave, we took up the clothes and shoes we had discarded in the
house. No problem there, but then Suzannet discovered that his pistol
was missing. Someone as adroit as our pickpockets in the Ile de la
Cité must have slipped it from his belt on the way to the house. Here
was a serious problem: a native with a loaded firearm. M. de
Bougainville's face was tense with anxiety as he tried to make Ereti
understand that something important had disappeared from Suzannet's side. I stepped forward, slapped the pistol in my belt. Ereti nod-

ded. Then I pulled it out, and went "*boum, boum!*" with my mouth. Ereti nodded again.

"Suzannet. I don't think they understand. Show them what it means to be shot. Play dead when I pretend to fire on you."

I aimed the pistol at Suzannet. "*Boum, boum!*"

I hadn't known that our marine had the talent of a Boulevard actor. His eyes rolled up, his head whipped back, he staggered in a circle grunting *aie, aie;* then his knees buckled under him, he threw up his arms, and fell full-length on the mat before him. An impressive job.

M. de Bougainville's face was caught somewhere between hilarity and a frown. He nodded vigorously at the prostrate Suzannet, then closed his own eyes and folded his hands in prayer on his chest, as if in imitation of the sculpted portraits that ornament royal tombs.

Ereti nodded again and looked with distress at Suzannet, who now rose looking a bit sheepish. Then began the interrogation of his serving men. All looked blank, and were clearly denying the allegation. One of them Ereti even grabbed by the shoulders and shook vigorously, but to no result.

"We can only hope for the best," said M. de Bougainville. "Gentlemen, to the launch."

As we trooped back toward the beach, the crowd began to gather around us again, at first quietly and at a respectful distance, then pressing closer and becoming mirthful. They seemed an irrepressible people. As we came down through the coconut grove, two young men, one holding what looked like one of our blockflutes, arrested our progress with a gesture and invited us to sit on a grassy patch beneath a palm. I could see that M. de Bougainville was anxious to be back on board, but he feared disobliging. So after a moment's hesitation, he accepted. We sat in a circle. Then began a song. To our astonishment, the man with the flute put it not in his mouth but in one of his nostrils. It produced a sweet and plaintive sound, confined, I think, to three notes. The song unfolded slowly, gracefully. No doubt this was the local Anacreon, singing of the pastoral bliss of his people in their Golden Age. The scene was charming beyond the fantasies of our most imaginative painters in France. O Watteau, O Boucher, I said to myself, where are you? Never did you dream that your imaginings and desires could be so realized on this earth!

The song came to its quiet end. We sat in silence. It was M. de Bougainville who spoke first: "*Et in Arcadia ego.*" He did have a talent for finding the appropriate phrase.

We rose and completed our walk to the shore. But as we loaded the boats the natives continued to press round, then to clamber in. The launches were quickly overloaded. M. de Bougainville's order came, quick and decisive.

"No more than four per boat," he called.

So d'Oraison and I counted four men who had established themselves amidships—they included our singer—and firmly escorted the others over the side. They obeyed docilely. Then we were off.

Captain's mess that night was a strangely festive affair, with each of us trying to demonstrate every politeness to our visitors. We showed them our sextants, our compass, our spyglasses, our cutlasses, and our plumed dress hats. They walked in a daze round the cabin, fingering everything. We said the name of everything they touched. They quickly understood the game and started giving us their names for parts of the body and the face. But of course we only grasped a tenth of what they said; real communication was impossible. Things kept disappearing into their hands and the folds of their robes, but were restored as soon as we demanded them back. They were light-fingered, evidently, but all in innocence. They just didn't seem to have our sense of personal property.

As the meal was ending, M. de Bougainville asked Véron, Commerson, and La Porte to give us some music, as they had occasionally done during our stay at Montevideo. The flute, the violin, and the cello kept in a locker were brought out and tuned, and the three of them scraped their way through some version of a divertimento by Lully. Our guests seemed pleased. Then all hands were brought on deck, and M. de Bougainville ordered a fireworks display, composed of the rockets and fireballs he had, with his usual resourcefulness, stowed on the ship.

Up whizzed the rockets into the soft starry night sky. Then they burst into an umbrella of red, white, and blue tracers that rained over the tranquil lagoon, illuminating for a split second the beach—where we could see natives massed along the water—and giving a confused glimpse of the majestic wall of palms and the fantastic mountains behind. Then they fell, making the calm water dance with myriad points of light. Our guests were trembling, their mouths open, their faces expressive of both fear and delight.

What a night. Here we were at the ends of the earth, entertaining with those delicious artifices used to amuse the Court at Versailles a people we had met only that afternoon. Our guests gave every sign of polite manners, of wanting to be friends, of wanting to please. Yet, at the same time they stood at the rail nearly naked, wrapped only round the waist with the pareu, while we were swathed in clothing. And while our intercourse with them was courteous, full of smiles and deferential gestures, we could not speak together. We did not know them.

IX

Early next morning, an outrigger was alongside. Ereti and three men, carrying a piglet and four trussed-up chickens, clambered up the ladder and onto the deck. Under Ereti's arm was Suzannet's pistol, undischarged and apparently unharmed. M. de Bougainville bowed, and accepted the pistol and the gifts with evident relief and satisfaction. Here was an auspicious beginning for our stay. A people with a conscience.

But there was not much time for further niceties, since M. de Bougainville had already ordered all boats lowered and loaded with our water casks. They needed to be repaired, scraped, and aired out to rid them of the sulphurous smell left by the water we had taken on in the Strait. And in the longboat La Porte was carefully stowing the twelve men sick from scurvy. I could hardly bear to look at them, with their whitened skin and bleeding gums, though I was to see much worse later on, when three quarters of the crew were sick and we almost died from starvation before we reached Buru, in the Sea of Ceram.

By the end of the morning, all was ready and we set off in four boats for the shore, landing at the mouth of a sparkling river that looked to promise pure water. We unloaded all the supplies needed for an encampment, and began to pitch our tents. Ereti observed us without comment. But in the afternoon, as our bivouac was beginning to take shape, he was back with the white-maned patriarch and five other men, who all seemed to have the dignity of local chieftains. It took us some time to understand what they wanted, though their gestures were quite unambiguous: they wanted us to leave. As M. de Bougainville and the chieftains exchanged signs and gestures, we thought we understood that what was most important to them was that we sleep on the ships—one of them lay on the ground and closed his eyes, and the others pointed to the *Boudeuse* and *Etoile,* towering over the canoes that had once again gathered round them. Then they pointed to the sun, to the river, to our water casks, and smiled. It seemed that our daytime visits were acceptable, but before the entrance of one of our tents, they scuffed their feet and frowned.

Here was a quandary. We needed a camp on shore if we were to restore our sick, cut firewood, fill our casks efficiently, and trade for the fruits, vegetables, and livestock we needed to continue the voyage. Our capacities for dumb show were now put to the test. M. de Bougainville made motions of sawing wood, of pouring water into a cask. He even tried to suggest some notion of a reciprocal trade, a this-for-you-and-that-for-us. Soon Commerson, d'Oraison, and I found ourselves running to the stream, hacking at the nearest palm tree with imaginary axes, exchanging pebbles with one another. We must have had the air of a trio of amateur comedians at a country fair. A half hour of this, and we were exhausted and sweaty.

The chieftains withdrew, to sit in a breadfruit tree grove some fifty yards away. They held a council. I could see the discussion was animated. All of us, I think, awaited the outcome in high anxiety.

Then they were back. Ereti traced the movement of the sun across the sky, again and again, with a questioning expression. Then he turned up the palms of his hands, and shrugged his shoulders.

"I think he wants to know how many days we plan to stay," Commerson spoke.

M. de Bougainville nodded. He held up the fingers of his two hands, then closed them, then opened them again.

No comprehension showed in Ereti's face.

Then d'Oraison, inspired by the trading exchanges we had been carrying on with pebbles, had an idea. He quickly scooped up two handfuls of pebbles and brought them to M. de Bougainville.

"You could count them out, sir."

M. de Bougainville nodded. He put down the pebbles in a pile, then began picking them out one by one, to align them neatly at Ereti's feet. Eighteen pebbles. So that was the time he thought we needed in Tahiti. He pointed to the sun, swept his hands across the sky, then pointed down to those eighteen white pebbles, which lay like the token of our fate in the sand.

The chieftains appeared to understand, but they did not respond at once. Again, they withdrew to confer in the grove.

When they returned, it was not Ereti but another man—short, broad-chested, and with a stern face scarred on one cheek by what looked like sword wounds—who stepped forward. Ahutoru, he named himself. He reached down and slowly, deliberately, began picking up pebbles from the end of the row. One, two, three, four. This was beginning to look serious. Five, six, seven, eight, nine. Then he stopped. Nine pebbles remained aligned in the sand. It was as if the Fates had cut the days of our life by half.

I thought that M. de Bougainville would have to resign himself to so clear a directive, but our Captain was not so easily overawed. He reached out his hand to the chieftain and took back the nine pebbles that had been removed. He knelt in the sand and restored them one by one to the row. He proposed no compromise. Eighteen pebbles again.

Another colloquy by the chieftains. We did not speak during their absence but only shifted uneasily and glanced at one another.

When they returned, Ereti was once more in the lead. He stretched out his hands over the eighteen pebbles, smiled, and nodded. Was nodding a universal sign, I found myself wondering, or had they so quickly learned to imitate it from us? Then he held up his

hands, palms forward. After a moment's hesitation, M. de Bougainville understood, and held up his palms to Ereti's. A gentle slap of the
palms, and all was concluded.

Now there were smiles everywhere. Almost instantaneously, joy
reigned again on Tahiti. Men and women appeared, seemingly from
nowhere, gliding out of the shadows of the groves. Ereti led us a short
way down the shore, where we found a large open house, more like a
shed, in which three canoes were pulled up. He ordered the canoes
removed, and gave us to understand that the shed was ours for the
time of the eighteen pebbles.

We laid out our camp between the river which, upstream, would
be used for filling the water casks, and a smaller stream, along the
beach closer to where we first landed, near the path which led inland
to Ereti's house. We struck four of our tents and pitched them under
the shed. Here we put our sick, thirty-four of them now that the
greater number from the *Etoile* had been landed. M. de Bougainville
ordered a guard of thirty armed men for the camp, and landed a
dozen more rifles for the protection of the men who would be filling
the casks and cutting wood.

D'Oraison and I decided we would henceforth sleep ashore. We
had our tents pitched side by side, back from the beach in a shady
grove, and we sent back to the ship for our necessities. M. de
Bougainville announced his intention of spending the first night ashore
in honor of our hosts. When Ereti understood this, he came, escorted
by five others, to join us. One of them was the broad-chested
Ahutoru, who we were given to understand was his younger brother,
though they didn't look much alike. Happily, Ahutoru's earlier stern-
ness had given way to smiles. A crowd of the curious followed, but
when Ereti reached the limits of our camp, he made it clear to them
that they were not to enter our precincts. Thus it was a select company that gathered at nightfall for dinner round our campfire. We
feasted on roast pork and fish, with mangoes and coconuts. M. de
Bougainville had sent for a decanter of wine from his dwindling stock
of good casks, and we poured a Vosne-Romanée into coconut bowls

for the occasion. Ereti politely tasted the wine, but he did not drink it. This precious nectar from the slopes of Burgundy, from that rich and fertile land once more puissant than France itself, seemed an odd and exotic intruder as we sat on our straw mats under the rustling palms, gazing across the beach at the magnificent lagoon where our ships lay to anchor, with the rollers breaking on the reef beyond. Cease from labor, everything whispered to us. Happiness is here.

After dinner, Ereti with gestures and scribbles in the sand told us that he wanted a repeat of the fireworks display of the night before. Though M. de Bougainville was reluctant to waste too much gunpowder in such a cause, he did not want to disoblige. A messenger was dispatched to the *Boudeuse,* and half an hour later a rocket shot from the six-pounder on her foredeck high into the black star-strewn night. It burst, lighting for an instant the incredible splendor of our surroundings. It was as if a flash of lightning had shown us to be on the stage set of a most exotic opera, something for one of M. Perrault's fairy tales. Or for those *Fêtes of Hymen and Love* in which I had applauded Sophie two seasons ago—was that right?—in another world. Our artificial fire, our *feu d'artifice,* here in the land of the natural. Where the natural was as wonderful as the beguiling Sophie. Here was some extraordinary junction of two worlds held together for a moment by a wonderful illusion.

I couldn't at the time sort this all out. We were strangers in a natural paradise that for us exceeded the fantasies of our most visionary poets. Yet, for our hosts, dwelling habitually in paradise, we must represent something far beyond the most fantastic of their imaginings. We came from a world truly unimaginable to them; our gunpowder magic was something they couldn't begin to grasp the causes of, much less the more sinister side to gunpowder. Then what must we not be able to grasp about them? Would we really ever get to know them at all? The natural, when you find it, may prove even a greater mystery than artifice.

Ereti and his companions squealed in fright and pleasure. From us French came something like a deep sigh of wonder and contentment.

And then we went to bed. When I lay down on my sleeping sack—

too warm to crawl into it—I found I was wakeful though tired. The night was still, with the utter cessation of those sounds and motions I had become so used to: the pitch and rock of the ship, the creaking of beams and planks, the flap of canvas overhead, the slap and gurgle of the waves alongside. Now it was only the soft play of the breeze along the sides of the tent, the regular and gentle lapping of the water on the edge of the beach, and then, as a distant background, the roar of the breakers out on the reef, a sound both soothing and somehow disquieting, as if to say: once here, you cannot return outbound again. Cease from voyaging.

I slept, but at first light, movements at the entrance to the tent awoke me. I was bolt upright before I was entirely awake, to see Ereti's smiling face, and next to it the broadly grinning face of a woman.

"*Tayo.*" Ereti pointed to the woman. Then, as I must have displayed a face of sleepy incomprehension and puzzlement, he became more explicit. He pulled off the wrap covering the woman's upper body, then reached and undid her pareu, so that now she crawled naked into my tent. Ereti's face was a spectacle of hilarity as he slapped his crotch. Then he was gone.

The woman had now stretched herself full length beside me. Alas, despite the deprivations of nearly half a year at sea, this would not do. She was old and flabby. Her flat breasts sagged sideways, her belly was round and wrinkled, her grinning face like parchment. She was, I learned a few hours later, one of Ereti's wives—only the chieftains, I believe, are allowed more than one—and thus his offering her to me was a sign of homage and some sort of recognition that he and I both belonged to aristocracies. Even on the spot, I knew that this unwelcome gift was to be treated with respect. But what to do? I imagine that some of the men on board our ships would have felt that any woman in such a situation was worth having, and that the exercise of the genitals had become an end in itself. But I was young, and despite my training as a soldier, still delicate and idealistic where the passions were concerned.

So I smiled and nodded at the woman, then rolled over on my side, to turn my back to her. Soon I felt a tentative hand on my shoulder. I turned my head back to her, smiled again, and shook my head, then closed my eyes and attempted to show that I wanted to sleep. It made the point. She desisted. We must have lain thus, side by side—but my backside to her—for the better part of an hour. But I could not fall asleep again with her troublesome presence. Above all, she made me long for one of those young native women with the firm bodies and flashing eyes, like the one who had come on deck the day before. I rose, dressed only in my breeches, and stepped out.

The sun had just lifted above the eastern horizon, out over the barrier reef. The morning was fresh and cool. Turning to the west, I found the tops of the two majestic mountain peaks illuminated by the morning light, while mists lifted from their foot. The flash of a waterfall showed high up on one of the mountains. Between the foot of the mountains and where I stood there seemed to be cultivated fields as well as groves of breadfruit. To my right was the lagoon, with the *Boudeuse* and the *Etoile* two strange and looming presences, somehow out of scale with this world. Not so much out of scale, really, as aesthetically wrong: too solid for this vaporous atmosphere.

I turned inland, moving slowly along the track that started from the shed where our invalids were stretched in rows. Shadows lay dark in the groves. But the path was well worn, and I walked on without stumbling. Light was now in the tops of the palms above me, and birds were beginning to sing. A bright green parakeet flashed across my sight. Soon the path joined the bank of the stream. It was clear, and deeper than I had imagined, flowing swiftly and eddying round boulders and into pools, like one of those upland streams in the Ardennes where as a boy I used to spend patient hours waiting for a trout to rise to the hook. I followed the path upstream as the light spread downward on the tree trunks, gilding their bark a rich ochre.

The path made a turning, and I stopped in mid-stride. Boulders strewn in the stream just ahead had formed something close to a dam, and on them were spread three pareus. From behind the boulders came sounds of splashing and laughter. Some European instinct of modesty made me stop and hesitate. I did not want to be the voyeur in paradise. But in a moment I knew that I was not going to turn back without at least a glimpse. I stepped forward softly: one, two, three, four steps. Then I could see over the boulders. In a clear pool, three young Tahitian women were bathing. But not as our Frenchwomen bathe, delicately lowering their limbs into the water. They were totally immersed, diving to the bottom, rising to spout water from their mouths, laughing and calling to one another. Their bodies rose and arched through the surface, like the dolphins we saw at play from the ship's deck. A glimpse of golden buttocks, then the flash of breasts breaking the water, and a fleeting vision of the shiny dark hair between the thighs. It was too beautiful for words, heartbreaking in its enticement. One of the three women in particular seemed wonderfully lovely, distinguishable from the others in no way I could describe—they all looked physically alike to my European eyes—but endowed with a certain extra litheness and grace. I realized I was aroused again. The temptation to strip off my breeches and plunge in with these nymphs was almost irresistible. But I also felt ashamed of the impulse. Their play was innocent; who said they wanted a man—a stranger—with them? Perhaps the laws and customs of the country decreed that women bathed alone. What did I know? Perhaps I would be breaking basic rules and bringing to an end the peace that reigned with our hosts.

I turned back down the path. Then I turned again, to keep my eyes toward the pool as I walked backwards down the path, reluctant to turn away from this vision of delight.

Do I sound childish? I wanted adventure; I wanted glory, the pride of winning a name for myself. But in my dreams of beauty and desire, I was still an adolescent. The poets of today might call me a romantic—though at the time we didn't know there was any such thing. Now that I am older, I don't want to deny that vision. I want to hold it—and all of that stay in Tahiti—in my romantic enchantment of the moment. I want to recollect it as it was then, in the freshness of the early morning of life.

When I reached the beach, I found M. de Bougainville had the day's work already well under way. He was tracing the outlines of a simple fence that he wanted built, from the bamboo-like canes that Ereti's men were bringing us in bundles, around the area of the camp. A group of four sailors had been assembled, with axes and cross-cut saws, to travel inland to cut trees designated by Ereti. The launch was on its way back to the *Boudeuse* to pick up sacks of nails, axeheads, fake pearls, mirrors, buttons, and the other trifles that we would be trading for fruit, chicken, piglets, fish, and the local cloth. I must say that as this trade became established over the next days I was deeply ashamed of our offering such trash for the produce of this rich and happy land. All I can say in excuse of my compatriots is that the Tahitians really seemed to prize anything we gave them, and that what they brought us in exchange they obtained with very little labor.

The command that man must earn his bread by the sweat of his brow seemed never to have taken effect in Tahiti. Consider the breadfruit tree. Its fruit is fat and rounded, like the *boules* of bread our peasants eat. When it is ripe, one simply plucks it—this only involves knowing how to shinny up the tree trunk, which the natives do far more agilely than we—then puts it to bake in the oven. The Tahitian ovens were holes dug in the sandy soil, lined with rocks, in which they made a fire. When the fire was done and the stones were heated, the breadfuit was put in. Half an hour later, it was ready to eat, and very tasty. They cooked pigs and large fish in the same way, while they grilled the smaller fish over an open fire. Then there were the coconuts, bananas, plantains, yams, sugar cane, yellow apples, nuts like chestnuts—all of which the earth yields without labor. They feed their pigs and fowls, they fish, they do a bit of planting and harvesting; but much of the day is simply spent in conversation, in relaxation, in pleasure.

They worked when they needed to, and certainly they were the greatest help to us in gathering and transporting logs. And when they saw Commerson looking for herbs to feed our invalids, they joined in and brought to the shed both herbs and fresh shellfish, which they take to be a sovereign remedy for the sick. What they wanted most of all from us in return was nails and axeheads. They had no iron or any other sort of metal. All their tools, their weapons, and their fish hooks were made from stones, from hard ebony wood, or from shells. The axeheads they immediately knew how to use. The nails they used not for carpentry—they did their joining with tough tree vines laced through holes drilled with sharp shells—but for fish hooks, which they bent and barbed most ingeniously. Curiously, though they had no iron, they knew at once that they wanted it. They even had a word for it: *aouri*. Here was a mystery that we could not penetrate.

Our camp was becoming a place of bustling commerce. It was not to my liking, and I didn't feel like helping Commerson in his "herborizing." Besides, he had plenty of native volunteers. I found d'Oraison polishing his neat folding spyglass before his tent. I noted in amusement that he had now discarded his ensign's uniform for the pareu.

"You look well in that, only a shade too pale and white to suit it properly."

He looked a bit sheepishly down at the reddish-dyed cloth around his loins. "It was part of what they gave us last night. I've another, if you'd like it."

I didn't hesitate. My breeches were clinging to my legs in any case, and I had been wondering how to make myself more comfortable for the longer hike I now had in mind. I stripped, and stood immodestly at attention as d'Oraison awkwardly attempted to wind it round me, as the natives do, so it would be snug at the waist and fall easily over the thighs. The cloth was soft and supple. I felt a surge of excitement at this new freedom in near nakedness.

"Now," I said, "what if we were to strike inland?"

"Right. I'll just ask the Captain's permission."

Still we followed the law of the sea, even though we were now on land, in a world where the rules of the *Boudeuse* seemed utterly inapplicable.

M. de Bougainville raised no opposition to our plans, but he addressed a parting homily to us: "Remember, we know little about our hosts. They appear friendly, but everything could change in a moment's time. Watch out for the ships. A squall, and we might have to move them to a safer harbor. Three guns mean all hands back on ship immediately. And watch out for the women. They look mighty available, but you can't tell what it means. You notice they eat separately from the men. Ereti tells me that to eat in mixed company is *tabu,* which means it can't be done."

This was the first time I had heard this word. "I can't see that much of anything else is *tabu* here."

An ironic smile flickered across his thin lips. "Perhaps you've never found anything *tabu,* Prince."

I flushed. An illusion to my taking Sophie?

He continued: "But you just can't tell. You won't know it's *tabu* until you do it, and get yourself in hot water."

"Yes, sir. To be sure, sir."

Interesting how this man who had been my rival for Sophie's affections had become my commander and guide from whom I now accepted instructions on how to behave with women! A true commander, I thought, since one simply assented to his word. I found myself wondering whether I could ever grow up, ever become such a leader of men. A lieutenant in combat was one thing; your men had to obey. Called upon to command an expedition like this one, would I get such instinctive obedience?

D'Oraison and I parted from M. de Bougainville with joy in our hearts, and prepared for our promenade.

X

WE STARTED up the same path I had taken earlier that morning, hoping to follow the stream deep into the interior. I was curious whether d'Oraison had received a guest like the one Ereti brought me.

"Any visitors to your tent last night?"

"No. Why?"

"Ereti brought me a woman near dawn. But she was old and ugly."

"Brought you a woman?"

"Yes, brought her to the tent, stripped off her clothing, and suggested that I was to make love to her."

"Hmm. He of course has several wives. Maybe one of the ones he's done with."

"If he had wanted to pay homage to me, he might have sent one of the younger ones."

"And the outcome?"

"Chaste."

"How did you get out of it?"

"Polite indifference. I hope I've not hurt any feelings."

"I can't figure it out. The women all seem to be available. But are they offering themselves, or is it the men who are offering them to us? And why?"

"Hospitality taken to its logical conclusion?" I suggested.

"Or an act of propitiation?"

"Because they realize that we could destroy them?"

"Maybe. They appear both proud and fearful."

"Our fireworks," I said, remembering that moment of fantastic display the night before. "And Bournand told me he brought down two pigeons with his fowling-piece, just to demonstrate to them the danger of our weapons."

"So that for them, we are those men who can kill at a distance. A sad character to have."

"Dominion of the earth," I reflected, "will belong to those who shoot farthest and most." I don't know where this thought came from, nor why it suddenly troubled me so. I was a soldier, after all. Yet I was used to fighting against other armed combatants, not these sweet and loving and defenseless Tahitians.

"But it's almost as if they knew our power to hurt and destroy as soon as we landed. As if they had seen it before."

"Maybe it was just the size of our ships. And then that fireworks display. Our Captain knows how to be impressive."

D'Oraison looked gloomy. "I don't want to impress. I want to know them as equals. Really to know who they are, how they think, what they believe."

"Likewise. But it's not clear to me that will be possible. However friendly we may intend to be, we're the intruders."

The philosophical meditation we had talked ourselves into was dissipated as we walked on. We soon were past the boulders and the bathing pool I had seen that morning, and emerged from under the shady groves into a kind of lush meadow. How I wished for the talents of a painter with the landscape that opened before us! It wasn't like a European landscape; there was no undergrowth to speak of, no low bushes. You could see through the groves of trees, see through the different planes of the landscape, take in several scenes at once. Across the meadow lay another stand of breadfruit and coconut trees, with neat houses, thatched with palm leaves, placed among them. Pigs and dogs lay sleeping or rooted about in a vast fenced area at the end of the meadow. Then, behind this tranquil scene, rose the mountain, a green cone, treed to its very top. We could now see clearly the cascade that descended in a plume from its side, no doubt the source of the stream we had been following. And on the morning breeze was the scent of flowers. Truly a perfumed land.

We trekked toward the houses in the grove, but we did not approach undetected. Soon a dozen, then twenty of the villagers were around us, mostly women and children, their smiles sparkling, with the usual cries of "*tayo, tayo!*" Once again, hands reached out, touching. I was pleased to be rid of the worry of my pistol, and indeed to have no pockets from which anything could be taken.

We shuffled on the beaten earth in the middle of the group of houses, uncertain what to do next. Now I wished I had brought a bag of trinkets, despicable though I found them, to distribute to the natives.

A tall and robust man with an expressive and friendly face emerged from under the eaves of one of the houses, and held up his hands, palms forward, to greet us. Then with a sweeping gesture he invited us to enter.

In a moment, mats were laid for us. And before we could protest, another meal was under way. This one, at least, was a kind of light collation: fruit, a jug of clear water, pieces of breadfruit, more of the *mahi* paste. I was eager to move on in our explorations, but I had no desire to hurt our host's feelings. And seated cross-legged in our pareus, d'Oraison and I began to unwind. I even began to feel a certain instinctive bond with these people with whom we could still hold only the most minimal communication. Our host had been joined by three other men, whether members of his household or neighbors I could not tell. When we had eaten our fill, one of them left and at once returned with a three-hole wooden flute, which he proceeded to play from the nose, in a kind of meandering song which was not displeasing. Then a mat was spread in the very middle of the house, and a young woman appeared.

She was dressed only in the pareu, bare-breasted and lovely, looking at once demure and somehow wise to the ways of the world, at least insofar as the ways of the world concerned her beauty, her desirability, and what she was supposed to do. I glanced at d'Oraison. His eyes glinted under his heavy black eyebrows, contracted under his scarred forehead; his nostrils were quivering. The girl stood in the middle of the mat, then raised her arms to hold them for a moment in a kind of circle. It was a gesture of breathtaking beauty. I noticed once again that Tahitian women—and likewise most of the men—have smooth armpits, from which they have plucked out the hair. She stood there as if she were going to begin a dance. Then, with a simple smooth move-ment, she unwrapped her pareu and let it fall. She stood before us completely, enchantingly naked. Now I could see in detail what had only passed fleetingly before my eyes with the woman who had stood naked on the deck of the *Boudeuse* two days before. Her buttocks were covered with intricate dark filigrees—designs we learned to call *tat-too*. It was disconcerting yet lovely, a kind of arabesque detailing that part of the body as if to say, this is worthy of attention.

Her body was both compact and graceful. From beneath her high breasts, the belly fell in a smooth, firm curve to the thighs and the glossy black patch between. Blood beat in my temples. I was ragingly excited. Now she stretched herself on her back on the mat, and struck her chest with her open palm. The invitation could not be clearer. The world had narrowed itself to my desire. Yet, at the same time my pe-ripheral vision took in shufflings at the edges of the house. It was filling with both men and women, smiling, gesturing encouragement, eager to witness the spectacle. Now palm fronds and flowers were thrown on the mat. The girl, her knees raised, ready for love, lay embowered. I could smell the perfume of the gardenias. Paradise was now.

But I couldn't. I could not drop my pareu and go to her amidst this crowd. Stupid and disabling prejudices of our civilization! How could this lovemaking, so cleary and innocently invited, so obviously celebrated by the villagers, be any more guilty than rendezvous I had known with Marie-Isabelle, who received me in her boudoir, all curtains drawn, wearing a négligé all in lace and ruffles? I thought about how Marie-Isabelle would allow me to slip her garments off, her blue eyes growing deeper in their coloring from desire, with little gestures of modesty overcome by her impatience for pleasure. It was all very knowing, and all very private. It was furtive love, its secrecy part of its very essence. Here, I was invited to be the object of public spectacle and celebration. Why not? Why not, indeed. In my philosophical old age, I often ruminate on that scene. I can still summon up the mixed feelings of burning arousal and the insuperable barrier of shame. Exposure perhaps more than shame. The incident has no importance in itself in a life that has brought many other adventures and pleasures. Yet it was so strange. I panted to be able to let myself go, but I remained rooted to my spot on the matting. So did d'Oraison. We smiled, we clapped our hands, we nodded our heads. But overcome with the false shame acquired in the salons of Paris, we could not throw off our trivial excuse for clothing and make love to her.

I think we would have sat there forever like Ulysses' men, incapacitated by this ingenuous Tahitian Circe, had she not finally risen from the mat, rewrapped her pareu in a rapid gesture, and left the house. I could not tell from her expression what she thought, but her dark eyes, flashing a few moments ago, looked veiled. Had we brought disgrace on her? Did she feel that she had failed before the eyes of the villagers? Would we be the cause of sarcasms directed to her by the other women? Or would they assume that the white men on the big ships were impotent? I was convinced by now that some of our sailors must have found a way to establish commerce with the women of the commoner sort. But here were the Prince of Nassau-Siegen and the Chevalier d'Oraison presented with a young and ravishingly beautiful girl—and unable to perform. We must have looked like idiots. My ears burned with shame.

When my excitement had sufficiently subsided, I rose, held forth the palms of my hands, bowed, smiled, nodded. D'Oraison was quickly at my side. We bowed again. The crowd fell away as we slipped out of the house and moved up the path through the village. We left, walking at a fast pace. Neither of us spoke. The path was taking us upwards, on a slope that was becoming more abrupt, promising the approach of the mountains. I realized I was panting, and came to a halt.

"Are you all right?" d'Oraison asked.

I managed to smile. "I'm all right. Just feeling ridiculous, and frustrated."

"A fast walk calms you down. I think our Oratorian Fathers at school would have approved."

"That's just it. Why do we have to behave as they would dictate?"

D'Oraison shrugged. "As the twig is bent."

"But I don't want to be bent. Why allow yourself to be bent?"

"We are products of the highest civilization that mankind has invented. Ask M. de Voltaire. We have created luxury, marvellous inventions to make our lives easy and pleasurable."

"Yet we can't take a beautiful Tahitian girl who offers herself to us."

"Love requires mystery."

"Does it? Mere prejudice. Why have we made a mystery of what is after all the most natural thing in the world?"

"Civilization, Prince. We've improved on nature, and have to pay the price."

"Maybe the price is too high. M. Rousseau probably has it right. The progress of civilization is a disaster so far as happiness is concerned."

D'Oraison looked scornful. "M. Rousseau thinks like a resentful lackey. He's envious of a society to which he doesn't belong."

I shook my head. "He's more than that. You know, I've actually read him. He makes more sense than you realize."

"You're not about to become a disciple of M. Rousseau, are you?"

"I don't know. Look, would I have left everything I had in France to come on this voyage if I weren't in some measure a believer in his ideas? Well, no, not truly a believer, I don't mean that, but fascinated by what you get when you strip away civilization, to find the natural state."

"I saw you as an adventurer, Prince. Now I find you a sentimental philosopher."

"But look at us," I gestured. Clad only in our pareus, our hair dishevelled, our bodies beginning to take on color from the Tahitian sun, we did not look like paragons of civilization. D'Oraison's face and arms had long since become deeply tanned; now his body was turning several shades darker. With his hairy chest and fringe of dark beard, he was beginning to look like someone's idea of a castaway. My blonder skin was turning a ruddy color.

"You look like Robinson Crusoe," I said. One of the few novels approved by the Oratorians during my youth.

"Who never was offered a female Friday."

"Ah, but he was English. The fair sex is not their strong point."

"So we French must be lovers around the globe?"

"Don't we owe it to the reputation of our realm?"

We had managed to restore our good spirits, but I knew that I now lived with an obsession that would have to be satisfied. I had to find a way to a more private kind of rendezvous with one of the Tahitian women.

XI

Our trek led us up through more rich and fertile land, then over a rocky plain and into a deep, rich cleft where the stream ran, faster now. High above us, we could just make out one of the waterfalls, descending in an uninterrupted plume from the mountainside, mist rising from where it disappeared behind the trees. We dangled our feet in the rushing water of the stream until we were cool. Then we made our way back to the camp, making a detour around the village where we had given so poor an account of French manhood. Dusk was gathering, the campfire was blazing, and preparations for dinner were under way. We found Commerson, who had now pitched his tent ashore, sorting flower specimens that he would put into his press.

He peered at us over his spectacles. "Been exploring?" he inquired.

"Yes, inland."

"And what did you see?"

"Things of indescribable beauty." I glanced at d'Oraison, and we both laughed. "And what news from the shore?"

"The Captain's upset. There's been more thievery going on. Besides some petty items, like Bournand's snuffbox, Véron's sextant has disappeared, which is serious. The Captain has been expostulating with Ereti about it."

"This is distressing," said d'Oraison. "They seem to be practiced pickpockets."

"Look," Commerson replied, turning from his flowers to gaze into the distance, as he was wont to do when he waxed philosophical. "There's no evidence they steal from one another. They appear to live in perfect harmony. It's just that they find our things new, marvellous, and irresistible."

"But still they're not theirs. Can't they understand that?" said d'Oraison.

"Maybe they just don't have our sense of private property," said Commerson. "Maybe they don't recognize *mine* and *thine*."

"They share everything in common?" I suggested.

"I think so. They fish together, gather the breadfruit and the coconuts together, and share the produce. It seems to be a society of each for all, and all contributing to satisfy the needs of each."

"Still, theft?" asked d'Oraison.

"Look," said Commerson. He let his spectacles drop, and settled back on his haunches in preparation for serious talk. "The concept of theft depends on a notion of property which is ingrained in us. They simply don't have it. Why, I saw Ereti himself try to lift my scissors this morning. When he saw that I saw what he was doing, he gave them back. At the same time, he's ready to give us the clothes off his back. Even his women. They're willing to share everything, including that which we Europeans guard most jealously."

"The Prince and I know something about that," said d'Oraison, a bit sententiously, I thought. "But we don't know what it means."

"It means that they delight in the act that we all delight in, but we have managed to make it furtive—a sinful pleasure. Too many centuries of Christian moralists. Hypocrites, rather."

"But how can a people live without some moral code?" d'Oraison asked.

"Who says they haven't moral codes? Don't they live in well-ordered communities? Do you see any sick, or any wounded from fights? Do they kill one another? No, they live in the most basic respect for life." Commerson was warming to his subject. "Their god is love, and the act of lovemaking is a festival for the nation, since it produces the greatest of goods, a new life. They live without modesty and without guilt, for they have not lost sight of the path traced out for us by nature."

I thought back to the scene in the villager's house that forenoon. "Tell me: why do you think they offer their women to us foreigners?"

Commerson shot an inquisitive glance at me. "Speaking from personal experience, my lad? No matter, I shan't pry."

I protested that my experience was thus far wholly platonic.

"But not likely to remain so, I wager. So much the better. You are just what they want, Prince. You are young, handsome, vigorous, well-built. They want your seed. Just as I will plant the watermelon and cantaloupe seeds I brought with us, your seed in the native soil would produce wonders. A cross between their native beauty and the ingenuities cultivated by France."

I blushed at this. I was not used to being considered as a kind of stud animal.

"And maybe that's what they think they need: an admixture of European blood. Because now that we have discovered them, other white men will follow. And some of them will not come in peace, as we have, but as conquerors and slavemasters, like the Spanish gold-grubbers in South America. Then the Tahitians will need the wiles of Europe if they are to survive."

Commerson had now talked himself into a dark mood.

"So that what we see here will not last in this happy state?"

He shook his head. "They will come—our compatriots, and the Spanish and the English and who knows who else, the cross in one hand and a musket in the other—to declare themselves owners and rulers of these blessed isles, and they will corrupt them in the name of the march of civilization and progress."

"And then this putative son of mine, bred in the womb of a Tahitian girl?"

"May be the only one who knows how to beat the Europeans at their game. Or maybe no; he may become the inner source of corruption and treachery, the one who panders to the Europeans' greed and lust for conquest."

"A fine future you paint for this son of mine."

"Who knows? Perhaps he would grow up a thorough Tahitian, with only a slightly lighter tinge to his skin to indicate his far-off paternity. And maybe he will be happier than the sons you breed in France. Look at the distress we create through our notions of property, even where women are concerned. For what woman in France is truly free?"

"They seem free enough to me," volunteered d'Oraison. "I mean, at least in the society we frequent. I don't know about fishmongers' wives, or peasants."

"An invidious distinction to begin with," continued Commerson, a momentary look of contempt passing across his face. "But see here, are your marquises and princesses really free? Yes, they can have lovers in their boudoirs; yes, they can permit themselves late-afternoon rendezvous in someone's *petite maison*. But everything must be surrounded by dissimulation. Everything is spoiled by jealousy, by possessiveness. The most ridiculous of all is marriage: the promise to remain faithful to one person for the unknown number of years one has still to live! It's unnatural. Here, a woman is free to give herself as she chooses. And she is honored for it."

"You don't know that," said d'Oraison stubbornly.

"But I think that is what Ereti was attempting to explain to the Captain earlier. The *vahine,* the girl, can do anything she wants. When she's married, she has to ask her husband's permission."

"And when they have children?" I asked.

"Look at them. Clearly they adore their children. But children aren't all tangled up in questions of property, of inheritance, of legitimacy." Commerson stopped here, with a slightly startled glance at me. He clearly hoped he hadn't made a wounding illusion to the problem that obsessed my childhood. But that obsession belonged to a once and future life. It wasn't part of the present hour.

Still, he had broken his own exalted mood. He affixed his spectacles to his nose and turned back to his specimens. "Look how beautiful," he said. "Now that you have become an explorer, I suppose I shall have to bring Baret on shore to help in the collecting."

"I think for now I prefer the flowers in the *vahine*'s hair," I replied.

As we made our way to the campfire for dinner—a relaxed and informal one, now that M. de Bougainville had gone back to the ship—I realized that I was now thoroughly obsessed with the notion that I must find a way to bring a young woman into my bed. I needed to know what lovemaking on Tahiti was like, how it compared with the Parisian kind. Apparently a number of our sailors had managed brief rendezvous despite the work to be done. Surely I could manage it. But who, and where?

Judge me not severely on this head. I know how trivial and self-indulgent my desires were. But understand, too, that this was about something more than just bedding a Tahitian girl. I was aroused, of course. Wildly. How could I not be, with this paradise coming upon us unexpectedly after the long sea voyage? But it wasn't simply the satisfaction of my arousal that I wanted—at least, not satisfaction in a simple sense. Something more was at stake. Maybe you could say that I took sex to be my contribution to our mission of exploration. I couldn't leave that to the forecastle of the *Boudeuse*. A man more refined, more articulate than our simple sailors was needed to make the island women's acquaintance.

This sounds fatuous, I know, and my whole obsession with the women of Tahiti no doubt does too. But I brought no expertise to our voyage—I was not a scholar or geographer or naturalist; I held no post of command. M. de Bougainville had reminded me of that often enough. Yet, I had some capacity for lovemaking, I thought. And that, it occurred to me, was one way to get to know an otherwise unknowable people. At least, there was a kind of knowledge involved in physical intimacy, perhaps a way to understanding of these remarkable people we couldn't otherwise be intimate with, we couldn't really know. As a young man whose life had been spent in military combat and sexual conquest, I knew which form of my limited experience I wished to bring to the islanders. It would at least be a more benign approach than warfare. The Prince of Nassau-Siegen would make his expertise the practice of sex as a form of communication, then. Though before the end of our stay I was to make the trial of a very different kind of experience, one that put me to the test in ways I had never dreamed.

Ereti joined us again for dinner. We were beginning to make some slight progress in communication. Commerson, especially, and La Porte had a certain gift for picking up the native words.

Ereti arrived with one of the small native dogs under his arms, a round, roly-poly kind of thing. As the roasted piglet was coming out of the oven—we were happy to let the Tahitians do our cooking for us—he gestured toward putting the dog in the oven. This seemed some kind of cruel joke. Then he indicated he wouldn't roast the dog just now, but at the next setting of the sun. This was some relief, but it didn't entirely end our consternation. So we would have to eat roast dog?

"You know," Commerson commented, "I think these dogs are vegetarians. I noticed some this morning, grazing on roots and such like with the pigs."

"Is it possible?" I asked. "Whoever knew a dog that didn't eat meat?"

"Their very mouths show they are carnivores," said La Porte. "Look at their teeth."

"But have you looked these dogs in the mouth?" asked Commerson. "Maybe they're different."

We couldn't pursue the investigation on the spot, since Ereti had now released the dog, which scampered away.

Commerson now proceeded, to my considerable embarrassment, with a conversation in which he tried to make Ereti understand that the Prince of Nassau-Siegen, a very great personage in the land beyond the seas, and with a handsome face, was in need of a *vahine* to share his tent.

Ereti's eyes narrowed.

"Careful," I said to Commerson. "I didn't tell you about what happened this morning."

"What was that?"

"He brought one of his wives, of a certain age, round and ugly, to my tent before dawn. I think I was supposed to take her."

"But you deserved better, eh?"

Ereti in any event didn't seem to take Commerson's request on my behalf as insulting, so far as I could see. I couldn't even tell whether he understood it.

There were no further fireworks that night, only the unimaginably bright stars reflected in the bosom of the tranquil lagoon. I sat alone at the water's edge, letting the water lap at my feet. The night was so soft I didn't need to seek any other clothing to supplement my pareu. I was tired from our long walk, and relaxed by the good food. Yet at the same time I was excited, my body alive. I sat long before I told myself that I must take some rest. As I crawled into my tent I wondered if dawn would bring another visiting woman, and whether this time she would look like the girl who had offered herself on the mat in the village's house rather than the apparition of the previous morning.

But I awoke alone. Again it was early. The sun, a glorious crimson disk, had just sprung from the water's edge, turning the breakers on the reef a rich gold. I found myself stiff from so much walking the day before—leg muscles atrophied from too many months at sea, I decided. What I needed was a sea bath. Or no, a bath in that bubbling pool up the stream where I found the three young women yesterday. Do they go there every morning? I wondered. Even if they do, I can wait my turn.

The idea of a bath was now enhanced by the vision of the three nymphs. I set out up the path, now fully awake, my heart beating fast. Dark shadows enveloped my feet, while above my head the treetops were bursting into life. Streaks of color flashed through the branches. Another day in paradise. I recalled those eighteen pebbles aligned in the sand. Take away two. A reprieve from voyaging—but only for another sixteen days.

I made myself walk deliberately, stretching my hamstring muscles at every step. But when I came to the boulders across the stream, my heart was pounding. I approached cautiously. No sounds of laughter reached me. I felt disappointment, but also relief. I came closer, my hand reaching to loose my pareu. Then at the same moment I noticed there was a single pareu stretched along the far side of the boulder, and I saw a head break the surface of the water.

To my surprise, I recognized her: she was the girl whose grace and expression had especially struck me the day before. Today she was alone. Her dripping face was startled for a moment. Then she laughed, and dove beneath the surface again.

I hesitated. Beware the *tabu,* I said to myself. But the blood racing through my body and flushing my face was too strong for reflection. I unwound the pareu, slung it on the boulder. Then, almost without measuring the distance, I leapt into the pool.

A rush of cold water surrounded me as I sank. I was cooled down in an instant. I touched the sandy bottom with one foot, then rose spluttering to the surface.

But I was alone. Where was she?

A laugh behind me. I flailed about until I faced her. Black hair plastered to her face framed her laughing mouth with its small and perfect white teeth. Her dark eyes, too, seemed full of laughter and delight. I trod water as best I could—I was not a great swimmer—and smiled back. I could see her body foreshortened in the clear water, her breasts with the dark brown nipples just below the surface, her legs moving gracefully down below, and the dark patch at the meeting of her thighs.

"*Tayo,*" I ventured.

A peal of laughter. "*Tayo,*" followed by a string of syllables that meant nothing to me. Then she dove again.

I dove after her, reaching out before me. She wriggled and spun like a fish. I just managed to touch an ankle. Then she was at the surface again. I followed her, breaching like a whale, I thought, compared with her smooth motions.

I reached out to touch her shoulders. "*Vahine,*" I tried. More laughter.

Then her face became serious. It was a truly beautiful face, narrower than most others I had seen on the island, with delicate high cheekbones framing the intense dark eyes. With three quick strokes she moved to the shore, and then stepped up to the bank. Now I saw there was a pile of coconut leaves, where she sat, dripping.

The moment, it suddenly occurred to me, was critical. Now or never, I said to myself. Take the risk, or you'll forever regret it.

I swam awkwardly to the bank and stepped forth. I noticed I was fully aroused again.

I suppose that decided it. As I let myself fall into a sitting position beside her, so close that my wet buttocks touched hers, she simply reached out a hand to my dripping chest. I in turn touched her breast, unbelievably smooth and elastic. Her nipple was hard under my hand. I kissed it. I kissed her mouth. Then she fell back, gently pulling me toward her.

They call it carnal knowledge. Those words, redolent of the Oratorian Fathers who had disciplined my childhood, went confusedly through my mind. That was it. All the foreignness fell away. I was in her; it was just as it had to be; it was wildly exciting yet familiar; we were man and woman together, all barriers gone. Here at the ends of the earth, under the tropical sun beginning to strike warm on my shoulders, with a woman whose language and very name and nature were unknown to me, I found that we all make love in the same way. The two of us couldn't speak together, but we could sigh together, cry out together. There was the great paradox. We couldn't communicate. Yet I felt that in some way we had the deepest communication possible. I felt we had breached the lonely confines of the body; did she sense this too? And when it was over, it seemed that peace fell on us from the gilded palms overhead as we lay intertwined.

We lay quietly for some time. Then I began exploring her body, her skin golden beneath my touch. I turned her over, and followed with my fingers the curlicues of the tattoos on her buttocks. We made love again, more slowly, deliberately. Then she splashed into the pool again, and I followed clumsily.

On the bank again, a serious silence ensued. We tried some conversation. Her name, so far as I could get it, was Ité. Of Charles she made something like Sholé. Ité and Sholé sat on the bank of the pool, now fully lighted by the sun, as bright-plumed birds dipped down to the water. I think I could have sat there all day, though I was beginning to feel stirrings of hunger. But she rose and wrapped herself in the pareu. It was evidently time to go. She took my pareu from the boulder and stretched it in her arms, then quickly, expertly—but with a brush of her hand across my genitals, accompanied by a peal of laughter—she wrapped it round me, far better than I could do myself. We stood gazing at one another, a rosy-colored man and a gilded woman. Her head was at the level of my chest, tilted upwards with an expression of grave curiosity. You could tell it was an intelligent face, full of unasked questions, the eyes quietly appraising my own face. Delicately, she ran her hand over my blond hair and bristling chin, followed the line of my nose and then my lips. She smiled as if pleased.

We walked hand in hand as best we could on that narrow path. As we came toward the edge of the beach another path forked off to the right. She dropped my hand, and indicated that it was her path to take. She beckoned for me to follow her. But now I hesitated. I still wasn't prepared for a scene of public lovemaking, if that is what she, or her people, had in mind. And I would by now be missed at our camp. I shook my head. I pointed to the shore. Then up to the sun, then to the east, and made motions of the sun rising from the sea, and pointed back to the pool. She looked disappointed, but nodded. Then she was gone before we could have any further explications.

I stood looking after her. How stupid of me not to have led her to my tent, to show her which it was, so she could join me there at night. Yet, no. I didn't want to expose her to the stares of our men. She was no camp follower to be the butt of jokes round the evening fire, or even the subject of Commerson's commentaries. She was too precious for that. For now at least, this was my private affair. If that meant lonely nights in the tent, they would be followed by radiant dawns.

I tried to assume a serious expression as I strode into the camp, but I must have looked more beatific than I wished. The gazes from the company round the fire were distinctly interrogatory. D'Oraison was too discreet to ask his questions publicly. But Commerson went right to the point.

"Visitations to your tent this morning?"

I shook my head.

"Matutinal rendezvous in the woods, then? Eh?"

I dropped to the sand without answering, and poured myself tea from the simmering teapot. We had long since run out of sugar, and I still hadn't quite become used to the bitter taste. But it was bracing.

Commerson considered my refusal to speak for a moment, then grunted. Apparently, even he could be tactful on occasion.

"Big dinner indicated for tonight," he said. "Ereti has promised us roast dog."

"Maybe we'd better lay in some ship's biscuit, just in case," said d'Oraison.

"No," Commerson replied. "The true philosopher welcomes all experiences. *Nihil humanum a me alienum puto.*"

"My Latin's gone a bit rusty. Be a good fellow and translate."

"The humanist's credo. Nothing that is human is foreign to me."

"Good," I said. "That's right. No matter how strange and different, they are like us. Deep down, they are the *same* as us."

A piercing glance from Commerson. "Depends what you mean. The same? When they see the world entirely differently, from a different latitude and longitude, when their language divides up the world differently, when they worship different gods—if they worship any at all, which I hope they have the sense not to? Ereti was explaining to me that there are five different words for our one word *wave,* depending on its size and shape. And roast dog?"

I struggled with this for a moment. I couldn't of course say what I really had in mind, describe how once I was in Ité's body all difference was erased, how there was a communication there that made all our strangeness to each other fall away.

"It's a simple thought," I tried. "It's just that we are made the same. We have the same bodies and the same heads. We are humans, not dogs, roasted or unroasted, nor are we monkeys. We're set on this earth with the same needs and wants and problems. We may invent our *tabus* in different ways, but the situation is the same."

"Good," said Commerson, as if he were my catechism teacher. "We're all two-legged creatures, having sometime in the distant past parted company with our cousins the apes, and come down from the trees to walk on the earth. And we all must eat, sleep, fornicate, and reproduce. The givens are the same. Only each milieu—with its climate, its vegetation, its game—calls forth different responses. For the Chaouans, a nomadic life on the cold plains of Patagonia, following the tracks of the guanaco, sleeping in leather tents. For the Tahitians, a life of ease with fruit hanging from every bough, and love on everyone's mind."

"Your history of the earth," said d'Oraison, "is not quite as it was taught by the Reverend Fathers at Saint Thomas Aquinas."

"Of course not. But surely we're beyond those nursery tales. We're amidst what your Fathers would call heathens, and they're a damned sight better off without the Cross and the Trinity and the Pope and the stinking corruption of Rome."

La Porte had now approached, and had been listening. "But we know nothing about their religion. It may be as repressive as ours."

Commerson flung his arms wide, his eyes shining. "They have no other god than love," he solemnly proclaimed. "Venus reigns supreme. The Isle of Cythera, where the Greeks imagined Venus was born from the sea."

La Porte persisted. "You don't know that. Wait and see. There may be a darker side to things. I've seen scars on some of the men that must come from battle wounds. And I think that was the explanation I was given. Mars is here, as well as Venus."

Commerson brushed aside the objection. "A thriving, healthy people, as fair to behold as any in Europe, in a landscape of dazzling beauty, with manners as gentle and refined as you could hope for. Doctor, accept your place in paradise. It's the only one you'll ever know."

La Porte smiled. "I'll do my best. Now I must go to my invalids, who haven't yet realized they're in paradise."

"*Vade atque vale,*" Commerson dismissed him. "I am awaiting Baret, since I know these young gentlemen will be pursuing their researches into Tahitian *mores* rather than helping me in the pursuit of positive knowledge."

Baret came over on the launch from the *Etoile* about an hour later as d'Oraison and I were planning a hike that we hoped would take us up the side of the nearest mountain, which the Tahitians called Orofena. D'Oraison feared it was farther away than it looked. As it turned out, our trek to the mountains would come only later, and then it wouldn't be a simple exploration. Instead, it would be the most critical situation we had to face.

Baret stepped from the launch just outside the palings that now marked the perimeter of our camp—more symbolic than anything else, since you could easily stride through them. The usual group of Tahitians were by the shore—they gathered for every arrival from our ships.

Then a strange thing happened. Little Baret had just taken a timid leap from the boat to the sand, his jacket flying behind him. He stood, looking for his master, as the Tahitians crowded round. "*Tayo, tayo!*" came the accustomed cries. Then there was a shout of "*vahine! vahine!*" As we watched idly from the camp we could see that the group of Tahitians, men and women, had pulled off Baret's coat. Now, despite his struggles, the waistcoat was flung off, and they were busy unbuttoning the shirt. Just as they had done with M. de Bougainville's cook,

I thought. But why now, since they've had plenty of assurances that we have the same natural parts as they?

How mistaken I was. As the shirt opened we perceived two soft little pear-shaped breasts with pink nipples. We stared in astonishment. Now the breeches were lowered, and the undershorts. *Vahine,* indeed. Baret was a woman. All the boyishness, the delicacy, the something slightly effeminate we had half-noticed about Baret, but dismissed without much attention, struck us full in the face. Baret was a woman. Had always been a woman. Commerson had travelled all this way with a woman in his cabin. The sly fox!

Now all eyes were on Commerson, who had risen, his belly quivering over his breeches, his face aghast. But he offered no explanations on the spot.

"Gentlemen," he said, "to the rescue of the fair sex!"

And he began to run, his spindly legs looking much too frail to carry that protruding belly. We followed, quickly outdistancing him. D'Oraison was the first to reach Baret, quickly dispersing the Tahitians. Baret stood nearly naked, her breeches and drawers down at her ankles, pulling the remnants of her shirt over her bare chest. D'Oraison gallantly looked the other way as poor Baret reclothed herself as best she could. She looked up piteously at Commerson as he arrived, out of breath, and took her by the hand.

"When I took her on at Rochefort, I thought she was a boy." He glanced at each of us in turn, but without meeting anyone's eyes. "She was dressed as a boy. I had no reason to doubt she was a boy. It was only later, much later . . ." His voice trailed off.

D'Oraison scowled. He looked outraged. But I found myself bursting into helpless laughter, and in a moment d'Oraison's mouth, too, cracked into a broad smile. It was both outrageous and ridiculous. Forever after, Commerson could only say the same thing. She was dressed as a boy. He needed a valet. He thought she was a boy. It was only much later . . . (But where? In the North Atlantic? In the Malvinas? in Montevideo? in the Strait?) We never believed him. I don't to this day. The old voluptuary, anticipating a voyage of forced celibacy lasting two or three years, had simply made sure he had his pleasure always to hand. No wonder he preferred the relative seclusion of the *Etoile* to the much more select company of the *Boudeuse*!

Bournand now volunteered to take the bedraggled Baret back to the *Etoile*. Commerson parted from her with all the dignity he could summon, with the order that she was to be moved from his cabin to the nearby quarter-deck. But I have no reason to believe they didn't renew their nightly rendezvous later on, after our stop in Batavia, when Commerson left the *Boudeuse* to take up his place once again in the *Etoile*. Baret continued to dress as a man, since she had no other clothes, and anyway it was more suited to the sailor's life. Even when she ventured back to the island, three days later, she didn't try the pareu. Probably just as well. I could not forget the contrast of her pasty white body, with those pink little nipples, like the insides of a rabbit's ears, and the sandy-colored down between her thighs, to the rich golden skin of Ité, the full, dark nipples thrusting from her round breasts, the glossy black hair which my hand had caressed. Baret stripped bare made me thankful my skin had taken on color from the sun. A poor, bleached-out race we Europeans, whom the centuries had made fit for the drawing-room, not the beach.

XII

M. DE BOUGAINVILLE was back on shore in the early afternoon, bringing with him bags of seed that we were to plant on Tahiti. He opened them before Ereti, and scribbled in the sand some approximation of the trees and fruit that each would produce. Ereti was quick to understand, and ordered a cane fence thrown up around a spacious area near his own house. Then four of our men set to work turning up the soil with hoe and spade. The Tahitians gathered around, admiring our gardening instruments. They brought out their own, which included a kind of hoe with a hard flint head, and a sharp rake-like tool made of coral. Thus we prepared a kitchen garden, where the next day we sowed wheat, oats, barley, rice, corn, onions, and a few other of the plants that every French householder knows. In my twilight years, as I spend more and more time cultivating the roses of my own garden, I often find myself wondering what has happened to our Tahitian garden, and whether it has fulfilled its promise of adding to the native stock of roots and yams. M. de Bougainville also presented Ereti with a pair of ducks and a pair of turkeys, male and female of each, with high hopes of a new race of comestible animals on the island.

I frittered away the afternoon keeping M. de Bougainville company as he oversaw these domestic arrangements. I longed to find my way back to Ité; yet, at the same time, I did not want to bring her to the attention of my compatriots. I knew nothing about Tahitian society, but I sensed she was of a finer sort than most of the young women who hung around our landing beach. My thoughts kept coming back to her face: the clear, candid eyes under the black eyebrows that gave her glance a fine intensity, the graceful curve of her mouth as she smiled at me. I thought I could sense depths of feeling, a kind of nobility of character in her. At least, she already was becoming precious to me. I waited until late in the day, when work ceased and preparations for dinner began. An oven had been dug in the sand, smooth stones placed as linings, and a fire built within it. Ereti had returned, as promised, with the roly-poly dog, which he proceeded to kill by suffocating it, simply holding shut its mouth and nostrils. Commerson watched with fascination; d'Oraison looked slightly ill. Then Ereti singed the dog over the fire, the way we do a chicken or a goose, and one of his men fell to butchering it.

At this point, I slipped away from the camp. I didn't know where to look for Ité. I wandered through the houses set about in the nearest grove. You couldn't really speak of villages here. Houses appeared to be simply strewn under the shade of the grove, and when you had another grove there was another sprinkling of houses. There was no principal street, as in our French towns, and no shops for baker, butcher, and greengrocer. Instead there were paths that wound through the trees and among the houses, always under the shade. There were no shops, and therefore no buying and selling. And as consequence—or cause—there was no money. Suddenly that obvious fact hit me: money played no part in Tahitian society. Though maybe we were introducing that notion among them through our trade, which M. de Bougainville had ordered well regulated, in that coconuts and breadfruit were to be paid a half-dozen for a fourpenny nail, a pig costing a sevenpenny nail, and so on. This at least served to restrain our men from reaching into the nail barrels for fistfuls, and thereby possibly creating an inflation in the currency. But that was just it. Why did we want the Tahitians to think in terms of currency and rates of exchange? D'Oraison told me that the sailors were offering seven-penny nails to willing girls in exchange for sex. That sounded too much like prostitution. Our iron nails for their golden bodies. And who could even say that such barter for sex given was even necessary? Hadn't d'Oraison and I been offered a beautiful woman free? And Ité? That maybe was different. But still, we had all seen women clearly made available, at least to our first in rank. Despite his habitual reticence on such matters, M. de Bougainville indicated that Ereti had offered him a more appetizing wife than the one who had visited me. Of course, we were the "chiefs"; maybe the common sailors had to pay where we didn't.

Had we come here then just to corrupt—to corrupt everything, including that love which the islanders seemed to hold as the central joy of life? Commerson's words came back to me. But was he right? Why was love so freely offered? Did the women choose freely, or were they coerced by men fearful of our huge ships and our gunpowder? Would a price eventually be exacted from us in exchange? Or from the Tahitians? I recalled a conversation with La Porte at the Captain's mess the night before we had anchored here. M. de Bougainville, with his usual foresight, had asked for an unambiguous report on any venereal infections among the men, promising to quarantine on board any man who might bring this scourge of our seaside taverns to an island where it was unknown and where it could work ravages. La Porte had assured the Captain that he had long had this in mind, that he and Vivès had recently inspected all the men on both the ships (a pleasant task, I'm sure), and that they were free of infection. Yet, could he be certain?

My prowl through the houses had produced no sign of Ité. Troubled, and irritated at myself for not having fixed another rendezvous before we parted, I searched out the path that led from the grove toward the stream. Maybe she would go seek me at the pool in the stream. I found the path without much trouble, followed it until it joined the path I knew already, turned to the left. Soon I was at the boulders. Now there were more pareus spread out—five of them. Later, I learned that the islanders bathed twice or even three times a day, a habit I quickly adopted for myself. Ité was there with four of her companions, laughing and splashing. When she saw my head above the boulders as I stood hesitating to approach closer, she beckoned to me. So I went and sat by the bank.

One by one, they came from the pool, streaming with water. The other four were young, like Ité—how old was she, in fact? I wondered—with the same elastic bodies, and similar tattooings on their buttocks. For just a moment I felt disoriented, uncertain which was my lover. I found myself wondering whether you could use the tattoos to read marks of identity, a sort of personal signature, so you knew which woman was which. But could they read? I had seen no signs of writing.

Ité resolved my doubts in an instant by stepping forward with a smile. Of course it was she, distinguishable from the others by the lithe gravity of her step, by her proud bearing. She stood unashamed before me, so very beautiful. Her smile faded, however, and suddenly I found her expression to be inscrutable. Was it pride in her new lover I saw in her eyes? Curiosity? A sense of challenge? Our encounter that morning had seemed so easy. But as she looked at me, her face now serious, questions returned. What did she think of me? Why had she chosen to give herself to me? Was it courtesy simply? Sexual desire alone? Curiosity for the unknown? Something else entirely, that I could never understand? For a moment I stood abashed before the woman I wanted to love, realizing that despite the intimacy I had felt that morning, she was a stranger to me.

Then her smile flashed forth again, and raising herself on tiptoes she rubbed her face against mine. The cool, wet face sent currents racing through my body. Her companions sat naked on the coconut fronds by the water's edge without any sign of self-consciousness, smiling and talking as I embraced Ité. I wondered if Ité might be ready to begin our lovemaking right there, under the eyes of her companions. But I delayed, holding her close to me but keeping my pareu on, despite an ever more urgent need to be rid of it. So Ité pulled me into a sitting position on the bank. Soon the other women rose, rewrapped themselves, and departed after exchanges of conversation that left me without a clue to their meaning, though there was much laughter. Then we were alone.

Darkness falls swiftly in the tropics, and it was pitch black when Ité led the way back down the path, and parted from me at the fork. I stumbled on till I picked up the light of the campfire. Dinner was well under way.

"We've saved you some roast dog," said d'Oraison. "Moreover, it's delicious."

Commerson gave me one of his appraising glances but said nothing. I think he may have been feeling a bit subdued from that morning's episode with Baret, whose absence from the circle I now noticed. Expiating her loss of disguise back at the ship, I supposed.

La Porte spoke from across the campfire. "It tastes like the best roast lamb. Try some."

I took a piece from the wooden platter. I tasted it gingerly, but they were right. Delicious. I found I was ravenously hungry. I think I managed to eat almost as much as Ereti that night.

Somnolence was settling over us. Our efforts at conversation with Ereti had lapsed. I was considering how I might politely leave him for my tent when I became aware of a patch of illumination glowing out on the dark water. It was coming toward us, from the far shore of the lagoon, behind the ships. D'Oraison nudged me. I nodded, and watched as the shape of an outrigger defined itself before our eyes, paddled by a dozen men. It was lit with some sort of torches, their light both fitful and intense in the velvet blackness. I watched, fascinated, as the canoe moved toward us, swift and nearly silent. Then it swung sideways to the beach and moved past us. A dozen torches, wooden batons topped with resinous nuts that burned brightly, with a plume of smudge wafting from them, were set along the outrigger's sides. The paddlers rested, their dark wooden paddles dripping and glinting in the torchlight, their faces intent in the shadows under their dark manes. It was a festive sight, like a carnival barge I once had seen approaching down a Venetian canal. Then it moved on, leaving a slim silver wake.

"*Oopu,*" said Ereti. "Fish."

Commerson nodded. "*Upea?* he queried, "*matau?*" These were the words for net and for fish hook.

Ereti shook his head. "*Patia,*" he said, followed by something I couldn't grasp. Then he was on his feet, gesturing to us to follow him.

We trooped along the beach, ghostly white under our bare feet. The outrigger had now come to shore at the mouth of the river that marked the far limit of our camp, the river that led up to the pool where our water casks had been taken for filling. Now the men had disembarked; each had taken a torch in one hand and a slim spear in the other, and begun walking in the shallows of the river, so carefully and quietly their feet made no splash as they moved forward. Ereti pointed to one of the spears. "*Patia,*" he named it. Then he gestured to Commerson, d'Oraison, Bourand, and myself to come to a halt on the bank of the river.

The torches held low over the full, flowing water cast a dozen circles of dancing light. They swung in slow arcs, and moved forward slowly upstream. Under the arching branches of the mangrove trees, it was another scene of glorious theatrical spectacle, astonishingly beautiful. Then I saw a spear dart from a hand. A furious splashing in the water. A split second later, the hand grasped the end of the spear again. On its point was impaled a wriggling fish, which the man quickly unspitted and shoved into a cloth bag slung from his left shoulder. Another spear leapt forward. Another prize. What skill. What beauty. In the spectral illumination, a muscular arm would flex and jab forward; a slim spear would shoot forth. Sometimes it would be pulled back empty. More often, there would be a moment of roiling water and a beating silver fish on the end of the spear.

I fixed my eyes on the spectacle as the men moved up the stream. The patches of light became more and more distant, the strikes of the spear indistinct. Then they were gone. We did not wait for their return downriver. We trudged back to camp silently, bade Ereti goodnight, and went to our tents.

I slept well. At morning light I was back to the pool. Ité was there, alone, waiting for me.

At noon that day, we received a ceremonial visit from Tuteha, who seemed to be the chief of another part of the island. We were given to understand that he had travelled several hours to meet us, and that he was a grand personage. Grander than Ereti, I think. At least, he came with a more considerable entourage, bearing an abundance of chickens, pigs, fruit, and cloth. And he was the tallest islander we had met thus far, a good six feet, with broad shoulders and a muscled chest as well as a considerable belly. He visited the camp only briefly. When he learned that Putaveri—this was the closest Ereti and his compatriots got to Bougainville, and so our Captain had been dubbed by them— was on his ship, they embarked in two large outriggers to pay their respects. At the end of the afternoon, we heard a six-gun salute fired from the *Boudeuse,* which gave us a sense of M. de Bougainville's estimate of the dignity of his guest.

The next day, we returned the visit to Tuteha. Led by Ereti, we walked for three hours, most of the time in open country, under a sun that made even my light dress too much. Putaveri (as d'Oraison and I now called him between ourselves) had insisted on wearing his frogged waistcoat for the ceremonial occasion, while his valet carried his coat, and he was awash with sweat by the time we made a halt at the upper margin of a meadow, in the shade of a stand of breadfruit trees.

We sat in the grateful shade and looked back on the ground we had covered. The sea—blue, immense, infinite—wrapped round the horizon, shading off into a haze where it met a nearly indistinguishable sky. Offshore, the barrier reef seemed to extend along all that we could see of the island, marked by a ragged white line where the waves broke. Then the lines of the beach: white near where our ships, no longer visible from here, lay at anchor, gray and even blackish farther along. Volcanic, no doubt. Then the groves of coconuts and breadfruit trees, where here and there I could just make out the roof of one of the houses strewn amidst them. Then a mix of cultivated fields and breadfruit plantations, the fields a dazzling bright green, the plantations a darker, shiny green, with crests rustling in the breeze. Flowers grew along the edge of the meadow we had just crossed, and the breeze brought us the heady scent of gardenias. Colors were everywhere, moving in the breeze, flitting on wing across our sight. Down to our right, you could make out how the island narrowed down to a kind of isthmus at what they call Taravao. The island then widened again into little Tahiti, the smaller of its two parts. To our left, the land fell toward the fertile valley of the Vaituoru River, which we would follow down to Tuteha's dwelling. Behind us, the majestic mountains.

"Look," said La Porte, who had given himself a day off from the invalids, already begining to improve from a diet of fresh fruit and fish. He handed me his spyglass. "Down there, where the beach curves."

I steadied the glass. There. Canoes, drawn up on the beach, but immense ones, far bigger than the outriggers we had seen so far. These had double hulls, lashed together with planks in between. They must be seagoing canoes, with high poops and bows, and huts of woven reeds set on the planks near the stern.

"Ahutoru," I called. He was squatting on his haunches a few yards away. I gestured toward the great canoes, and looked questioningly at him.

He fixed his bright eyes on the distant objects, and his face became grave; then it was almost a scowl. He started to explain. I didn't understand. Then he pulled up the side of his pareu, exposing on the inner face of his right thigh a long shiny purple scar. I glanced from scar to the canoes, uncomprehending.

La Porte spoke. "A battle scar, I think. I've seen others on the men. I believe he's trying to tell us those are war canoes."

War. I turned to La Porte, grimaced in anger, and pretended to strike him and beat him. La Porte in reply grabbed a stick from the ground and made a dumb show of skewering me with a spear. We looked at Ahutoru. He nodded grimly.

"So they do have wars," I said, reluctantly. "Who do you suppose with?"

"Other islands, perhaps," said La Porte. "They must be able to navigate on the open sea. Commerson supposes they must have come here originally by sea."

"They must be fine navigators," said d'Oraison, who'd been listening. "Imagine just finding this spot in the immense ocean."

"They know their stars," said La Porte. "Ereti was telling us their names for them last night."

I rose and moved off. Somehow I was disturbed by this talk of navigation, of other islands, of the sea that had to be crossed. To me, this island was beginning to seem like the best home I had ever known. I had few enough reasons to feel I belonged in France, where my very right to my name was still contested. Tahiti was home to Ité, to the intensest and most peaceful pleasure I had ever experienced. Her ready smile, her lithe and noble body, even the occasional inscrutable gravity in her dark eyes were intensely present as I stared out to sea. It is true that our verbal communication was still limited to a few nouns, that there were vast regions of the unknown in her. And yet, I felt that I knew her—and she knew me—already better than any other woman I had been with. Sophie? Marie-Isabelle? They and I understood one other perfectly on the level of social banter and erotic needs, but nothing more. There was a generosity I felt in Ité's eyes and her touches that promised another kind of understanding. The idea of embarking on our ships, of sailing away from Ité seemed incongruous. Where else in all the world could I ever find such happiness?

M. de Bougainville rose and signalled our departure. Another hour of walking brought us to Tuteha's house, larger but otherwise little different from those we had seen. Banana fronds were dropped at our feet. Lunch was spread before us, with piles of plantains and bananas, roast pork, and grilled fish. I was getting used to feasting. Following the meal, we lolled on our mats, and the women appeared.

We offered gifts of our usual trinkets, plus a handful of nails. To Putaveri was presented in return what must have been one of Tuteha's prized wives: a young woman of regal beauty, tall, her skin nearly as white as ours though far smoother and more beautiful, her striking face set off by a tiara of gardenias. Three flutists struck up a tune. I exchanged glances with d'Oraison. This again. I was curious to see how our Captain would handle it.

M. de Bougainville rose and bowed slightly to the woman, then invited her to sit at his side. He looked slightly flushed, but his dignity was unruffled. If he found a way later on to take better advantage of the consort offered him, d'Oraison and I were unaware of it.

We meanwhile had been presented with our own women, less young and beautiful than our Captain's, but thoroughly desirable. Had I not discovered Ité, the feast, the music, and the afternoon sunlight gilding our mats and the golden bodies next us might have roused me to action. Fidelity didn't seem to be a concept prized by the islanders, so far as I could see, but I was thoroughly satisfied with what I had found. And I never could shed French customs enough to conceive of lovemaking in public. Though in a speculative way I once again found myself wondering, why not? It was clear that the Tahitians felt no shame in the public display of their pleasures. As Commerson had said, they know no other god than love.

As we sat contemplating our companions a tall young man—I thought he might be Tuteha's son—offered us an example. The young woman with him had unwrapped her pareu and lay naked on a mat, her eyes shining. He unwrapped his covering, and entered her. I glanced over to M. de Bougainville. I knew the sometime lover of Sophie Arnould was no more a prude than I; he stared in fascination at this erotic spectacle.

They say that earlier in this century, at the Court of the Regent

Philippe d'Orléans at Saint-Cloud, evening parties became wild debauches, where these satiated aristocrats would order spectacles in
which men and women coupled before them. Then they would take to
their own couplings, scattered on divans in a vast drawing room, not
bothering to withdraw to privacy. As I watched the couple of islanders
in their bliss I thought of those reports of the Court of Saint-Cloud. I
had never seen a man and a woman making love before my eyes. It was
arousing, yes. It was slightly comical, too, when you gained a moment's detachment from it and saw it as two bodies engaged in weird
motions. Yet also—I can't explain all these contradictory thoughts—it
was the most natural thing in the world, a man and a woman enjoying
one another. If I stayed here long enough, would I achieve their ability
to take pleasure so simply? So innocently? For that was it. Their innocence was radical. I wish I could make you understand that this had
nothing to do with pornography. Nothing to do with the debauches of
Saint-Cloud, nor with my afternoon transactions with Sophie and
Marie-Isabelle. I had been so proud of these—not so long ago, but in
what now seemed a distant past—but now they seemed almost
worthless, frivolous. Could we Europeans ever be innocent again?
Were we truly fallen creatures, as the Fathers used to tell us? But why?

The couple reached the climax of their bliss. Three or four of the
spectators threw flowers at their couch. M. de Bougainville, d'Oraison, La Porte, and I were all clearly in a state of disarray. I wondered if
our captain was ready to disappear into the woods with his consort.
But as the music subsided, and the couple rewrapped their pareus, M.
de Bougainville brought a conclusion by rising to order our departure.
It was a long walk back, though more of it would be downhill than in
coming. I could not tell whether Tuteha was displeased that we had
not put his women to better use. In particular, I wondered if Putaveri
had given offence by doing nothing with the regal wife offered to him.
But these were things we would never know.

Led by Tuteha, we trooped down to the beach. Here, there was no
reef offshore, and the breakers came thundering directly on to the
beach. M. de Bougainville noted that there were canoes drawn up, and

wondered aloud how they managed to launch them and beach them in such waves. Then we saw a sight that gave us some idea. A dozen boys, proud young adolescents in their first manhood, were out swimming. When a breaker came upon them, they dived under it, rising to the surface beyond it with infinite ease. They had dragged an old canoe out beyond the breakers. Then two of them stood in the canoe, while the others steadied it, stern out to sea, and pushed it forward in front of the onrushing swells. The breaking wave then caught the stern of the canoe. It rose high on the wave, its bow pointed down, so that you thought it was going to plunge under the water. But no. The long canoe shot down the wave like a rushing wagon out of control on a steep hill, swift and beautiful, the two naked boys holding their balance in the stern. Twice we saw them shoot all the way into shore in the most graceful soaring motion, until the canoe grounded and they leapt off into the shallows, to drag it back again. Then they started over. Several times, we saw the wave break over them in mid-career, bringing the canoe to a shuddering halt, its bow raised skyward. Then the boys leapt overboard and pulled the canoe back out. Again and again they started over. Then once again, the perfect wave, the perfect run toward the shore, the canoe rushing foward on the crest, to subside into the sand. I watched, fascinated. What wonderful sport.

M. de Bougainville finally called us away, with evident reluctance. But we had a long trek before us. The journey back was wearisome. We all looked forward to stretching out in rest, and for myself I hoped there would still be time for a visit to the pool in the stream. But as we approached the camp we found that the usual four sentinels had now been doubled, to eight, and that they seemed to have abandoned the relaxation they had become used to for a state of alert.

Bournand, Suzannet, and Commerson were with us the moment we passed by the sentinels. Clearly they had been waiting for us.

"Wretched news, sir." It was Bournand who spoke. "There's been a native killed, with a musket ball."

"Shot? But how can that be? The men are forbidden to leave the camp armed. You know that. They all know that."

"Yes, sir. But so it is. The man's been shot."

Now Commerson spoke. "It's only too true. Suzannet and I went to his house to make sure. A musket wound in the chest."

"And he's dead? Nothing to be done?" This was La Porte.

"Past your remedies, Doctor. He's dead."

M. de Bougainville swore aloud. Never had I seen him so angry. "Assemble everyone who's been ashore today. And then bring in the guard, one by one."

"Yes, sir. Shall I send to the ships for an accounting of who came in in the launches?" Bournand asked.

"Do that. Without delay. We can't let this thing fester."

"A cowardly deed," Commerson said. "Despicable. And why? At what provocation?"

"Theft, I would suppose," said M. de Bougainville.

"Theft, indeed! Is there anyone of our ship so barbaric as to think theft should be punished by death? Shame, shame."

"I cannot understand it. My orders were strict and precise. No retaliation against the natives by our men. All problems of justice to be referred to me."

"Once happy island, now may you wish that you had never welcomed these visitors to your shores! Better to have brandished your spears, like those natives who lined the shores on Spear Island! You offer us love; we reply with gunshot!"

Commerson was off on one of his tirades. Annoyance passed across M. de Bougainville's face. He had no time for philosophy at present.

He moved to the center of the camp. Dinner was forgotten for now. There would be no visit to the pool that evening. Our camp was now transformed into a court of justice, with a long list of men to interrogate.

The court continued until well after dark. Then, the mystery still unsolved, we officers—M. de Bougainville had included me among them this time—began again in the morning. Fifty-four men were interrogated: thirty of them from the camp, twenty-four who had come in from the ships that day. We made no progress. No one confessed. No one could point a sure finger at anyone else. M. de Bougainville's brow was furrowed; he spoke less and less.

Meanwhile, he had sent d'Oraison and Bournand with presents to Ereti, who himself appeared at the camp at the end of the morning. He appeared calm, and made no reproaches so far as we could tell. But with him was an old woman—wife, or mother, of the man killed?—who stood before us and took a shark's tooth and struck her scalp with it several times. Blood spurted from the scalp wounds, and she wailed piteously. Ereti watched her, silently and solemnly, making no attempt to restrain her. It was horrible. La Porte stepped forward, but we all understood that it was not for us to intervene. The spectacle lasted for some ten minutes, then it was over. She stanched her wounds with leaves she had tucked in her belt, then she was gone. Ereti stayed to lunch with us. It was evident that the shooting had not altered his friendship for us, or at least his desire to maintain good relations.

M. de Bougainville ceased to pursue the inquest, reluctantly. But he was anxious now, and ordered that the work of repairing our casks and collecting our water go forward without delay. Our scurvied men were visibly better—almost no cases of bleeding gums were left—and I sensed on our Captain's part a resolve to be gone before the end of the time allotted us by that row of pebbles in the sand. To say my heart was sore would completely miss the point. I grieved; I was torn asunder within. I asked myself whether I should not simply disappear into the interior when that command came to ready for departure. After all, I had chosen to make this voyage. I could choose to make it cease when I wanted. And then? Stay in paradise, at least until the next ship called from Europe, however many months or years ahead. Why not, I kept asking myself. Why not?

XIII

ONCE IN MY LATER LIFE, after I had been married for six years to my beloved wife, Charlotte, Countess Sangouska, I tried to tell her about Ité, about love in the South Seas, about what it all meant to me. Charlotte and I were not only husband and wife, or perhaps I should say not so much husband and wife—in that Charlotte remained strangely chaste, almost detached, in our most passionate moments—as we were intimate friends, bound by a fierce and total loyalty that set our marriage apart from the vicissitudes of my military life. Our souls were transparent to each other, and we spoke without reticence—about most things, at least.

We had breakfasted in the morning room. Its windows looked out over the deer park, and beyond that the fertile fields of the estate. These endless acres of the rich Ukraine were part of the peace that Charlotte had brought me after my agitated quest for glory. A marriage of elegance and plenty and retirement from the world's muddled affairs, which was what I wanted and needed. It was September, and the wheat fields stood tall and golden, ready for harvest. Already, peasants with their scythes were making their way toward the nearest meadow, and a hayrick drawn by two slow oxen trundled down the road from the barns.

"I shall have to go join the harvesters today, to cheer them on."

Charlotte considered. "Don't you think you might spare yourself that? It will be very hot today. A day for staying in the shade, and letting me read to you."

"The heat never bothers me. You know that. Tahiti cured me of worry about the heat."

"Ah, but didn't you run about in Tahiti in nothing but a loincloth, like the natives?"

"Yes, to be sure. But a pareu wouldn't do in the wheat fields. Too scratchy, I should think."

"And then," said Charlotte, a bit archly, "our Ukrainian peasant girls are handsome enough, but hardly your brown, bare-breasted island wenches."

"They weren't brown. They were nearly as fair as you or I. Only with a marvellous golden tinge to their skin."

"So I suppose you find me bleached out, do you." This was said in a tone of mock bitterness in which I thought I detected a shade of the real thing.

I reached to stroke her blond hair—the very color of the wheat fields—but she spun her head away and pushed back her chair.

"I believe my dear girl is jealous of my life in a previous existence, in a world I sometimes think I knew only in a dream."

"I'm sure I can't compete with your dreams."

The conversation was taking a bad turn. Rather than changing the subject, as I should have done, I tried to explain.

"This was a woman with whom I couldn't talk, who couldn't even pronounce my name, who called me Sholé. Our only communication was through our bodies. It was just that I thought I had found a form of paradise. One that could never have suited me forever, of course. I had my life before me—my career, my fame to conquer. Time didn't exist there. I had to return to Europe, to history. To become what I now am. But it was unforgettable. It . . . it was quite astonishing"—I wasn't ever going to deny the wonder of that time with Ité, even to Charlotte—"but it wasn't anything like the love between us, my dear."

She had reimposed serenity on her fine features. "I should think not, my own Charles. A little heathen peasant girl, tattooed and anointed with coconut oil! Indeed!"

Even in the best of marriages, there are things that can never be understood. It is better not to try.

The sun was already warm on my shoulders as I walked down the path to the meadow. I stopped to shed my waistcoat, and hung it from a bough of the pear tree near the garden gate. I found myself plunged into another revery. Could there have been a permanent union that included what I knew with Ité? Or was that kind of knowledge antithetical to marriage? Could you be that way and also talk about it? And bring it into the time of calendars and calculations and future planning and historical memory? Or was it destined to be a luminous point in life, warming still but never to be quite recovered? Words spoken by Commerson came back to me: the real, the true paradises are perhaps only those we have already lost.

After that morning of fruitless martial court, I set out in the afternoon to search for Ité, whom I had not seen for over twenty-four hours. As I wandered in the grove of trees beyond the first group of houses I came upon a platform lashed to the trees at about the height of my head. There were no beds in Tahiti, yet this looked like a bed, lashed to the tree trunks, and with a thatched canopy above it. As I came closer I found it was indeed a bed, covered with coconut matting. On it lay a man, the one killed by the musket ball, evidently. He was wrapped in cloth, only his face visible. His hair was carefully groomed, pearl earrings in his ears. But already he smelled. I approached cautiously. The stench kept me at a distance, and also the fear of violating some *tabu*, since evidently this was a ritual of Tahitian burial. A hatchet and a spear and some coconuts lay alongside the corpse. And insects of various sorts were scurrying over the face. There he lay, first victim of our arrival on these shores. Sorrow and rage gripped me at this wanton destruction of our peaceful and loving hosts. How could Frenchmen be such uncivilized brutes?

The body continued in the days following to lie in its bed lashed to the trees. This wasn't a laying-out in preparation for burial. The Tahitians don't commit bodies to the ground but to the trees, where they leave them to rot and dessicate. When the bones are bare, they transport them to the *marae,* a kind of pyramid, though not very high, made of gigantic stones. Ahutoru explained this later. But by then, I had already, to my horror, encountered a *marae.*

Late that afternoon, in the second group of houses inland from our camp, I found where Ité lived. It was a house like the others, open at the sides, with a thatched roof; yet, it was larger than most, and it seemed to me particularly inviting, somehow in the choicest part of the grove, with the dappled sunlight playing on the threshold and the mildest of cool breezes playing under its eaves. When I came upon the house, Ité and two older women—her mother and an aunt?—were seated in the shade cast to the eastern side of the house, weaving those fine cloths of *tapa.* They looked up at my approach. Then one of the older women—handsome, with silver hair, and a refined, intelligent face that certainly looked like Ité's—turned to Ité and spoke quietly, though, it seemed, emphatically. Ité bowed her head gravely a moment, then smiled and nodded. She rose, so light and graceful, and stepped forward, to rub her cheeks against mine. I held her against me, her naked breasts pressed against my bare chest. She wore a gardenia in her hair; its scent was in my nostrils. Her whole body felt fresh and clean, stronger and more muscular than any I had known before her. My desire for her was so overwhelming that I thought I could almost conform to Tahitian custom, and make love to her on the cool mats of the house. But I had no idea what was expected of me.

Then the woman I took to be Ité's mother rose and left, while Ité held me by the hand and led me inside. The other old woman promptly brought a pitcher of water and pieces of mango. Then the mother was back with a tall, lean, well-knit man, his hair streaked with gray. Ité's father, evidently. We held up palms to one another, calling each other *tayo*. His face was dignified, almost solemn, his manner seemingly more formal than what I had seen with most Tahitians. We ate and drank. I tried my Tahitian vocabulary, which now included about a dozen words, as they nodded and smiled and said things I could not understand. I found myself thinking of it as a strange visit to my in-laws, whose language I could not understand but who evidently blessed our union. Our communication was limited, but the warmth and dignity of their reception was evident.

By the end of the afternoon, under the long shadows, Ité and I had left the house. She seemed to know what I longed for; it seemed to be what she wanted, too. She led me down a track that connected with the path to the pool above the boulders. When we reached the bank of the pool, she wound her arms around me and held me to her, with what felt like the greatest tenderness. I held her head in my hands and gazed into the dark liquid eyes that looked up at me. They were not laughing now, but deeply serious and passionate. This was beginning to feel like something important, something that was not just dalliance with a Tahitian girl, but romance with Ité. When we made love this time, it was long and tender. Then we bathed in the pool, and made love again. Then she parted from me, and I made my way back to the camp.

D'Oraison, Bournand, La Porte, and Commerson—they had become our regulars on shore, who didn't go back to the ships at night—were gathered around the fire, where a huge slab of fish was grilling, supported by an ingenious set of stones.

"Tuna," noted La Porte. "They're as good as our Breton fishermen."

It smelled succulent. My appetite, whetted by swimming and sex, measured the fish with satisfaction.

Commerson signalled to me to sit by him.

"Amusing yourself?" he asked.

His words had the strange effect of bringing me suddenly to the verge of tears.

Commerson looked at me for a moment with astonishment. Then, with a tenderness I hadn't known in him before, he asked, "What is it?"

What *was* it, in fact?

I shook my head. "I don't know. But it's those pebbles, aligned in the sand. I don't want to go."

Commerson thought a moment. "In love?"

I nodded. Suddenly it was a relief to confess it. I realized I hadn't even recognized it. Yes, I was in love with a golden girl. I had never known such happiness before.

"Won't that pass?" Strangely, he was not mocking me. My plight evoked something deep within him.

"I don't want it to pass. Not now, anyway. There's never been anything like it."

"I understand. But you're not going to spend the rest of your life on a Pacific island, Prince. You bear a great name. Great things lie ahead for you."

"What? If the European peace continues, a life of garrisons, card games, duels, and whores. Except on leave in Paris, where it's more elegant but furtive liaisons. If the peace is broken, we're back to what we knew in the Seven Years' War: mangled corpses, famine, pestilence."

"I thought you were too young to have been in that war."

I shook my head. "I saw the last year of it as a cadet. That's how I became a captain. I love my uniform; I love the glory of morning on the battlefield. But—I don't think I could have said this before now, I didn't know it before now—I loathe the close of the day. The screaming, the dying."

"Peace surely is better. And even in peace, you can rise to a position of command. We've lost most of our possessions in Canada and India, but still there's Louisiana, there're vast possibilities in Asia, there're things we may yet discover on this voyage."

"Glory. What is that compared with peace and happiness?"

"Sometimes glory is to be preferred to peace, even to happiness. Those have a way of not lasting. You need to find out who you are, what you can do."

We were interrupted by La Porte's pronouncing the tuna done. He served it out on wooden platters, and we burned our fingers and our lips in our eagerness to eat.

Commerson returned to his subject as soon as he had eaten his fill.

"With a bit of luck, Prince, you'll live into the next century. Imagine. The nineteenth century. Who can say what the spread of enlightenment will bring? An age of peaceful competition, perhaps, with our great powers setting aside the sword to pursue understanding of the wonders of the universe. Rulers enlightened enough to raise the people to a level of education and civility never before seen. Everywhere the notion of the useful triumphant. The Church and its inquisitors relegated to oblivion, like some nightmare of childhood."

"Do you believe all that?"

"No, of course not. Or maybe. A few more rulers like Frederick of Prussia, and it could be done. But no. Mankind is too immersed in destruction. It's too in love with death."

This was a striking thought. I didn't quite understand him, and yet in an odd way it made sense.

"That's right. But here it's different, no? These islanders don't love death. They love love, and all it brings."

Commerson assented. "They are instinctively of the party of humanity. They live what our philosophers babble about. Look at their love. They've abolished jealousy, coquetry, all the falsities we've attached to passion. They declare what they want. They follow the penchant of their heart and their senses. They have said yes to everything we have been taught to deny."

"That's it. And why have we been made to deny it, to hide it, to wear a mask during the day that we take off only at night, or in the boudoir?"

Commerson shook his head. "I suppose it all comes back to the Church, that old hag of European history, that witch that feeds off her young. *Inter urinas et fæces nascimur,* said old Saint Augustine. Love for those Fathers who shaped the Roman Church was an obscenity, tied to parts of the body they could not contemplate without shame."

"That's right. They don't like the body; they don't understand it. But why?"

"The source of corruption, of impurity. And itself condemned to corruption. So that they must fantasize the existence of an ethereal and eternal soul."

"No soul, my friend? A thoroughgoing materialist?"

"And why not? Isn't the material universe grandiose enough? Isn't your body a thing of wonder to you? Aren't your arousals the greatest joy you know? Isn't being with your Tahitian wench, whoever she is, the height of bliss?"

I nodded. "Yes, of course."

"So why fight it? Why substitute for these real joys some chimera of a future happiness promised by old men who believe in the mortification of their ugly flesh? How can they have persuaded all of Europe that their perverted imaginings are the truth? Why have we let them dupe us in this way?"

I shook my head. I couldn't quite keep up with Commerson. A moment ago he had been telling me that Tahiti and Ité were an insubstantial dream I must give up; now he was making European glory seem a deceptive illusion, almost a nightmare. And certainly I couldn't find an answer to his riddle. "It must have served someone's interests," I suggested.

"Of course. The interest of the rulers, of the oppressors. Of those who wanted to keep the majority of mankind in a state of infancy, so that they could grab everything for themselves."

"But did they need everything?"

"No, they didn't need it. They wanted it. And the more they got it, the more they wanted more."

"But why?"

"I don't know why. The *libido dominandi*. That wretched will to power. You've read the great Jean-Jacques Rousseau, Prince. Look at what he says about property: the first man who said, this is mine and this is thine, and had a neighbor so foolish as to believe him, sealed the fate of mankind. The rest follows inevitably: wars, rulers, frauds, charlatans, the division of the world into those who have and those who want. Even women as property. Marriage as property rights. Jealousy, infidelity, all the rest."

"And these islanders have avoided all that. So it's not man that's corrupt. It's man in our European society."

Commerson's exaltation relaxed for a moment into amusement. I felt his large, callused hand rest for a moment on my bare shoulder. "If the House of Nassau could hear you now, they'd think you were some changeling. A radical philosopher switched for a prince in the cradle."

I smiled bitterly. "They don't need to think that, since they are convinced that I am a child of nature in any case. A bastard."

Commerson, faced with this delicate topic, thought a moment. "If you are, be proud of it. Let nature be the guide of bastards. If you're not, trust nature anyway. She's the best guide we have."

"Then why should I not stay in this happy island?"

"You think I've simply proved your point?"

I nodded, deeply serious again.

"In philosophy I have, Prince. But that is not reality. Even Jean-Jacques knows that we cannot return to the world of our origins, to the first society, to the Golden Age. We are what we are: the weary and self-conscious products of the old world. There's no going back."

"But why not? This is no philosopher's utopia. This is real. It is here, it is now. Why leave it?"

Commerson was uncharacteristically silent. The fire had burned low, and the stars now stood above us with a soft intensity. They were mirrored in the quiet water of the lagoon. The smell of hibiscus and gardenia reached us on the gentle breeze.

"Because," he finally spoke, "you are not it, and it is not you. What do you really know of the Tahitian soul? What will you ever know, even if you stay here for years, for a lifetime? And who knows what dark places lurk even here?"

"Like what?"

"Well, those war canoes, for one thing. We don't know what bloody struggles they represent. We've arrived at a moment of peace. How long will it endure?"

"But surely they don't want war, even if they must defend themselves at times. You can tell they love peace."

"There's darker still. If I understood correctly what Ereti was explaining to us today, they sometimes have human sacrifices—in the *marae,* their temples—when they need to propitiate their war god. They kill a captive, or a servant."

I shuddered. "Dark enough, if it's true. But are you sure?"

"I don't know. It doesn't really matter, does it? The point is we know nothing of their beliefs, really. We see, we observe, we touch. We enjoy. But what do we know?"

"We know something through the body, surely."

"Something, yes. But do we even understand their bodies?"

"What do you mean?"

"Well, the meaning of those tattoos, for instance? I watched the tatooing of a girl this afternoon. Pretty cruel."

"Tell me."

"They use a black soot, which they get from burning the candle-wood nut. They scoop it up on a kind of serrated comb, made from a shell. Then they jab it deep into the buttocks, so the blood starts forth. The girl must have been about twelve. A cute thing she was, lying there naked. She looked eager enough to have the tattoo-maker begin. But five minutes into the operation, she was sobbing and trying to pull away. Two old women had to hold her down. It wasn't pleasant."

I grimaced, thinking of Ité held squirming as those designs were worked into her thighs and buttocks. "You say she was only twelve?"

Commerson nodded. "Some sort of coming-of-age ritual, I imagine. Boys have it too."

"Yes, I'd noticed."

"But we can only speculate on what it means. What do we know about this kind of symbolism inscribed on the body? We can't read it."

"Maybe not," I said stubbornly, "but that doesn't prevent the body from being itself, and being like all bodies everywhere, so there can be a communication there. Between the body of a man and a woman."

"Yes. But that can't wholly satisfy, Prince."

"Why not? Aren't you the materialist?"

"Yes. But the clay of which we are made has developed other desires we cannot now renounce. To know, to understand. To philosophize. To make ourselves understood to one another, and to the generations to come. That is where the materialist predicates his immortality—in the future."

I pondered. "Here there is no future. There is only now, unchanging."

"Exactly. And could you stand it forever? To give up the future?"

"The future be hanged."

"I know, I know. The future is a hard taskmaster, one who makes us renounce all sorts of present gratifications. And yet, perhaps, also the very motor of progress, of change, of betterment."

We had talked ourselves into a kind of stupor of understanding. At least I could go no further. I couldn't think anything through with clarity. I was wretched, though at the same time replete and sleepy.

The stars looked close enough to touch as I made my way to the tent. But they offered no counsel.

XIV

THE FIRST RAYS of sunrise fell across my face. My mind was awake and alert instantly, but my body felt pleasantly sluggish. Something was unknotting in me. It was as if something had resolved itself during the night, something that had taken place in my body itself. It wasn't a decision. When I thought again on the choice I had to make, anguish flooded through me. It was simply a postponement, a relaxation, excusing myself from decision for now. Life now was in and for Tahiti. Maybe I had learned the art of temporizing between the well-regulated demands of Marie-Isabelle and the tempestuous desires of Sophie, keeping things in a kind of chaos that was not disagreeable so long as it didn't get out of hand. As finally it did, I reminded myself. But it was an art that was to serve me well in command. Once you had determined that you knew more or less the strength of the enemy units and where they were positioned, you went to bed knowing that you had done all you could for now. That there was no point in worrying it any further. You knew that the necessary decisions would get made when they had to be. It was the preternatural calm before a decisive battle.

I was becoming better at wrapping my pareu, so that it fell easily from my hips. I was onto the path up the stream in a moment. When I reached the boulders, once again there were three pareus spread out. Now I didn't hang back. In a moment I was naked and splashing in the cold water of the pool with Ité and her two friends.

It was as if they had conspired to play games with me. One of them would break the surface behind me, putting her small, soft hands on my shoulders. When I swung round to meet her, another came underwater from the front, to grab my feet. Then the third swam through my legs and breached in front of me, laughing. I reached out for her, but she was gone, twisting and diving away. Now the one at my shoulders was wriggling through my legs, and the one hanging on my feet had surfaced behind me. They sported like dolphins. I didn't know who was where. I didn't know which was which at moments, then Ité would rise before me for a wet embrace. Then it again became a blur of splashing water, gilded in the sunshine, and golden wet bodies breaking the water's surface in a peal of laughter, or gliding beneath in movements of heartbreaking grace. Flashes of breast, of rich brown nipples, of smooth muscular legs.

When they were tired of their sport, all three put hands on my back and shoulders to propel me to the shore. I was breathless, half drowned. Excited too, of course.

They pushed me down on the pile of coconut leaves. And now with hands and mouths they began exploring my body. I glanced at Ité, troubled that we might be breaking some trust between us. But her face was laughing; she and her friends appeared to be all together in playing a game. Hands stroked the bottoms of my feet, then the undersides of my knees, then the inside of my thighs; a mouth was on my chest. I was wild with excitement. I think I nearly fainted from pleasure. Finally, I reached out urgently to Ité, to pull her down on me.

I don't think we lay still more than a few minutes before their explorations began again. If I loved the golden smoothness of their skin, they seemed to be enchanted with the pink blondness of mine. Never in my life has my body felt so adored as it was that morning. They explored every inch, with smiles and laughter and little exclamations of pleasure.

"*Patia,*" said one of them as she reached gently between my thighs. Spear, I remembered. That was good.

Ité laughed aloud and shook her head. "*Ure,*" she said. "*Ure.*"

A less metaphorical description of the thing in question? It wasn't very spear-like at the moment, though I sensed it wouldn't be so relaxed for long.

I reached out and touched Ité's breast. "*U,*" she said, smiling. I let my hand slip softly down her skin, to rest just as the glistening black hair began. "*Tia,*" she said.

Now a hand had slid to my buttocks. "*Tuaio,*" said a soft voice.

Ité's hand was in my hair. "*Huruhuru,*" she said. She put a handful of my wavy blond hair next to her straight jet black hair. "*Navenave,*" she exclaimed. I knew that meant *beautiful.*

Her companions stroked my hair. "*Navenave,*" they repeated. So it seemed to be fair hair that was my particular asset. Their hands wandered through it. I felt two hard damp nipples against my back, two more against my chest, a third pair against my thigh.

But it is useless to try to describe it all. It was indescribable in any case. Ité appeared to preside quietly at our revels, as if pleased to have her lover the center of attention and the object of the pleasure they so generously meted out. I can't even say how many times we began again, or what finally brought us to an end. The base of my spine ached from pleasure. I fell asleep in the dappled shade, for how long I cannot say, either. When I awoke, they were dressed, their hair combed and adorned with flowers. They were sitting, watching me. I somewhat anxiously sought Ité's eyes: was everything really all right? Had pleasure been followed by shame or remorse? Ité's radiant face told me I was worrying about French ideas, not Tahitian ones. I let them wrap me in the pareu—even that could produce no excitement now—and we went along the path again, to part at the fork.

Our camp was in a midday somnolence. Evidently I had missed lunch. D'Oraison was not to be found. Bournand and La Porte were napping under the shade of a stand of palms. The sand was hot underfoot, the beach dazzling in the sun. At the water's edge, the launch was drawn up, with a sailor hunched under its bow, keeping lookout with his eyes closed. He was unarmed in any case, since M. de Bougainville had restricted the carrying of firearms to the camp sentinels. We were at peace with the islanders. And peace seemed to hang over everything. The two ships in the lagoon appeared immobilized in a mirroring lake. Only the line of the breakers on the reef, and the dull roar they gave as a bass note in the otherwise silent scene, suggested a world beyond.

I made my way through the camp, past its boundary, and on along the upper limit of the beach, in the shade of the trees, looking for something left over from someone's midday meal. I nearly stumbled over Commerson, who was seated where the shadow of a clump of palms spread over the sand. With him was Ereti. Commerson had placed near him a large open notebook, with quill and inkstand next it. His spectacles were on his nose. Was he sketching specimens? But I saw no specimens. What he held in his hand was a sharpened stick, with which he was making marks in the sand. As I stood behind his shoulder I made out the words *Ereti tayo.*

When he had done, he read them out, his stick following the syllables. "Ereti tayo." Then he pointed his stick at me, and nodded. "Read them."

I repeated, "Ereti tayo."

Ereti nodded and looked pleased, but puzzled.

Commerson took up the notebook, dipped his pen, and carefully wrote out in block letters: Ereti tayo.

He passed the notebook up to me. "Ereti tayo," I solemnly read.

Commerson took the notebook back and passed it to Ereti. "Read," he said, pointing to the words.

Ereti looked smiling at Commerson, then at me. "Omaté tayo, Sholé tayo," he said.

Commerson frowned, shook his head, and pointed to the words again. "Ereti tayo." Then he wrote out: Omaté tayo, Sholé tayo. He pointed to the new words. "Read."

Ereti looked smiling from one of us to the other. "Omaté tayo, Sholé tayo," he said, without looking at the words.

Commerson was stumped for a moment. Then he wrote out: Putaveri tayo. He said nothing, passed the notebook to me.

"Putaveri tayo," I read aloud.

Ereti looked disconcerted. When the notebook was passed to him, he looked from the page out to the *Boudeuse* at anchor, then turned to us.

"Putaveri?"

Commerson nodded, and brought his attention back to the notebook. Under the word *Putaveri* he drew a little stick picture of our Captain, with his epaulettes and his sword at his side.

"Putaveri . . . come here?" Ereti asked haltingly in our own language.

Diligently, though by now I saw his lips were compressed in discouragement, Commerson wrote out: "Putaveri no come here," and passed it up for me to read.

Ereti hesitated, his eyes shifting from one to the other of us. "No?" he said. "No Putaveri?"

Commerson set the pen down in perplexity. "This isn't working," he said. "How do you suppose you can get across the idea of what writing is for?"

I shook my head. "If you don't need it, then it's not for anything."

"But anyone could see it's useful, if you just get the idea. How else to transmit ideas over a distance? And to preserve thoughts?"

I was silent. The dry sand was trickling back into the first indentations made by Commerson, making the letters vague. Soon they would be illegible.

"No writing, no history," said Commerson. "No way to keep the simplest chronicle of what happened over the course of a lifetime, or during the reign of a chief."

Or on a beautiful morning in a shaded pool in the stream, I added to myself. "Is history necessary?" I found myself asking, feeling a bit idiotic.

Commerson stretched himself. "I don't know. I don't know. For progress, yes. For happiness, probably not. Life without history. Quite inconceivable to us." He was silent for a moment. "Still," he said, "I feel as if the one thing we could teach them would be writing. Far more useful than our nails and axeheads."

Then I had an idea. I crouched, dipped the quill in the inkwell, and, approaching Ereti gently, I wrote on the smooth, hairless skin of his ankle: Ereti tayo.

He was startled. Then he smiled. "Tattoo," he said.

I nodded, and pointed to the writings on the page. "Tattoo," I said.

So we were in agreement on this much. Now, if writing was tattoo, could tattoo be deciphered like writing? Was there a message there? My mind slid back to the three pairs of lovely black-laced buttocks with which I had played that morning.

But our writing lesson could progress no further. Ereti's eyes were by now closing. Commerson removed his spectacles, closed the notebook, and capped the inkwell. Soon they were both stretched out in the shade, their eyelids heavy. Ereti's smooth body, majestic in its bulk, wound round by a rich red pareu, lay next to Commerson's white-clad round belly and spindly legs. Both of them had weathered, experienced, clever faces, now relaxed. Their eyes closed. They slept, like two oddly assorted twins in their shady bower. Ereti began to snore, and soon Commerson's deeper-pitched snore came in counterpoint.

I continued on my search for food. Finally, I had to make do with two mangoes and a coconut I found in the launch.

Toward evening, as I sat with d'Oraison and watched the sun sink behind the shoulder of the mountain, there was a commotion at the boundary of the camp. We looked over. I recognized the parents of Ité and sprang to my feet. Behind them stood Ité herself, dressed in a fullness of raiment I had never seen before: a rich red cloth draped from her shoulders, belted with a sash around the waist, her hair encircled with gardenias. A large, perfect pearl glittered in one ear. Behind her came two servant girls, teuteu, carrying bundles of cloth.

The sentinel let them pass, and they came directly toward me. Now

d'Oraison and I were joined by Bournand, Suzannet, La Porte. And
Commerson was making his way from the entrance of his tent.

Ité's father held up his palms to mine. Then the two servants came
forward and set down their bundles. They proceeded to take up each
piece of cloth—there must have been ten or a dozen of them—and
spread it at my feet, silently and solemnly. It was clearly the finest
tapa, like fine muslin, dyed hues of rich red and yellow. I watched in
grave silence, apprehensive.

Then Ité herself stepped forward. She untied the sash at her waist,
unwound it, and laid it on the pile. Then she lifted off the cloth covering her upper body—it had a hole for her head, like the indians' pon-
chos in Buenos Aires—and laid that on the pile as well. She stood
before me, naked to the waist, breathtaking in her youth and beauty, a
shy smile on her face.

Her father took his place next to her and began a speech. Sholé and
Ité, I understood, were to be joined. They were to travel to a place he
gestured toward, up beyond the beach—I supposed he meant his
house. They were to lie there—he laid his head on his wife's shoulder
and closed his eyes. They were to stay there many, many revolutions of
the sun—he was now tracing an arc across the sky. And Sholé was not
to go back to the ships—he pointed to the *Boudeuse,* frowned,
stamped his foot.

Even before he began his speech, the truth had begun to dawn on
me. This was a formal proposal of marriage, an alliance with the house
of Ité's parents. They had come to show that they were people of sub-
stance—of the *arii,* as we learned to call them—and brought the
dowry of cloth in token of this. And I was to move into their house, and
stay there forever. And never return to the ships. Cease from voyaging.

My companions were glancing from Ité to me. I felt my face burning from embarassment and doubt.

"Well, you would make a handsome couple." This was Commerson,
who had come up behind my shoulder. "And no doubt produce a race
of superior people, who would become the princes and princesses of
Tahiti."

Commerson's words pricked d'Oraison to action. "What do you want us to do?" he asked quietly. "Shall we escort them away? I don't want you in any trouble. Beware the *tabu*."

I could not speak. My mouth was dry. I was mortified. I was flattered. Ité stood there, heartbreakingly beautiful, her grave eyes upon me. I had to say something, do something. But what? I found that I was perfectly divided in my mind. How could I say no to what was offered me? Yet, how could I say yes? I wanted to sink beneath the sand. I, the Prince of Nassau-Siegen!

"The crossroads of life, Prince." It was Commerson again. "Choose. The knight without fear and without sin stands at the crossroads. One path leads to war, struggle, glory. The other to peace, happiness, love. A gothic etching."

His words did me good, if only because they showed the choice to be impossible. I could only temporize myself out of this.

With a gesture, I invited Ité and her parents to sit by our campfire. We would feed them dinner. Then we would see. I turned from the gifts of cloth, leaving them in a pile on the sand. I was not accepting them. But I put my arm lightly round Ité's shoulders, and we smiled at one another.

So we sat, largely in silence, as the sun was quenched behind the mountain and the campfire blazed into life, and the stars came out to dot the lagoon with light.

Ité and her mother and the female *teuteu* drew apart, to eat separately from the men. Her father sat with Commerson, d'Oraison, Bournand, La Porte, Suzannet, and myself. Ereti came to join us. There was little attempt at conversation. A deep solemnity fell from the air. For me, it seemed that everything in my experience had come to be concentrated in that dark evening on the beach. The gentle breeze cooled my bare chest, while the sand was still warm beneath my legs. Physically, I felt an exceptional sense of well-being. Well fed, well exercised, my skin now lightly tanned, my spirit relaxed from bathing and from sex, I felt closer than I had ever before to my body. It was as if my body was gaining new knowledge, of itself and by itself. I had begun to understand the islanders' rituals of the body, their bathing several times a day—how much better the *Boudeuse* would have smelled if its crew had followed this practice!—their near-nakedness, their anointing of their hair with *mono-ahi,* oil of coconut scented with sandalwood. I thought I had come to understand even their tattoos. Whereas we Europeans put all our love of ornament into clothing and accessories, the islanders expressed theirs on the body itself, indelibly, as if to say: it is only real if it's there in the state of nakedness. You must strip me naked to read my message. Only round my waist, on my backside, once my pareu is off, can you know my identity. And wasn't this right? Wasn't anything else mere disguise?

I remembered Marie-Isabelle, that pale body on the red damask sofa. All white and pink, never having known the sun. Think of it—never having been naked out of doors. An entirely different kind of nakedness. Those elegant breasts, slung low on her chest, finished in soft pink nipples. The marks of the corset down to her waist, so narrow and refined. Even the light brown hair where her thighs met, in a way the product of centuries of breeding, a repudiation of too much nature. In lovemaking, she was avid enough—though never abandoned like Sophie—but somehow our episodes on the sofa were only parenthetical in her clothed existence. Her natural state was to be fully dressed, bejewelled, surrounded by accessories as by admirers. Not the same thing at all.

Marie-Isabelle, summit of my conquests, a love that any young man could be proud of. Lost, of course. Yet, maybe my long absence would work as an expiation of my fall from grace? Perhaps we could start again on my return. No, she would be with some other lover. But other possibilities would present themselves. Hadn't Françoise, the Marquise de Listomère, during the rout at her château near Mont-morency just a week before my departure, given me all the usual indications that she was ready to succumb, if only I would make a proper declaration of passion? All the signs were there: her constricted breathing as we danced together, her blush as I led her onto the terrace following the quadrille, the way she held and pressed my hand as we parted. She even told me when I could find her at home. While her reputation may have been slightly tarnished by her adventure with the

Chevalier de Beauchêne, she would surely make the most amiable of mistresses. In the Tahitian darkness, I could evoke her flashing brown eyes, their promise of pleasures over the edge of the known. Almost more than Marie-Isabelle and Sophie, it was Françoise de Listomère who had given me pangs of regret as I set out for Nantes.

What was Ité compared with these women—and all the other enchanting and elegant figures lined up at the quadrille at Montmorency? What was I thinking of? Yet, when I brought my mind back to Ité, sitting somewhere beyond the flickering circle of light cast by the campfire, my body stirred with a passion I had never felt on my native soil. I felt again the cool, muscular smoothness of her thighs against mine, the thrust of her breasts against my chest, the eagerness with which she embraced me. There was a generosity in her lovemaking, an openness to intimacy that made me trust her instinctively and made me feel, too, that we had only begun to explore a vast sphere of delight. Blood began pounding in my temples.

I rose without conscious decision and groped from the firelight into the darkness. In a moment, my eyes adjusted. I found Ité, her mother, and the two *teuteu* seated near the limit of the camp. They smiled, and rose, too. In a moment, Ité's father was beside us. Quietly, simply, without a word spoken, we passed the sentinel and made our way up the beach. I followed as they turned onto the track leading up into the grove. They walked slowly but without hesitation on the dark path. I stumbled a few times, but kept pace. In a quarter of an hour we were at their house. It was pitch black under the thatched roof. The fronds hanging over the eaves rustled in the breeze. The *teuteu* disappeared. Ité's parents became vague shapes on one side of the house, unrolling their mats, putting themselves to bed silently and quickly. On our side of the house, Ité rolled out the mats, five layers of them, and a lighter fabric to pull over us. Then she came and stood before me. She smiled up at me, but her eyes looked deep, grave, almost solemn. I held her lightly in my arms, searching for a word that would express my understanding of the moment. Nothing came to me. She slipped from my embrace, unwound her pareu, and reached to loosen mine.

XV

Dawn in ité's house. Later, in fact, than my awakenings in the tent—the grove sheltered the house from the sun's rays, and the thatched roof created a cool shade. Ité was sitting upright, naked still, her eyes shining. I looked past her across the floor of the house. No one else to be seen. She was on her feet in a moment, and wrapped her pareu. Then she took mine and wrapped it round my waist, but not without caressing my thighs and giving me a wide smile as she did so. Then she took my hand, and we were soon on the track to the pool in the stream.

It had rained during the night. The ground was damp and firm. The leaves dripped splashes of cold water on my shoulders and down my back. A cool wind gusted through the trees, but the sun was warm. The morning was fresh, with the smell of creation.

As we approached the boulders I was startled by a deep boom. A glance at Ité. She looked like a doe in the Forest of Fontainebleau that has picked up the scent of a predator. Then another boom. The cannon of the *Boudeuse*. We stopped and waited. Then a third. This was M. de Bougainville's signal for all hands to return to the ship. What was this all about? I waited to see if there would be more. Perhaps a salute to Tuteha, or some new chief who had made his presence known. I knew our Captain wouldn't idly set off his cannon—and not only to conserve gunpower. He respected the island's peace; he disliked any unnecessary display of our weaponry.

We stood uncertain in the path. I knew that if M. de Bougainville intended the cannon shots as a signal, he would repeat it in five minutes' time. The wait seemed interminable. Then, there it was again. One. Two. Three.

I turned to Ité. My face could not have been more anxious than hers. I put my arms around her and rubbed my face against hers. Then I kissed her on the lips. Her face was taut, her eyes troubled as they scanned my face for an explanation. I tried to indicate with gestures that I must go, but would return soon. She nodded, but clearly I did not dispel her anxiety. Nor mine. She clung to me, her mouth on my neck, her arms clasped firmly to my shoulders. I could feel her strength, her purpose. She did not want to let go. Gently, I placed her arms at her side and turned to go, cursing myself for what seemed a ridiculously misplaced sense of duty. I wasn't, after all, a regular member of the ship's crew. Yet this call for all hands to return to ship meant something grave. I turned back several times as I loped toward the beach. Ité was still immobile on the path, her strained face lighted by the sun falling through the palms.

The camp was pandemonium. The longboat was already loaded and had just shoved off. Men were tumbling into the launch. There might just be room for me. A glance at the shed that housed the sick showed me that La Porte still was there, no doubt intending to stay with the dozen or so men who still were incapacitated. And the sentinels remained at their posts. Probably the watermakers were still at their casks, up the river. A glance out to the ships. What was happening? Now I could see that the launch of the *Etoile* was already halfway out to that ship. And now, as my eyes swept over to the *Boudeuse*, I saw the problem. Her stern was swinging in a wide arc, sweeping menacingly toward the *Etoile*. Evidently, the stern anchor line had been cut. Bournand had told me that the bottom was all coral, and our anchors were all on ropes, not chains. I ran toward the launch. A sailor made a place for me on the bow thwart even as he pushed off with an oar.

Now I could see a splash off the stern of the *Boudeuse.* Another anchor thrown out. But the wind was freshening from the south—it had regularly blown from the east thus far—and the stern of the *Boudeuse* continued its arc. Evidently the new stern anchor had not set yet. As the sailors laid to their oars we all gazed toward the two ships, waiting for the sickening crash that was bound to come. Both ships splintered? Our return to France cut off? What then?

But now the mizzen topsail of the *Etoile* broke out high up the mast. In a moment the wind filled it, and the stern of the *Etoile* began moving away from the approaching hull of the *Boudeuse.* La Giraudais had raised his sail and brought in his stern anchor just in time. Now I could see his bow anchor coming up. The *Etoile* moved forward. The high stern of the *Boudeuse* swung past the *Etoile*'s stern with a few feet to spare. Saved, for the moment.

The *Etoile*'s launch was now alongside the ship. We were close enough for me to see the crew in the launch reach up and take the end of a side anchor line thrown to them from the deck. Then they laid to their oars, and made it to the side of the *Boudeuse* just as we came up under her bow. So the *Boudeuse* was going to tie to the side anchor that had been out to the east of the *Etoile.* Meanwhile, La Giraudais, some fifty yards away, dropped his bow anchor again, and lowered sail.

As we climbed up on the deck of the *Boudeuse,* orders followed. A crew was dispatched in the longboat to fish the lost anchor. Meanwhile, the *Etoile*'s launch was sent back to fetch the spare 2,700-weight anchor from her hold. The longboat came back with most of the lost anchor rope but without the southeast anchor, irretrievable in thirty fathoms of water. And the stream anchor was gone too, its buoy sunk as well. Then M. de Bougainville gave orders for the *Etoile*'s launch to move out to the north, to see whether there might be another passage through the reef to the northeast, which would enable our ships to pass out of the anchorage without making the impossible maneuver of turning against the wind to go out the way we had come in. He ordered the mizzen staysail and foretopsail made ready, so that we could take advantage of any wind that might move us up toward the northeast.

But by the end of the morning, the wind dropped, then passed to the east, where it continued, steady and moderate. We took advantage of the situation to remoor the *Boudeuse,* with the spare anchor from the *Etoile* and another light anchor set to the southeast. The *Etoile,* lighter than the frigate and apparently by good fortune anchored on a sandy bottom, seemed to be safe enough. We all waited out the afternoon in anticipation of the results of the the the exploration undertaken by the *Etoile*'s launch, and in making our ship ready to move to an anchorage outside the reef, if this proved possible.

But I knew that an anchorage outside the reef could only be temporary, a preliminary to our real departure. I felt trapped, caged on the ship's deck. I must go to Ité. Wasn't she now, in some sense, my wife? Hadn't I spent a wedding night in her house? That night of course changed nothing, in any official way. I hadn't taken possession of a virgin after a ceremony where she had been dressed in white and given away by her father. Ité was surely no virgin; she had had other lovers before me, probably starting at a very young age like the other Tahitian girls. How old was she now? How to tell? But the point was that she had chosen me above all other lovers, given herself to me. In her young pride and dignity, she had pledged herself to me. She had sensed that we were a match, and she was right.

In France, she would have been considered a fallen woman, a maid no more, unsuitable for a proper marriage—at least if her previous liaisons were known. I had always assumed I would marry a virgin. How did I feel about her experience? Confused, yes, but also delighted. She met my desire openly, frankly, without second thoughts or false modesty. She knew what she wanted. And she wanted me. Would a virgin know that? And wasn't it better for her to have had her experience of other men before knowing me? Better, that is, than what I knew from Marie-Isabelle, married at a virginal sixteen to old

Comte de Lesdiguières, who promptly impregnated her with two children but then turned to his court intrigues, teaching her nothing about lovemaking and bringing her no satisfaction. So that as a married woman she began her sexual explorations with men like me. Better, perhaps, to have fallen as a maid and then to become a faithful and loving spouse, as Jean-Jacques Rousseau seemed to maintain, with his usual perversity and paradox, in his novel *Julie*. Did I really believe that? I did not know. But my limbs ached for Ité's touch.

I paced the deck in anguish. I came to rest at the port rail, near the bow. I noticed that my hands were gripping the polished wood so hard my knuckles showed white. Then, as I stood staring at the shore with sick longing I became aware of a boat that had pushed off from the beach and was headed toward us. It was the little pinnace, the only boat we had left on land, pulled up under the hospital shed. As she approached, I saw it was La Porte at the oars. What had made him desert his charges? The fear the ships would leave without them? Surely he knew his commander better than that.

The pinnace made her way toward us with agonizing slowness. Even the gentle east wind kept pushing the light craft off course. When finally she was alongside, I could see La Porte's face was etched with anxiety.

"What news?" I called down to him.

"Bad news," he called back. "Very bad. Where's the Captain?"

I turned and told one of the midshipmen to alert M. de Bougainville. He arrived as La Porte clambered up the rope ladder.

"Grim news, sir. Three islanders have been killed. Stabbed to death with bayonets, sir. And everyone has fled. The whole colony is deserted. They've left their houses. They've fled. They were carrying spears. We saw the last of them taking the three bodies with them."

"Bayonets? Are you sure?"

"Sir, believe me. I've seen all sorts of wounds in my life. Only a bayonet could make these. The islanders don't have weapons that could make such gashes."

"But who could possibly? And why?"

"I suspect the sailors we left in charge of the water casks. The islanders must have been caught at some piece of thievery."

"But my orders were explicit. No physical brutality in response to thievery. The islanders just don't understand it as we do."

"I know, sir. A clear infraction of orders."

M. de Bougainville looked trapped. For the first time in our voyage, I saw him hesitate. Here, his ships were in danger. On the shore, the remains of our camp, including the invalids and the watermakers, might be on the point of undergoing an assault.

His hesitation didn't last long. He summoned Duclos-Guyot and gave him orders for moving the ship if the *Etoile*'s launch came back with a favorable report, for securing the mooring if it didn't. Then he assembled the dozen marines left on board and ordered them to load their arms. Suzannet, de Kerhué, d'Oraison, and myself were to go as well, and carry charged pistols.

As we set out in the longboat and the launch, M. de Bougainville explained his plan. Our camp lay between two streams—the one that led upstream, to the pool I knew so well; the other, larger one, a river really, where the watermakers were at work—about half a mile apart. Behind the camp, under the trees between the two streams, much of the area was covered by a mangrove swamp. So that there was a decent perimeter that could be defended, especially since the islanders were without firearms. On the fourth side of the camp was of course the beach, and the lagoon, which could be raked by the cannon of the *Boudeuse*. If it was to be war, we would be in a strong position. But of course our purpose in any armed conflict would not be to conquer the natives but to get off our sick and the filled water casks—the most vital thing—with as little loss as possible. And whatever other provisions could be gathered. Who knew where and when our next landfall would be?

I listened, heartsick, to these preparations for combat. Could we really make war on the Tahitians? On our friends and companions and lovers? How had our dream of paradise become a nightmare? I cursed the riffraff of the docks and taverns of Nantes who had brought this upon us. I cursed all Bretons, all sailors, all men of war.

The bow of the longboat grated on the sand. We waited, arms at the ready, for the launch. When she had beached, we filed out over the bow and took up a vee formation on the sand. To the right and to the left, the beach was empty. No islanders in sight.

La Porte, from the launch, joined M. de Bougainville in the center of the vee.

"Who is it you suspect of this blackguard's deed?" asked the Captain.

"Follow me," said La Porte.

We moved swiftly up the beach. Past the invalids' shed, where the dozen men remaining raised their heads and propped themselves on elbows to watch. A sentinel crouching under the far corner of the shed rose, presented his rifle, and saluted.

"This is the man who brought the report," said La Porte.

"Right. Well done, my man. What happened? A theft?"

"No, sir. Not really. A quarrel. The men were trading, you see. They wanted to pay two nails for a pig—just a little one, sir—and the natives refused. They wanted more."

"Go on."

"And our men took the pig anyway. Then the natives were joined by others—there must have been eight or ten—who were trying to get the pig back. There was a melée, sir. All very confused."

"And?"

"And our men fought back with their bayonets, sir. And then there were three bodies on the ground. Dead, I believe, sir. The natives took them away."

M. de Bougainville looked like the personification of a thundercloud. "How many of our men were responsible for this?"

"Four, sir."

"You're sure of them?"

"So it was reported to me, sir. I'm quite confident that's correct, sir."

"Who reported it?"

"I can't really say, sir. One of the natives, sir."

"One of the natives? Whom you trust?"

"Yes, sir. A young woman, sir. She had no reason to lie. She . . ."

"Right." M. de Bougainville cut him short. "Come on."

He strode off to the right, to the river of the watermakers. We followed. When we reached the river—which was maybe thirty feet wide where it cut the beach, and three to four feet deep, and flowing swiftly—M. de Bougainville gave his orders.

"Suzannet, take half the men and follow the other bank. Keep pace with me on this bank. De Kerhué, with me. M. d'Oraison, go with Suzannet. Prince, with me. La Porte, with me. The stream should cover our noise. No talking. When we come upon them, we encircle them, disarm them all. Then we take the suspects prisoner." He turned to the sentinel. "Keep just behind me, so you can identify them."

"Yes, sir."

"Right. Now over the river and let's get started."

We waited while Suzannet and the seven under his command splashed into the river, muskets and pistols held high in the air. The water in midstream reached above their waist, but the footing was sandy and sure. I found myself wondering whether d'Oraison's pareu would dissolve in the water. I felt quite unmilitary in my own. Still, better than soggy breeches slogging around the knees.

Suzannet formed up his men in single file on the other bank. M. de Bougainville raised his hand, then let it fall. We were off.

We moved cautiously along the margin of the river. Where the breadfruit and mangrove grew too close to the water's edge, we stepped into the river itself. It was now a stony and slippery bottom, still about three feet deep—deep enough to bring the filled water casks out on a raft, which was what M. de Bougainville intended and why he had chosen this stream for the watering. Our progress was slow. But the distance cannot have been more than a mile, probably less. Not more than twenty minutes had elapsed when we came on the dam—a natural dam, or built by the islanders, I don't know—which partially blocked the stream, leaving a clear pool of water on the other side. M. de Bougainville signalled a halt.

Below the dam, the raft was secured by two stakes and ropes strung to nearby trees. A dozen water casks were set on their ends on the raft; others lay on the shore of the pool. Two men were filling another cask in the pool, holding it under. Bubbles drifted to the surface and popped. Six sentinels were visible along the shore, two of them standing, resting on their muskets; the other four seated with muskets on their knees, looking vaguely into the trees. They were outnumbered, and unprepared. If we acted quickly, all should be well.

With a gesture to Suzannet, M. de Bougainville divided the sentinels into two groups: the two off to the right for Suzannet's platoon, the other four for us. Then he held his hand aloft for a moment.

His hand fell, and we sprang forward. The surprise was complete. Only the last sentinel in the line on our side had the chance to bring his musket to his shoulder. As M. de Bougainville shouted, "In the name of the King!" de Kerhué swung the butt of his musket at the sentinel's arm, sending it tumbling onto the ground. We disarmed the others in a moment. Two of us held each of them.

M. de Bougainville turned to the sentinel from the camp. Without speaking, the sentinel pointed his finger at four of the men in custody. The marines detached the manacles they carried hanging from their belts, and the four men were handcuffed behind the back. The other two were released.

Now M. de Bougainville detached six of our marines to reinforce the sentinels at the watering hole, and gave orders to speed the work of filling the casks in preparation for an imminent departure. Then we marched our prisoners back down the river to the camp.

M. de Bougainville had evidently decided to delay interrogation of the men until we reached the ship. Evening was approaching, and he was obviously still concerned about the safety of his ships as well as the situation on shore. But he brought us to halt on the beach, looking puzzled. He called Suzannet, d'Oraison, and myself to him.

"Here's the problem," he said. "We need to get back to the ships as fast as possible. But arresting these blackguards is only part of what needs doing. We need to show the islanders we're arresting them. That we are capable of distributing swift justice to the malefactors among us. That we are still their friends. But there's not a single islander visible."

It was true. The trading area at the edge of the camp, where almost always on days past some transaction had been under way, was deserted. And beyond the boundary of the camp, across the small stream, there was none of the usual movement of daily life. Several outriggers were pulled up on the sand; no fishing was going forward.

"Yes, we need an exemplary punishment," I suggested.

"But an example is no good with no one to see it."

"Do you suppose they're preparing an attack, sir?" asked Suzannet.

"Quite possibly. The remaining marines stay on shore, and I'll send another boatload of armed midshipmen to reinforce them."

I thought this was missing the point. Peace was what we should be after.

Then d'Oraison had a suggestion. "Even though they've disappeared, don't you suppose they may be watching us? Have pickets hidden in the groves? Or watching from the uplands?"

"Possibly. So what do you suggest?"

"Maybe if we show them the arrest, out in public, where someone will see it, maybe word will get back to Ereti and the others."

M. de Bougainville approved with a curt nod of his head. He looked round him. His eyes came to rest on the broad expanse of beach beyond the camp, the beach the islanders crossed to come to the trading post. "Out there on the beach, then. If they're looking at all, they should be able to see that."

"And what do we do?" I asked.

In M. de Bougainville's silence, d'Oraison spoke again. "Let's take off their manacles, march them out onto the beach, and then publicly, showing carefully what we're doing, manacle them again."

M. de Bougainville assented with a nod.

"Do we have a cat-o'-nine-tails?" I asked. "We could make show to flog them, there on the beach."

M. de Bougainville looked at me sharply. "Can't do that. That must be done on shipboard. Besides, we must question them, and give them a chance to answer before we apply punishment."

"Maybe the arrest will do the trick, if we make it solemn enough," said d'Oraison. "Maybe whack them with the flat of the sword."

M. de Bougainville nodded. "Your job, Suzannet."

So we unmanacled the four prisoners. Each of them was placed between two of us. Our solemn procession set out, M. de Bougainville in the lead. He had drawn his sword, and held it firmly before him. He looked like the figure of inflexible justice as he led us across the little stream and along the beach. We advanced almost as far as the beached outriggers. There, he called us to a halt. He turned to face the column that had followed him.

He brandished his sword in the air, cutting an imaginary filigree. "Gentlemen. In the name of His Majesty the King, do your duty."

The marines turned to the prisoners, manacles at the ready. The rest of us stepped aside so as not to block the view of any islanders who might be watching. The marines, rising to the drama required by the occasion, held the manacles high against the sky. With exaggerated gestures, they pinioned the prisoners' arms behind them and locked the manacles in place. Then Suzannet drew his cutlass and whacked each of the prisoners in the backside with the flat of the blade. It was both solemn and slightly comical. A bit of theatre, I thought, improvised on a Pacific beach, for an invisible audience. What we needed was a drum. A drum and a fife. The ceremony was soundless except for the clanking of the manacles.

"To the boats," said M. de Bougainville. "Slow march."

We marched the four wretches back over the stream. They were all placed in the longboat. D'Oraison and I piled with some others into the launch. The oarsmen pushed off. We left the eerily silent shore. The camp was now a fortified garrison, with the marines joining the sentinels already in place, pacing the boundaries of the camp.

Night was coming swiftly on. The campfire was lit, but none of the usual preparations for dinner were going forward. As we made our way to the darkening shape of the *Boudeuse,* stars began to stand forth in the deep violet sky. They danced on the water churned up by our oars. Was this the end?

XVI

For all the disasters of that day, I knew I couldn't appear at Captain's mess in my pareu. Changing hastily in my cabin into a clean shirt, underdrawers, and breeches, I noted how tanned my body now looked set against the white linen. Also, how sensitive it felt. The finest chambray shirt felt scratchy. My nipples were surprisingly sensitive as I buttoned the shirt. Ité had awakened new nerves. It was as if my blood now lay closer under the surface of my skin.

I had not set foot in M. de Bougainville's cabin since our arrival in Tahiti. Under its low beams, it now seemed a cage, an unlikely place for people to live. I wanted the rustle of palm fronds in the breeze, the dappled shade, the fresh feel of matting under bare feet. Dinner was moreover a somber affair, even though well provided with roast pork and fresh fish. The day had cost the *Boudeuse* two anchors, apparently irretrievably lost, and she was no better moored than before. The launch sent to look for a northeast passage through the reef had not yet returned. On shore, we didn't know what storm might be brewing. The four suspected killers were in irons in the brig, but we couldn't be sure that the islanders knew that, or whether it meant anything to them if they did. All this was the subject of endless, inconclusive talk among the Captain, d'Oraison, Bournand, and La Porte. Bouchage, who had from the start opted out of the shore party and spent most of his time on board with Duclos-Guyot, plied us with questions, which no one could answer. I myself felt useless. All I could think about was Ité, our mornings and evenings at the pool in the stream, and last night in her arms at the strange house which now could be mine. A night of love which was also a night of the deepest peace I had ever known.

I excused myself from the mess as soon as I decently could and went on deck. The dome of the sky was strewn with stars, the lagoon all silvery from their reflections. But over on the shore, all was dark except for the one fire burning in our camp. I thought of my tent still standing there, empty. A ghost camp, inhabited only by the sick and by the sentinels. No doubt they were pacing the sand in their heavy boots, treading our defense perimeter. Marking the dividing line between French and Tahitians.

The night wore on. It was useless to think about trying to sleep. Just the idea of going below to the cabin was intolerable. I was irritated, anxious, deprived. Finally I stretched myself out on the deck at the foot of the mainmast, my head on a coiled line—not comfortable enough for sleeping, but at least I could rest a bit, try to induce some relaxing of my tense muscles. Through the rigging above me, I pondered the stars. Such an immensity made our voyage to the South Pacific seem paltry and facile. Yet, what a difference it made. On this speck of a planet whirling in unending space, human creatures could live so differently from one another, believe in different gods, understand the very nature of the creation differently, understand happiness differently. And make love, both differently and the same. That was the amazing thing. To take Ité into your arms, to hold her to you, knowing that she was wholly other, believing things you couldn't even imagine, knowing hardly a word of your language and you hardly a word of hers, with no idea even of how to say "making love" in each other's language, yet to know also that the parts would be the same, and the same things would happen; you would fit together in the same way. All so well known, yet at the same time so new. This was incoherent. But thinking it warmed my loins and spread a kind of contentment through me.

I was awakened by rain lashing my face. It brought me to my feet in an instant. I started for the companionway and heard shouts from the poop deck. The wind. It gusted in from the starboard side. I could feel the *Boudeuse* shudder, straining at her anchor ropes. Instead of going below, I moved aft to the helm, where M. de Bougainville stood with Bouchage, whose watch it was, and Duclos-Guyot. Behind them, three sailors were leaning over the bits where the stern anchor was fastened. There must have been another group at the bow anchor.

"Get a spare anchor up on deck, starboard side. But don't throw it yet."

"Yes, sir." Bouchage summoned two sailors from their place by the rail, and sent them below.

"Have we enough anchors left?" I asked M. de Bougainville.

"Only two. More on the *Etoile*. But not enough if we continue losing them at this rate."

"All quiet on shore?"

"No signals." He was silent for a moment. "If they do attack, when do you suppose it will be? At dawn?"

I shook my head. The very idea of the Tahitians attacking seemed incongruous, absurd. Yet, I knew they had wars. I had seen those great double war canoes on our trek to Tuteha's house; I had seen Ahutoru's scar. La Porte had seen many more, and he had figured out that they came from doing battle with the men of a place called Bora Bora. And Commerson said they sacrificed to a war god.

"But I'm more worried about this," said M. de Bougainville as another blast of wind from the east moaned through the rigging and made the *Boudeuse* strain at her anchor ropes.

The sailors now had a spare anchor on deck and were eye-splicing a line to it.

But fortunately it wasn't needed. The squall passed as suddenly as it had begun. The rain stopped, the clouds scudded away, the stars stood out again. For half an hour, it was dead calm. Then a gentle breeze

picked up, coming offshore. The *Boudeuse* stood peacefully to her
mooring ropes.

I went below to put on dry clothes. Then I stretched out on my
bunk and slept fitfully for another hour or so. I was back on deck as
the sun lifted from the sea.

More trouble. The squall had done its damage, after all. Just after I
came on deck, Duclos-Guyot discovered that the anchor warp to
northwest had been cut under water. Just as he was ordering the
launch to go out to try to fish it, the hawser that held us on the *Etoile's*
stream anchor parted as well. Four anchors lost. Now we were holding only by the bow anchor and the springline to the southeast. The
ship began drifting eastward, toward the line of breakers along the
barrier reef. The squall had churned these breakers into a fury. They
loomed off our starboard side. A few more yards, and the *Boudeuse*
would be ground to pieces on the coral.

M. de Bougainville was now on deck again, his face haggard. He ordered the launch out to look for the two lost anchors, which it never
found, since the buoys had sunk with the anchor ropes—how, we
never knew. The wind had dropped. The *Boudeuse* rested peacefully on
the big anchor we had brought from the *Etoile,* and the sideline to the
southeast. Our last spare sheet anchor was brought up from below
and made ready in the bows.

Things were peaceful only for an hour. The brand-new hawser on
the bow anchor suddenly parted, sawed through by the sharp coral
deep below us. Now the *Boudeuse* was held only by the line to starboard. She began to sideslip in the light westerly airs, toward the
breakers. M. de Bougainville at once ordered the final spare sheet anchor thrown from the bow. Down it went, with a splash that reached
the deck. The rope ran out. Still the *Boudeuse* moved eastward. The
breakers were no more than twenty yards from our starboard side.

"Can't give it enough scope, sir. It won't set in time before . . ."

M. de Bougainville interrupted Duclos-Guyot with a shouted order
to raise the fore and mizzen jibs and let them luff.

"Wind," he said. "It's the only thing that can save us."

But for now there was only the gentle westerly breeze. And that was pushing us toward the reef.

"All the boats out?" M. de Bougainville spoke quietly now to Duclos-Guyot.

Duclos-Guyot nodded in reply. "All ready, except the launch. It's not back yet."

"All hands on deck."

The gong sounded. Men came pouring up the companionways. Still the ship moved eastward. No more than ten yards now to the breakers. No time, even, to start the boats towing the *Boudeuse* to the west. Not that they could hold her for long. Now I could see the wall of coral teeth as the waves receded with a throaty roar. Now the next wave came on, and burst in a fury of spray and foam. That was where we were headed. If not drowned, at least marooned.

The outcome looked inevitable. Already I was calculating what it meant. Months at least in Tahiti. To build a new ship? We couldn't all fit into the *Etoile*. Maybe dispatch it for succor? More months in Tahiti, until another ship could set out from France to rescue us. I wouldn't be the one to object. Ité's cool body flashed before my eyes. But first I had to avoid being ground to pieces on the reef. Time to think about dropping into the longboat yet? Not until the Captain ordered it, of course.

We watched in silence, helplessly, waiting to see whether the new anchor would catch, as we continued to drift slowly toward our crunching encounter with the reef. What must it mean to M. de Bougainville to lose his ship, I found myself wondering. That imbecile of a ship's writer Saint-Germain was now at my elbow, four large notebooks of his scribblings clutched in his arms, inkwell precariously balanced on top of them, quills emerging from the pocket of his coat. I think he wanted my help in carrying his precious notebooks, but I pretended not to notice. D'Oraison was now on deck—everyone was now on deck—and I moved to his side. La Porte joined us, carrying his medical kit bursting at the seams and with its mouth open. He had crammed everything he could think of into it.

"Prepared to abandon ship?" d'Oraison asked.

"No," I answered. "Nothing we need. We can live off the land."

"If we can get there," said La Porte.

"We can swim for it if we have something to hang on to. An oar, even a spar," said d'Oraison.

Yes. I didn't think I could make it swimming without something to buoy me up.

"Wind backing to southwest, sir!" Duclos-Guyot, at the helm, was the first to feel the ship respond to the change in the wind. She heeled a moment in the freshening breeze, then her bow slowly veered to port. She moved forward.

"Out topsails," M. de Bougainville ordered. "Bring in the anchors."

The topsails came out of their stops with a crack. The capstans turned, the men straining to bring in the anchors. We were moving. Slowly we edged away from the breakers, back up into the center of the lagoon.

The southwest wind lasted only twenty minutes. M. de Bougainville had to abandon any thought of moving out to sea. But it was enough to give us safety for the moment. By now, we had lost for good four anchors. But we re-anchored the last spare sheet anchor, and took another sideline from the *Etoile,* this attached to its large anchor. Then the launch was sent to fetch the hawser from the 2,700-weight anchor—its buoy was fortunately still in place. We bent another hawser to it and carried it out to the northeast, then returned the sideline to the *Etoile.* She had all along been moored on a less coral-infested bottom and, a lighter ship, had avoided our troubles. We were safe for now, while awaiting the results of the exploration for a passage out undertaken by the *Etoile*'s launch.

When the *Boudeuse* had come to rest again, M. de Bougainville called the lookout down from the crow's nest.

"What do you see on shore?"

"Camp looks fine, sir. Sentinels at their post. No sign of activity."

"And the natives? Back in their houses? Back at their usual occupations?"

"No, sir. No sign of them. Not a one."

M. de Bougainville surveyed the situation. I feared that he was simply going to order all the remaining shore party back on board in preparation for sailing. But he was too fine a man to slip away without seeking a better conclusion to our relations with the islanders.

"An embassy," he said. "I think that would be in order."

My heart bounded. An embassy—good. I looked toward the shore, gleaming white under the early morning sun. Farther up, the fringe of coconut palms and the noble crown of the breadfruit trees. Somewhere back behind that inscrutably beautiful setting were the islanders, our islanders, hidden in fear and hostility.

I stepped forward and saluted. "I'll go, sir."

M. de Bougainville contemplated me a moment. I felt in his gaze some of his old disdain for his younger rival for Sophie's favors, his insistence on maintaining an edge of distance that suggested I was somehow not yet of age. Untried, not yet ready for command. At this critical juncture, could he designate as his ambassador the youngest member of his staff? And a volunteer who didn't display the instinctive obedience of the mates and the marines?

Silent and anxious, I watched him glance round the afterdeck. Calculations were clearly going on in his mind. Who should command this vital embassy? Not Bouchage, who had spent too little time ashore to know the islanders. Not Bournand, who despite his competence on board was too unreliable in his dealings with people. D'Oraison, maybe, though his monkish ways had made him less popular among our hosts than I. La Porte, perhaps, especially since he needed to visit his invalids. Or Suzannet, whom he trusted implicitly. But something made his gaze come back to me. Maybe my rank. Maybe my innocence. Maybe because he knew about Ité and my Tahitian family. Yes, curiously, for all the little I knew about them, I had become our expert in Tahitian ways. It was startling to recognize it. I was really the best prepared for this particular encounter beyond the bounds of what we had so far known.

"Very well, Prince. It's your mission. Take d'Oraison and two marines—take Fouchet and Kerbron—with you. La Porte, go see your invalids, and prepare them to come back on ship. Suzannet, you're in charge of the watering party. See if they can be ready to bring the raft downriver this afternoon, tomorrow at the latest."

I saluted again. I took nothing, not even my pistol. The two marines were armed. I asked d'Oraison to bring his spyglass but to leave his pistol behind. In two minutes, we were seated in the longboat. We pushed off. We were on our way back to the shore.

XVII

THIS LANDING was unlike the earlier ones. No one on the beach to greet us. Utter silence. And the sentinels standing to attention as we ran the bow up onto the sand.

La Porte hauled out his medical kit from under the thwart, and trudged off toward the shed. Suzannet headed east to the river that led up to the watering hole. I assembled d'Oraison and the two marines, Fouchet and Kerbron, by the campfire.

"Remember," I said, "we go in peace. No use of firearms unless I order it, whatever the provocation. Keep the muskets pointed at the ground. I do the talking." I stopped for a moment. "No," I decided. "No firearms at all. Fouchet and Kerbron, leave your muskets with the sentinels. We go unarmed."

The two marines looked anxious, as if they were going to protest. I glanced sternly at them and turned away. They surrendered their muskets to the sentinel. Then we were off.

I led them down the beach to the left, then struck inland through the grove that shaded the houses nearest the beach. We saw no one. The houses stood empty, the palm fronds over the eaves rustling gently in the breeze. The livestock was gone as well. No hogs rooted in the pens. A lone rooster strutted outside Ereti's house, his head turning from side to side, his step hesitant. I ducked under the eaves into Ereti's house. Nothing there but the smooth matted floor. Even the sleeping mats had gone. The carved wooden idol against the post faced us, its lidded triangular eyes inscrutable, its phallus aggressively pointed at us.

"Cleared out completely." D'Oraison spoke softly at my elbow.

I nodded. "Utter panic, I suppose. Yet well organized, too."

We left this group of houses. I took them to the path which I knew led up to the next community, where Ité's house stood. Five minutes later, we came out into that grove. Silence, everything abandoned. I stopped in front of Ité's house. A water jug, split and fallen neatly apart into two pieces, lay on the sandy earth next to the pit oven, covered with stones. I wondered if they had left a pig or a dog roasting within. Nothing in the house but a pile of cloth neatly stacked in the middle. Where I had slept with Ité was simply part of the expanse of matting. I couldn't even have said exactly where it was.

"Where do we go from here?" d'Oraison asked.

"Where would they have gone?" I pondered a moment. "Where would you go if you felt threatened? Inland, I suppose. And up, into the mountains."

"But you know, they fear the mountains. Ereti told me they are full of the *tupapau,* the spirits of the dead."

"Yes. But maybe just because. Because they'd think that we were fearful of penetrating too deep into the mountains ourselves. What do you think? And anyway, where else could they be?"

"Taken to sea? Set off by canoe to one of those other islands they've told us about. Moorea. Huahine."

I nodded. "That crossed my mind. And if that's the case, we'll never find them. But they left canoes on our beach."

"But those aren't the oceangoing ones. When we reach the uplands, we should be able to see if the the big canoes are still beached farther up the shore."

I nodded, and motioned to Fouchet and Kerbron. We were headed inland, up toward the mountains.

I don't know that I could ever describe the sensations of that trek, up across the open fields, into another grove—more deserted houses—and on up. The day was fair, the sun growing hotter as we climbed, though when we paused to rest, the gentle breeze cooled us. Everything was serene. We were strolling through the Garden of Eden, but everything was wrong. This happy isle was deserted. And all through our fault.

From the high ground we now had reached, our view took in a sweeping line of the coast. Off to our right, we could see the anchorage, with the *Etoile* moored forward of the *Boudeuse*—two black hulks that never seemed quite right in the seascape. Heavy, even sinister, compared with the graceful outriggers. Both ships appeared quiet and secure. But I uneasily thought of the preparations for departure that must be under way. Just beyond the ships, the line of breakers on the reef where we had almost been ground to pieces that morning. What a different twist to our destinies that would have given. Maybe a better one.

D'Oraison had out his spyglass. "The *Etoile*'s launch is on its way back."

He passed the spyglass over to me. Yes, the launch was moving down from the north toward the anchorage. Through the glass, I could make out the splash of the oars. I wondered what news it was bringing.

To the east, our view of the sea was blocked by a promontory, with only the distant blue of the sea beyond. I turned to my left, looking northeast now. Here we picked up beach again. I moved the spyglass carefully over the beach. There. Yes. At the far end I found what I was looking for: the line of high-prowed double canoes, more than twenty of them, beached high on the sand.

I passed the spyglass back to d'Oraison. "Look," I said. "They've not left in their canoes."

He had found the spot through the glass. "You're right. Unless they embarked from somewhere totally different. But that seems unlikely."

"Inland still seems like the best bet," I replied.

I turned west, toward the mountains. The peaks of Orofena and Ao-rai, the two tallest of the island, rose magnificently before us, so different from what we knew. Imagine the Mont Blanc without jagged rock faces, without a snow-covered crown. And their shape, more like a cone, reminded me of a gothic painting I once had seen of the mountain of purgatory, crowned with the garden of the earthly paradise.

"We need to find the track on which we made the first part of the journey to meet Tuteha," I proposed. "Then, when we reach the Vaituoru River, we can try going upstream instead of downstream. What do you think?"

"That sounds reasonable. Unless we've found some trace of them before that."

We fanned out in a line, till Kerbron found the track. Then we formed a single file again, myself in the lead. The way was steeper now, and we kept silent. The sun was overhead, and we were beginning to feel the need for food and water. Once we reached the river, water wouldn't be a problem. For food, we'd have to make do with coconuts.

The path went on. Parakeets and cockatoos flashed bright green and crimson as we entered another grove. Then the path forked. We stopped. The left-hand path disappeared into the thickest grove of trees I had seen on the island. Was there something in there?

"Let's have a look over this way," I said quietly.

We took the left fork, and in a moment we passed into the deep shade of the grove. The sunlight was nearly blocked by the massed foliage overhead, and the breeze suddenly brought a chill. Then I made out the shadowy form of a kind of rock wall before us. I paused, my eyes adjusting to the gloom. When I moved forward again, I saw that we were at the foot of a sort of pyramid of smooth and fitted volcanic rock. It rose before us in layers, each set back from the one below it. Gazing up, I counted four tiers, ending not in a point but a high platform, maybe twenty feet above us.

At my shoulder I heard d'Oraison breathe in sharply. Then I saw it too. Along the back wall, at the top of this pyramid that never quite became one, stood a long row of skulls, the blank sockets staring out over us. Grisly. But now I recalled Ahutoru's efforts to tell me about the *marae,* the place where the bones of the dead were transported. Their temple to the dead. A place they held sacred.

I turned to d'Oraison to explain. But his eyes were still fastened on the temple's highest platform.

"Look," he whispered. I followed his glance. Yes, there was something else as well. Lying on the top of the platform, two indistinct forms.

Then I was pulling myself up over the first row of stones, across the first platform, then up to the next. Now I could see. Fear and loathing gripped my throat. I reached toward my belt for the pistol that of course wasn't there. I wished it had been.

"My God," d'Oraison gasped from behind me.

Stretched out on the top platform were two bodies. Young men, with smooth muscular bodies. Naked. They were trussed, each tied on a plank, their arms bound behind the plank, their legs tied together and to the plank. And each was encased in a kind of long basket, made of plaited coconut leaves, as if offered on a serving dish. They were dead, of course. But they weren't those killed by our bayonets. No wounds. As we gingerly climbed up to the top platform, we could see that their heads had been bashed in at the top. Neatly done, but dried blood showed the place.

Kerbron whistled. "What's this, sir? A sacrifice to the gods?"

I nodded slowly. "It must be. Commerson told me about it. Human sacrifices."

"And what for?" Kerbron inquired.

"To their god of war, I think. He feeds on the dead."

"Bloody heathens," murmured Fouchet.

I tried to puzzle it out. "Do you suppose it means that they've put themselves on a war footing? That this is a preparation for battle?"

D'Oraison nodded. "Seems likely. Look, they can't have been killed more than a few hours ago."

This was true. The corpses looked fresh. No signs of corruption yet. They lay there, exposed in their young manhood. Why them? I wondered. What had they done to get selected? Were they *teuteu*? Chosen by lot? The sun fell hot on my shoulders, but I felt a chill rising up my spine. I glanced quickly around me. Danger? Were we being watched?

D'Oraison must have been having the same thoughts. "What happens next, do you suppose?" he asked, his shaggy head moving in an arc as he scanned the landscape. His face looked drained; I noticed that the scar on his forehead had become more more intensely visible. "What kind of ceremony? Or have they had their ceremony already?"

There was no answering these questions. I stared, transfixed. So they really did have human sacrifices. I thought of Ité, her laughter, her gentleness, the power of her love. How was this possible?

No insects had found their way to the bodies yet, maybe because of the breeze that blew stronger in this exposed place. I looked up from the bodies to confront the row of skulls against the back wall. Some fifty of them, I guessed. Had they all come to be here by the same means? Something compelled me to look back at the bodies. Smooth, almost hairless except round the genitals, exposed to the sunlight. No more pleasures of the body for them. Cut off in their youth, to propitiate the war god. And because of us, of course. These, too, were victims of our clumsiness. But still, war was one thing. Deliberately killing your own people was another.

I forced myself to turn away. From this vantage point at the top of the *marae,* I could see over the tops of the trees in the sacred grove, out to the blue haze of the sea. I suddenly felt a tremendous weight of responsibility on my shoulders. I shouldn't have undertaken this expedition without guns. What did I know about how we would be received by Ereti and the others, if we ever found them? What had I been thinking of? Was I really fit for this command?

Kerbron's lips were moving silently; then he crossed himself. Fouchet looked haggard and pale in the bright sunlight. I wondered whether we should head back to the beach, regroup, arm ourselves, and set out in a larger party. But there simply wasn't time for that. Already, we were into the afternoon. And anyway, this was supposed to be an embassy, not a war party. We simply would have to take the risks.

"Time to move on," I said. "We need to reach the river before we parch."

One last glance at the corpses, and we started lowering ourselves down the terraces of the *marae*. I led the way through the sacred grove and back to the main path. We turned left and started climbing again. No one spoke.

We continued in silence. The sun was ever hotter on our shoulders. I wished I were back in my pareu. I stripped off my shirt and wrapped it round my waist, but there was nothing I could do about my breeches, which were clinging to my sweaty legs. We trudged on, panting now. The crest of the ridge was coming up before us. Finally we reached it. Before us, the land descended sharply to a thicket of trees. In them must lie the river. We moved faster now, swinging downhill with long strides. Soon we were under the shade of the trees. In a few moments, we could hear the gurgling of the river. I had to hold myself back from the temptation to break into a jog. Too dangerous on this narrow path. Another five minutes and we were there. One by one, we threw ourselves on the bank to drink.

"Not too much," d'Oraison warned. "We'll get cramps."

"We need something to eat. Any ripe coconuts?"

Kerbron proved the most agile at shinnying up the coconut trunks. After two false starts, he found one rich with fruit. As he shook and swayed the tree we soon had half a dozen.

A meal of coconut meat and coconut milk is not very satisfying, but it did give us the energy to go on. The question remained, though, which way? Downstream would take us to Tuteha's. Perhaps Ereti and his people would have gone there to seek refuge and join forces. On the other hand, wasn't it likely that if they had gone to Tuteha, he and his people had also decamped and headed for the mountains? A trip downstream, if fruitless, would put us in an awkward position. Already it was midafternoon. If there was no one there, we'd have to start climbing inland again, with evening coming on. And I knew M. de Bougainville couldn't spare us much time.

Going upriver, on the other hand, was a stab in the dark. That should take us closer to the mountains—but to find what?

There was no sure basis for a choice. But it had to be made. I rose. "We'll follow the river upstream," I announced.

No one raised an objection. We set out again.

Travelling up that river was like the experience of some dreams, like a nightmare, even. No path, only a narrow bank, scarcely wide enough to set a foot on, and blocked every few paces by roots that reached down into the stream itself, so that we would have to step into the swift-running water to continue. Back-breaking work, with no discernible sign of progress. We could see nothing. It was deeply shaded, and the banks looked continuously the same. We advanced, but we could not measure how far we had come. And we had no idea how far we had to go—if indeed we were going anywhere at all. No map, no guideposts, no markers. And yet it was heartbreakingly beautiful, too. Vegetation rioted along the banks. The smell of hibiscus and gardenia reached us from time to time. Birds flitted across our path. Brightly colored butterflies lolled through the air. We were four Frenchmen lost in a primeval forest. As we labored on, our mission seemed to me more and more absurd. Everything was a misunderstanding, starting with our landing on these shores. What were we doing there? What did we want? I had an absurd vision of the Comtesse de Lesdiguières, of her silk stockings and high-heeled pumps emerging temptingly from under the flounces of her skirt. What did she have to do with all this? Then I conjured up the throne room in Versailles, and the King in his majesty seated at the end of that long gallery, as I saw him the day I was first presented at Court. Were we toiling for him? What for? If ever he had a thought for the mission of the *Boudeuse,* what did it mean for him? He couldn't have imagined this. How could he?

We had trudged for well over an hour without speaking when I called a halt. The faces of my three companions were flushed and dripping with sweat, their legs were wet and muddy, their boots soaked. Kerbron and Fouchet squatted on the bank. I leaned back on a fallen tree trunk. D'Oraison carefully seated himself on a rock at the stream's edge. We rested for a moment in silence, listening to the heaving of our lungs and the racing of our blood.

"Listen." It was d'Oraison who spoke.

I made an effort. What was there to listen to?

"Do you hear something? Not the stream. More like a distant roar."

I paid attention. Something other than the gurgle and bubble of the stream? Yes, now I heard it. A distant hollow roar. Almost like the booming of the surf, only continuous, and more subdued.

"Yes. Now I do. What do you suppose it is?"

"Falling water, I'd guess. A cascade. Something different, anyway."

I rose. "At least something to look for," I said. "Come on."

We lost the sound as we started trudging forward again. But a quarter of an hour later we began to hear it even over the noise of our sloshing in the stream. Yes, it was definitely organizing itself into a roar. Another half an hour, and we rounded a bend in the stream to find a deep cauldron of a pool, into which another stream poured from the right-hand side. Where the two streams met, the water boiled and swirled. The silver flash of a fish leapt and fell back into the frothing water.

But the roaring sound was not from the pool. It was now distinctly coming from up on our right, from the stream that fell into the one we'd been following.

My decision was quickly taken. "Let's follow up to the right. That's certainly the high ground. The mountains."

D'Oraison nodded. We started up to the right. The stream ran almost level for a bit. The roar was becoming louder, deafening. Then through the thick cover of foliage there was a dazzling glimpse of white, a sheet of dancing white reaching up beyond the treetops. A few moments more, and we stood at the foot of the cascade, a long white plume falling uninterrupted from a hundred feet above us, subsiding into a mist of foam at its foot. It was breathtaking. It was alive, yet unchanging. It was like a divinity of the forest and mountain, their animating source. Then I remembered what Ereti had said, pointing inland to the mountain streams: *papa moe,* which I think meant something like sacred water. Fair enough, I thought. Sacred water. We've arrived somewhere. We're at the heart of something.

D'Oraison was trying to tell me something, but I couldn't make sense of it over the water's roar. I beckoned to him. He came over and shouted in my ear.

"What now? Do we try to go up the side?"

"Yes," I shouted back. "Nothing else for it."

He nodded. "Which side?"

I looked. There seemed to be no basis for a choice. "Any path?"

D'Oraison shook his head. "Not that I can see."

"Take Kerbron and try the left hand. Fouchet," I screamed. "With me," and I beckoned to the right-hand side of the cascade.

Fouchet and I slogged across the stream below the thundering foot of the cascade. For a few moments we were enveloped in a bright cool mist. Then we stepped inland from the boulders at edge of the cascade. The undergrowth was dense, but in a moment we were free of it. Room to walk under the trees. But the ground before us rose like a mountain face. Tree trunks rose from it; roots spread out over it. There was no sign of a path. We'd have to crawl up.

I signalled to Fouchet, and we pushed through the undergrowth back to the stream. No sign of the other two. We waited. We should have stuck together, I thought. No sense in dividing up a party of four. Are you fit for this command? I found myself wondering again.

Then d'Oraison was back on the other bank, beckoning to us. We crossed to him.

"A path?" I shouted.

He nodded. "A track, at least. Almost straight up. Find anything better?"

"Nothing at all. Let's give it a try."

It was definitely a path, narrow and tortuous, but recently used, I thought. You could see that the earth, damp from the mist of the cascade, had been trampled. I came upon some flowers sprouting by the edge of the track that had been crushed, also not long ago. They were still alive in the mud.

I turned back to the others. "Advance cautiously," I said. "We may be getting near."

But there was no way to follow my own advice. All our attention had to go into climbing, grasping at tree-trunks, swinging ourselves forward, slipping on the damp ground. There was no way to keep our heads up. And anyway you couldn't see forward—the ground rose too steeply, the path twisted and turned. We were all panting—you could hear it even over the roar of the water. If we walk into an ambush now, I remember thinking, there's nothing for it. Lambs to the slaughter.

The path made two hairpin twists in sharp succession, and suddenly I stumbled forward on level ground.

I had fallen on my hands and knees. As I rose to my feet, before me stood a vision such as I had never imagined before. A man—at least it had the bare feet of a man, and a bared right arm, which held a long plumed staff—but completely covered and masked. Folds and layers of matting covered him, but it was particularly the head that was awful, inhuman. A high collar of shiny black and white disks, a mask covering completely where the face must have been—I didn't even see any holes for the eyes. Then a high red knob atop the mask, with high spikes, a couple of dozen of them, radiating from it, like arrows tipped with feathers. Was this a vision of death? High priest of our undoing?

The figure stood motionless. D'Oraison, Fouchet, and Kerbron now emerged from the path and stood panting behind me. The figure stamped its foot. It brandished the staff. Then it let out a mournful call, a howl, a lamentation—I don't know what.

There was a stirring from the trees behind. A face peered out. It was gone. Another moment of silence, as we stirred uneasily, glancing round us. Through the trees to our right I could now make out the headwaters of the cascade, a pool where the water rushed forward to take off into the air. To our left, impenetrable forest. Ahead of us—I could now discern figures moving. In a moment a figure burst from the stand of trees. Ereti. He was carrying a branch of banana leaves.

He threw the branch at my feet. "*Tayo,*" he cried. "*Tayo maté.*"

I felt my knees, then my whole body go limp from relief. *Tayo.* We still were friends.

"*Tayo maté,*" Ereti spoke again. I could detect anguish in his voice.

"What's he say?" d'Oraison asked.

Maté. I tried to recall Ité's language lessons. Kill. Yes. "He's saying that friends kill, or we're killing friends."

I nodded vigorously to Ereti. Then I thought hard. "*Tayo . . . eno. Teparahi.*" All this accompanied by gestures in the direction of the shore. I was trying to indicate that these were bad friends who had done the deed, and whom we would flog. I made gestures of flogging; I showed my arms bound behind my back.

Ereti seemed to understand. But he made no move to come closer. He glanced uneasily at the priest-like figure, whose face we couldn't see.

There was a rustling in the trees. Then a group of women, a dozen, more probably, came forward and threw themselves on the ground before us. They cried; they wailed. Some of them had sharks' teeth, with which they struck their scalps, making the blood run down their faces. "*Tayo maté,*" they repeated. Then there were more of them. One clung to my legs—I thought I recognized Ité's aunt—then another, tears streaming down their cheeks. I raised them to me and embraced them; I held them in my arms. I was weeping with them. But Ité? I didn't see her.

I twisted round to look at d'Oraison. He, too, was surrounded by women. I could see his bristly head emerging from an indistinct mass of golden arms and shiny black heads. Fouchet and Kerbron were surrounded too. They held us; they embraced us. Our bodies were entwined. The rich smell of gardenias was everywhere. The moment was intoxicating, but still tense. The priest of death was still there, motionless, waiting.

Ereti, his face still solemn, swept the women aside. He took me by the hand and led me through a stand of trees. We were on a broad patch of level ground, at the end of which the land rose steeply up to the mountains. Here was the islanders' camp. Not a bivouac, but evidently a refuge used in the past. I saw three immense houses, like the sheds that housed their canoes and like the one used by our sick down by the shore. The pigs and dogs were penned together in a large fenced area. I found myself wondering how they had forced them up the path we had taken—or was there another? There were people everywhere. There must have been several hundred of them. As the crowd parted before Ereti I noticed, off to my right, a group of men prepared for battle. They carried lances, some of which must have been more than twelve feet long, slender and tipped with hard points. They were wearing a kind of matting I had never seen before, a sort of protective armor. But then there were others dressed only in the *maro,* the loincloth brought between the legs that I had seen fishermen and boatbuilders wear. These men carried slingshots at their waist. I detected a vast pile of rocks—their armory. Some of them were carrying sorts of maces made of wood, with sharks' teeth stuck in them, or simply the serrated backbone of the stingray. There were some fifty of these soldiers, I made out, ready for combat. So they were in fact preparing for war—a war in which this panoply of weapons would be blown to smithereens by our cannon and muskets. Pathetic images of gore arose in my mind. This must not occur, at all costs.

But now the strange priestly figure made his way through the crowd and stood before Ereti and myself. The hubbub of voices was immediately silenced. The priest stood stock still, his staff raised from the ground. His face was still masked. No features to watch and try to interpret. What did he want?

Ereti held up his open palms to the priest. Then he turned to me. "*Tahu'a pure,*" he offered by way of explanation. Then some more words, in which I grasped *marae* and *maté.* Evidently this figure had something to do with the sacrifice of those dead men we had found at the *marae.* I repressed a shudder. Why on this happy island did they

need this ghoul? And what was his power? I looked on him with instinctive loathing. And yes, dread too.

Ereti turned to the priest. "*Sholé. Tayo.*"

I could make out nothing more in their exchange. It was deliberate.
Each spoke in turn, slowly. Then a pause, during which the silence was
almost palpable. Then the reply, slow and solemn. There was a kind of
formal debate going on. I did not want to move, but I managed to
look back over my shoulder. D'Oraison, his face intent with question
and surmise in the frame of his black whiskers. He stood in a group of
ravishing young women, still clinging to his arms. Fouchet, his somewhat vulpine and intelligent face straining to understand. Kerbron, his
round Breton fisherman's face expressing wonderment, his mouth
hanging open. Someone had placed a gardenia in his unkempt curly
dark hair. An incongruous sight.

Long shadows from the mountain now covered the spot where we
stood. Night would soon be falling. The dialogue between Ereti and
the priest went on. Ereti had just finished a particularly long state-
ment. I waited for the reply. I wished I could see more than that blank
mask. It was too unnerving.

No reply came this time. Silence. It must have lasted for two or three
minutes, which at the time seemed an intolerable length. Then the
priest slowly turned. His back to us, he walked away, toward the far
end of the camp. The crowd parted silently as he moved through it.
Then he was gone from our sight. All that evening, I know I, at least,
waited for and expected his return. But we never saw him again, unless
he reappeared without his priestly robes and we did not recognize him.

Now Ereti picked up the banana tree branch and threw it at my feet
again. I reached down, picked it up, and threw it at his feet.

It was the right thing. A roar of joy came from the crowd, and cries
of *tayo, tayo!* Everyone was smiling, laughing, crying. It seemed that all
was forgiven. There again it was: that extraordinary capacity of the
Tahitians to forgive, to set aside injuries done them, and to pass from
enmity back to friendship without hesitation, without coolness or re-
serve. It was as if they could not stand not being loving for very long.

Then at the outer edge of the boisterous crowd I saw a familar grace-ful shape. People fell back to let her pass. Ité moved gently into my embrace.

The tropical night came on with a rush. Campfires were lit; roast-ing ovens were filled. Joy reigned. A large mat was spread for Ereti, and we were invited to sit down to a feast. When I saw we were in for a full Tahitian meal, I was vexed. By inexplicable Tahitian custom, Ité of course wouldn't be able to eat with us. And then, I really should be returning to the shore, to give M. de Bougainville news of our mis-sion. But in any case we couldn't undertake that journey at night, even if we furnished ourselves with the torches the islanders used in their night fishing. That would have to wait till morning. And anyway, the feast was part of our peacemaking. Ambassadors, I reminded myself, often have to partake of banquets. Part of the job. Just so long as I could find Ité later.

The feasting went on and on. Ereti surpassed himself. He ate three breadfruit entire, three small fish, fourteen or fifteen bananas, and a chop of roast dog, and finished it off with a large dish of *mahi* paste. I was famished and almost kept up with him—except for the *mahi,* which I didn't much like. D'Oraison, Kerbron, and Fouchet were also consuming vast quantities of food.

As Ereti was slurping down his *mahi* I started peering into the dark-ness in the hope of seeing Ité, though I knew nothing could be done about that until the meal was over. And now, just as the meal seemed to be reaching a conclusion, something unexpected occurred.

A group of islanders, maybe thirty of them, irrupted into the camp with loud cries. They brandished torches, the light leaping in wild shadows across the groups at their meals. There were shouts of joy. Dinner was summarily concluded. A large space was quickly cleared in the middle of the camp. Music began, with two flutists and two drummers. Then six young women, girls really, stepped into the cleared space and began a dance as the spectators pressed around.

They were naked to the waist. Below, they wore instead of the pareu a kind of long flowing skirt, covering their feet. The dance began slowly; they scarcely seemed to be moving their feet at all. But they made elaborate, delicate movements of the hands and fingers. Then they began a rolling, undulating movement of the hips—fast, faster, till they seemed to be whipping and twisting their bodies in a way no European ever could manage. It was disconcerting, but graceful. Exciting, too. The spectators were becoming more and more animated. Bright teeth gleamed in smiling faces amidst the planted torches. Faster and faster went the dance. Now one of the girls stepped forward, holding the sides of her skirt in her two hands. Then she lifted the skirt, her body whipping in its rolling motion. There was a glimpse of the glossy black between her thighs. Sighs of pleasure from the crowd. They clapped in time to the music. Now all of the girls were lifting their skirts. The audience appeared to be in ecstasy. Here was bliss represented before them. The dance became more and more frenzied. The lead dancer stepped forward again. She pulled at her skirt and simply dropped it to the ground, now naked except for the gardenias in her hair. She whipped and twisted. It was as if she were in the throes of lovemaking. The rest of them kept their skirts but held them open. I was wide-eyed, and excited.

So was everyone. That, it struck me, was the whole point. Just one more of their celebrations of the pleasures of Venus. The dance ended abruptly, and the dancers rewrapped their skirts, looking demure but with shining eyes and gleaming mouths. Then couples started drifting away into the shadows. Love was in the air. Ité slipped to my side. She pressed her pliant body against mine. She was breathing deeply.

Where we made love that night, I couldn't quite say. It was on a wadding of coconut leaves somewhere at the edge of the camp. It went on and on. It was magnificent.

XVIII

MARRIAGE may be the true mystery of life. As I grow old, and the circle of existence contracts, I think often of my beloved Charlotte. The two years since her death have been a time for reflection, a time of solitude and a melancholy, which is not without a sweet flavor at times. For two separate people to live in harmony seems to me a rare and wonderful thing. To know each other so intimately, to like the intimacy, to want to be entirely indulgent toward the other's peculiarities—this is surely a blessed state. And not so wholly natural as is often assumed. By the time I married, I was quite used to living on my own. And of course after marriage I was often gone for months on campaigns, missions often filled with danger. But every return to Charlotte was a return to order, to tranquil happiness, to a life that was transparent and serene. We complemented each other without trying, and our life together flowed smoothly, in deep and strong waters.

Why do I need to say this? Because I have to try to explain what Ité has to do with it all. In a curious way, that too was a marriage. I know this sounds absurd: an interlude with a Tahitian girl with whom my verbal communication was very limited, whose manners and customs were entirely foreign, in a context that barely made sense to me, can hardly seem to bear comparison with my many years with Charlotte. But, you see, it was its own kind of intimacy—a kind I can't say that I ever achieved with Charlotte. It was the intimacy of two innocent but knowing bodies. Innocent, in that whatever each of us may have done before on the couch of love, this was—for me certainly, and I think for her as well—our first exploration of all the intensest and most splendid pleasures two young bodies can give each other. Knowing, because we seemed to know what to do. By a kind of instinct, we led each other on to new caresses, new embraces. No doubt Tahitian women were trained to knowingness by their whole society. That dance, that *upa* in the camp, was just one of their many celebrations of using the body to pleasurable ends. And why not? Our cotillions are more decent, to be sure; yet they serve the same purpose in the great mating dance of young men and women. Only they are more hypocritical, veiling the ultimate object of the game. No doubt our civilization needs this veiling; it is part of our whole notion of progress. We must take some kind of pleasure in our denials. But why? Is it a good thing? Isn't it somehow bound up with all our enmities and aggressions? Somehow, those battles I was to fight on the shores of the Black Sea were directly related to the cotillions of Versailles. I can't quite work it out, but they were part of the same civilization of desire baffled, artificially constrained and thus made bigger, more unmanageable, more rivalrous and aggressive.

Anyway, that night with Ité following the *upa* was continuous bliss. I knew as it went on that I could not leave her now, that it would be madness, that I would regret it forever. I was beginning to know her, and I was discovering myself in the warm and live recesses of her body. I knew that morning would come sometime, that I would have to pick up my ambassadorial role once again, that decisions would have to be made. But the outcome seemed to me assured. I would stay with Ité. It didn't matter how. There would be a way. After all, once M. de Bougainville returned to France, Tahiti would be on the map. The way here would be charted. Soon other ships would call. Ships from all over Europe, when you thought about it. In fact, no doubt there would soon be too many, nations vying with one another to discover for themselves the pleasures of this enchanted isle. Commerson was right. Black hulks would anchor in our harbor, one after another. Tahiti would no longer be Tahiti. What could be the harm in staying? There would be a chance to go back to that other world, later, sometime.

When the rising sun reached our sleeping place under the trees, it was well past dawn. The islanders were up and moving about. Ité was awake and already wrapped in her pareu. I dressed quickly, and went to seek Ereti. Time to bring news to M. de Bougainville of the success of our mission.

Ereti had just finished a summary breakfast—bananas and a few pieces of mango—and was on his feet, giving commands. His brother Ahutoru, short and solid, had appeared from somewhere. D'Oraison was with him, looking quite unkempt. I wondered where and how he had spent the night. I understood that Ereti had something grandiose in mind. We were not to return to the shore alone. I found Fouchet and Kerbron, evidently dressed in haste, the latter with his *vahine* still clinging to his neck. I ordered them to form up and fall in behind Ereti.

And now our journey got under way. It appeared that simply the whole of the camp was to accompany us. Counting everyone was beyond my capacity as the islanders assembled behind Ereti. But certainly they numbered in the hundreds—maybe as many as five hundred.

We began our march, not down the steep track we had followed up the cascade, but by a gentler and broader path that set farther south, away from the mountainside, before descending in a wide arc to rejoin the stream we had followed somewhere above the branching that we had taken up to the cascade. We were a merry troupe. Smiles and

laughter and talk were everywhere. The dignity of Fouchet and Kerbron as marines was considerably compromised by the young women
who skipped down the path beside them, occasionally linking their
arms through theirs. Ité marched with me, her mother and father just
behind us. Ereti led the way. Glancing back, I didn't see any of the
men in war dress, and no weapons were apparent. The embassy had
become something closer to a carnival. I supposed I couldn't have
asked for anything better than this, though my mind was now thoroughly preoccupied with my own situation. How was I to make good
on my decision to stay on the island? How could I justify it to M. de
Bougainville, to Commerson, who would be sure to argue with me? I
had to make them understand I was not simply deserting their cause.
That it was vital that I stay. And besides, think of all I could learn from
staying on. I could make myself really proficient in the language. I
could penetrate the mysteries of their society. Learn of their gods,
their beliefs, of everything that made them such a civil and gentle people. Perhaps learn lessons that could be put to use in the old world.
Make it a place of greater peace and happiness.

The march downhill went quickly. We didn't have to pick our way
along the stream bed this time; the islanders knew a path just uphill of
the stream, which then crossed it to proceed downhill. We might have
found it ourselves on our way up. We continued at a good pace. Soon
we came out of the river valley onto open ground. When we moved
up to the crest of the ridge above the river, Ereti called a halt. The vast
crowd of men, women, and children spread out on the meadow and
flopped to the ground. Only now did I get a full sense of their numbers. Like some vast group of pilgrims, I thought.

From the ridge, I couldn't see our anchorage. But I could take in a
sweep of sea to the north of it. As I sat and gazed out, my heart suddenly was in my mouth. A ship was just off the edge of the land, under
sail, headed northwards. I knew what it had to be even before I had
called d'Oraison to me and quietly asked for his spyglass. Now I trained
it at the sea, taking my bearings from a promontory on the coast. Carefully I found the range. There it was. Yes. The *Etoile,* with most of her

canvas set, was moving up along the coast and out to sea. Evidently, M. de Bougainville had found the northeast passage through the reef he had been looking for. And had sent the *Etoile* out, to have her safe from the risks of that coral-infested anchorage. No sign of the *Boudeuse,* at least not yet. She must still be in the anchorage, awaiting our return. No doubt impatiently awaiting our return. If M. de Bougainville had despatched the *Etoile* to the open sea, it must be with the intention of following soon. He must be just about ready to sail. The water casks must be coming on board, the invalids too. Everyone was making ready for departure. Just waiting on us. And I had no intention of departing. I hoped to take some things from my cabin, but even that wasn't really necessary. Here on the island I could find all that I needed.

But somehow it wasn't that easy. It wasn't easy at all. The *Etoile* moving out to sea gave me a deep shock. In a moment, I felt sick to my stomach. What was this all about? I had known it must come; I had been thinking of nothing else for the last several days. I had resolved all this last night. Was it that I couldn't face M. de Bougainville? Then again, I didn't really have to. I could simply let the others proceed to the shore without me while I waited in Ité's house. Where she would come to me after the *Boudeuse* weighed anchor and cast her lot again to the uncharted seas.

But that would be cowardly, I decided. I had to explain, face up to M. de Bougainville and to my decision. Make it clear that I wasn't just skulking, like some deserter. He had entrusted me with the embassy, overcoming what I knew were his prejudices against me. I had to bring the embassy to a satisfactory close, show him that I was worthy of his trust. And that I understood the importance of that trust. That I was, after all, the Prince of Nassau-Siegen, born to command. Only after that could I be ready to claim my own right to happiness.

Ereti was now pestering me for a look through the spyglass. I left it to d'Oraison to try to get him to use it properly. I rose and paced about.

"We should get going," d'Oraison said to me. "The Captain will be anxious."

I nodded, and gestured to Ereti. He reluctantly gave up the spyglass—he now was looking at his feet, through the wrong end of the glass—and stood. The pilgrims straggled to their feet. We were under way again.

Down, down to a rendezvous at the shore, which my heart dreaded. My anxiety grew ever greater as we approached. Another hour's march, and we were in the group of houses where Ité dwelled. People stopped to pen their hogs and dogs. On to the houses in the grove nearest the beach. Then our party started moving out on the beach, spreading all over it. I noticed that Ereti and his brother and many others had cut banana fronds along the way, to signal peace to Putaveri, and several had brought gifts—coconuts, great bunches of bananas, chickens.

A glance to the left showed me the camp. Almost deserted. No tents left, and no heads to be seen under the invalid's shed. A pile of perhaps a dozen water casks at the edge of the lagoon, with five sailors resting on them. Just two more loads for the longboat, probably. The sentinels were still at their posts. The *Boudeuse* still lay at anchor, her sails furled. But now I made out that one of the boats had just pulled away from her and was headed toward the shore. Coming to pick us up.

As the launch neared I saw that M. de Bougainville himself was seated in the stern. I expected that. He wouldn't leave the final ceremonies of peacemaking to anyone else. Yet no doubt he came cautiously, intent to make sure that the peace was real. Now I saw that Commerson was seated next to him. Why hadn't he gone with the *Etoile*? No need for concealment now that the secret of Baret was out? Or was he going to join the *Etoile* later? There were also four marines. Armed, I noticed.

The launch was almost to the shore. Time to pull myself together. I was the ambassador, after all. I stepped to Ereti's side.

The launch ran onto the sand. The cries went up from Ereti and the crowd: "*Putaveri! Tayo!*"

Dignified and benignant, as always, dressed in his blue coat with silver epaulettes, M. de Bougainville stepped from the launch and held his palms up to Ereti's. Then they were embracing, Ereti rubbing his face against M. de Bougainville's, tears in his eyes. Behind the Captain stood two midshipmen holding large bundles in their arms. Now M. de Bougainville turned and took them, one by one. First he laid before Ereti and unwrapped a gleaming set of gardening tools, the best that our ironworkers in Saint-Etienne produce: a rake, a mattock, a hoe, two spades of different sizes. I was pleased. Here was something worthy of the islanders, something beyond the trinkets we usually had to offer. Ereti chortled with delight. The other bundle contained a rich assortment of silks, damask brocade and moire and supple *peau de soie*. Evidently our Captain had been safeguarding somewhere this very special set of treasures, and had decided now was the moment to dispense them. The women crowded round, touching them with expert and appreciative fingers. Joy illuminated their features. Bananas and coconuts fell at our feet; trussed chickens and two pigs were added to the display. Everyone was speaking at once. It was something like a country fair, under the bright Tahitian sun.

M. de Bougainville was now doing his best to explain, with much gesture and pantomime, that the four men responsible for the killings were in irons, and would be flogged that day on the *Boudeuse*. But Ereti and his people didn't seem interested, if in fact they understood. Peace was restored, and retributive justice didn't seem to have any place in it. Ereti wanted M. de Bougainville to understand that he was welcome to stay. He gestured toward the remains of our camp, he beckoned for men to leave the ship and come on shore, he pointed out toward the unseen *Etoile* and indicated that she should come back to the anchorage. M. de Bougainville understood, but shook his head.

Then Ereti remembered. Pushing people aside, he began picking up pebbles from the beach. When he had a large handful, he returned to M. de Bougainville, and began laying them in a row on the sand. Jostled by many shoulders, I couldn't get an exact count of how many there were. Maybe the original eighteen, maybe even more. Was he saying that we had not yet stayed the full extent of our original bargain—which was true—or was he indicating that we could and should stay even longer? In any case, that line of pebbles spoke for me.

Yes, why go now? All was well; peace was restored. We could look forward to golden days of plenty and pleasure.

But M. de Bougainville frowned. He bent down and swept up the pebbles, leaving just one lying in the sand. One more day. He pointed to the sun, then to the point of its rising in the east. Tomorrow morning we would leave. Then, as if to demonstrate the irrevocability of his decision, he started giving orders to move the launch down the beach to the stack of water casks and to start bringing them out to the *Boudeuse.* He was determined to leave, and determined to show he was leaving. As a final gesture, he brought forth from the launch a small plank of wood on which the ship's carpenter had engraved the name of the *Boudeuse* and the date of her arrival in Tahiti, and attached to that a sealed bottle containing the names of the Captain and officers of the ship. A formal act of possession of the island in the name of the French crown. By what right? I found myself wondering. Imagine a Tahitian canoe landing at Brest and laying claim to the kingdom of France. I glanced at Ereti, wondering what he made of all this, as M. de Bougainville was instructing a sailor to bury the plank and bottle in the sand under the shed that had housed our invalids.

Now the longboat arrived, with a group of sailors who set to cleaning up the remains of our camp, filling in the latrines and raking the sand. I drew Commerson aside.

"The *Etoile* has already taken to sea?"

"Putaveri ordered her to move out this morning, after her launch came back with the report that there's a good passage through the reef some distance to the north. I decided to stay with the *Boudeuse,* just to have one more trip back to the island."

I nodded. "We saw the *Etoile* from the high ground, this morning. And she's to wait for us there?"

"Yes. The Captain wanted one boat to be in safety. He's worried because he's got no more spare anchors if the hawsers start getting cut again."

"So he's really determined to be off? Why not just find a better anchorage? There must be one, somewhere along the shore."

Commerson gave me a sharp glance. "He's circumnavigating the globe. Tahiti is just a watering stop. He doesn't have your reasons for wanting to make it a place to stop and stay. He's not taking a summer vacation in the countryside, like you."

His remark stung me, as it was meant to. "It's not a vacation I'm looking for. This is important. We've scarcely begun to penetrate the ways of this island. We owe it to ourselves—we owe it to our countrymen—to come back with a full report. After all, this is the most extraordinary discovery of European exploration. A real paradise. Not some imaginary Eldorado, not some bogus Fountain of Youth."

Commerson raised his eyebrows. "Penetrate, eh? I guess I know what you've been up to."

I pushed past my annoyance. "Yes, that's part of it. That is a part of knowing them. It's . . ."

He interrupted. "I know, I know. And you're right, of course. This is important. Nothing the Spanish or the Portuguese or the English have discovered comes close. They only found riches to exploit, and destroyed whatever native peoples they found in their path. We've discovered human riches, social riches, a place where mankind has made life beautiful, a golden lesson to our world. We should stay. But nothing is to be done. We are leaving."

"But it's not right."

"Not right? That depends. For an old scientist like me, and a young lover like you, it's not right. We need time for exploration, for contemplation. To live with the people, to absorb their ways, to observe, to weigh, to evaluate. But Putaveri is different. He's a navigator. His place is on shipboard. He needs to push westward, to circle the globe, to make his report for further expeditions."

"But we don't have to go with him. I don't, at least. I could stay here. Surely another ship will be dispatched once he brings back his report."

Commerson became grave. "Yes, probably. But it could be several years from now. And you, Prince, will have consumed the best years of your life in timeless idyll, while time continues to march on in our world. You'd come back a stranger. You might never find your place again. The race for fame and fortune would have passed you by."

"I don't need fame and fortune. I have happiness here."

"Happiness. Is that what it's all about, my lad? The pursuit of happiness?"

"Of course," I said. "Isn't it?"

"I wonder. Yes, we all set out in the pursuit of happiness. But that can't in itself be the goal. It's too elusive. Once you think you've got it, it's never enough—you want more. We're a restless race. The goal can't be happiness in itself. It's got to be something like self-fulfillment, making the most of your talents, conquering your place in the world."

"But it's that restlessness I don't want. Peace, contentment. The islanders have more wisdom about these things than we."

"So it seems. Though d'Oraison has been telling me about those two trussed-up corpses with their heads bashed in, at the *marae*. There are more things here than you understand. Two or three or four years here, and you'd no longer be a vacationer, Prince. Invisible tentacles would reach out, to make you conform to their rituals, to their *tabus*."

Last night's dance flashed through my mind. "Yes, but I like most of the rituals I've seen. They affirm life, they say yes to pleasure, to the body, to love, to . . ."

"Prince, listen to me. I stand at the threshold of old age. Already, the body sometimes refuses my commands." I found myself thinking of Baret. He went on: "I know still the pleasures you speak of. But I know also they're not enough. You can strip off your clothes, you can go naked under the sun, but you can't strip from yourself that clock that we Europeans have built into us. It's innate. It's history. We are part of history—our discovery of this island is part of history. The island itself has no history. But it is our glory, and our fate, to make it part of history. We must return to the land of history, the land where these things—these discoveries—become part of the chronicle of humanity. It's . . . the point is, it's not enough for us to make the discovery. We must bring back the news. We must write about it, think

about it. Debate its meaning with our philosophers. Understanding—
that's what we're about. A curse, if you will, but it's us. No way to es-
cape from it."

I felt an immense weariness descend through my shoulders and
move on down through my body. My legs were weak. I had trekked
many miles in the last day and a half, and spent the night in lovemaking. I was hungry. And above all, I felt beaten down by Commerson's
arguments. He couldn't understand. How could he? The lover of Baret
and the lover of Ité could never come to terms on that question. And
yet Baret was part of the point: Commerson was not a man to discount the senses. But he was an old man, flushed under the Tahitian
sun, his face a mass of wrinkles and crevices beneath his smooth, high
forehead.

"Time to eat," I said.

"Yes," he agreed. "But a decision still has to be made, Prince. And
you'll do the right thing, I'm convinced."

Lunch was a festive occasion, under the shade of the palms at the
edge of the beach, a kind of *pique-nique* organized by our hosts, with
food enough to feed the hundreds of hungry mouths. We were well
into the afternoon when it ended. The longboat was ferrying off the
water casks. Only one boatload still remained on shore. The camp was
now clean. M. de Bougainville had ordered all hands on board by sunset. I went in search of Ité.

XIX

Darkness was coming on as Ité and I wrapped ourselves in our pareus—I had left my clothes at her house—and prepared to leave the pool above the boulders in the stream. The last boat would be leaving for the *Boudeuse*. Maybe it had left already. I had only to linger in the woods, and then it would be too late. I'd have secured my place on the island. Unless they came looking for me.

As we reached the fork in the path, and Ité held out her hand to lead me back toward her house, I came to a halt. I was wracked by indecision. I signalled to her to go on, that I would join her in a short time. Then I crept forward along the path leading to the beach. I stopped short before emerging from under the trees.

The longboat and the launches were gone. But the pinnace was pulled up on the sand. Where had she come from? Who had brought her? There was no one around.

I kept in the shadow of the trees and began to move sideways along the edge of the beach. I moved to the right, in the direction of the group of houses around Ereti's. No one was visible. I did not go as far as the houses, where I knew that dinner preparations must be under way. Now I turned and moved to the left. No one here either. I had almost reached the river that led up to the watering hole when I nearly stumbled on Commerson, stretched out at the foot of a breadfruit tree, his eyes closed.

I started to retreat quietly, but a hand reached out and grabbed me by the left ankle.

"Got you now." Commerson heaved himself into a sitting position.

I pulled my ankle free. But I did not move away.

"Prince, I got Putaveri's permission to come back with the pinnace. I rowed all the way in myself. For a last talk with you. He says you're perfectly free to do what you want. You came as a volunteer, at your own expense. You can't be called a deserter. But he represents to you, via his humble messenger—in the person of myself—that it just won't do. Greatness awaits you at home. Such is his message. He also wanted me to tell you that he was looking for an opportunity this afternoon to congratulate you publicly on the success of your embassy, but you slipped away. You know, I really think he's become very fond of you, though he has trouble showing it. He cares about you. He doesn't want you to throw away your life, your youth, anyway."

I wasn't quite prepared for this generous message. I had been ready to defy the Captain's orders, to hide away, to let him sail away cursing my obstinacy. His kindness made things more difficult.

I glanced out to the *Boudeuse,* now a dark hulk in the fast-descending night. The lagoon was a dark purple under the afterglow. Damnation.

I turned to Commerson. "What sort of deadline are you under from Putaveri?"

"No deadline. Only, we sail at first light. Or as soon as the wind comes up in the morning."

I pondered. The only decision I could come up with was no decision. "Let's go share Ereti's dinner."

"A last supper, eh? So be it."

We rose and walked down the beach toward Ereti's house. Darkness encompassed us. The only sounds were the scrunching of our feet on the sand, and the soft lapping of the water at the edge of the beach. The stars began to stand forth in the immense soft sky.

When we reached Ereti's, we were greeted with shouts of joy. Another full feast was under way. Mats were laid for us, jugs of water fetched, roast tuna fish presented on wooden platters.

"You know, Prince, it may be your duty to leave in another sense as well." Commerson picked up the thread of our earlier talk, once the fish was disposed of, as if there had been no break in our conversation. "It may be the right thing to leave these islands alone, without any foreign element. You'll be a disruption. Your children with Ité will project that disruption into the distant future. You'll teach them things they don't need to know."

"But you said yourself that after we are gone others will come. Others less well-intentioned than we. Adventurers, plunderers. Jesuits, missionaries. Those with a cross in one hand and a musket in the other. Maybe I could help them protect themselves."

He shook his head. "The only protection would be total isolation, standing outside the march of history. Once we've reported their latitude and longitude, it's only a matter of time."

"Then we shouldn't report their latitude and longitude. Make no report at all. Keep silence on our discovery."

"But you know it won't be that way. Putaveri is commissioned to report his discoveries. History is inexorable. Can't be reversed."

I squirmed. "Then I wish we never had discovered the island."

"That, too, is irreversible."

"You mean that the coming of history is the coming of corruption. Of property. Of mine and thine. Of jealousy, rivalry, and the artificial needs and desires that they create. We've already made the Tahitians thieves, maybe. Next, they'll be murderers like us. They'll lose nature as their guide."

"Easy, Prince. It's maybe not so very simple as all that. The Tahitians knew the art of murder before we touched their shores. They even murder in the name of their gods, which we, on the whole, do only in symbolic form. At least, at the present time. Nature? Yes indeed, nature. But nature, you see, permits everything and authorizes nothing in particular. Even murder is in nature, you know. Destruction. Nature couldn't go on without destruction. We move forward only across graves, whole cemeteries of them."

"But still, we have nothing better to offer as a principle than nature. Natural law. Do we?"

"No," said Commerson. "Of course not. It's what we have to try to come back to, as best we can, from our state of good and evil. But it's not so simple as fornicating in a hut, my boy. You get back to nature from where we are only through acts of thought and imagination."

"But when you encounter the thing itself, here, now, in this paradise?" I sensed that my voice was becoming anxious, desperate.

Commerson was moved, but relentless. "For us, the only true paradises are the ones we have lost. Paradise is an idea we carry in our head. It is that idea we are obliged to work with, to make it as real as possible. At least, to try to cultivate some bit of that garden."

I couldn't maintain the conversation. Commerson was overwhelming me. I rose. "I'll be back," I said.

But I didn't come back. Once away from the light of the fire, I couldn't rest until I found Ité. I knew the path well enough now to find it in the dark. Stumbling, my heart pounding in anxiety, I walked away from the shore toward her house. I found her sitting by the embers of a fire, waiting for me.

Later, sometime in the middle of the night, I woke. My body was relaxed from love, but thoughts were racing through my head. It was impossible to go back to sleep. I slipped quietly from under the mat covering us and went to sit just outside the house. The sky was an incredible display of stars. The soft air made them seem friendlier than at home or out at sea.

Earlier, when we had sat by the embers of the fire and I'd held Ité in my arms with a kind of desperation, she had understood my tense and desolate mood. Instead of taking me to bed right away, she sat with her left arm wrapped around my shoulder while using her right hand to point to the constellations above us. With her instinctive grace, she seemed to sense that only the starry vault of the night could, for a moment, take my mind from my present dilemma. She tried to teach me the names of the constellations in her language, and the legends that went with them. I thought I understood that Ta'aroa, the great spirit, dwelt in a dark black sky until he conjured forth the *atua,* the many gods, including the maker-god Tu, who eventually made man and woman. There were gods everywhere in that starry night. Not mine, Ité's—but why shouldn't they be mine? No reason. Except that they couldn't be.

Now, as I sat alone outside the house I became aware that the stars on the eastern horizon were beginning to lose their radiance. Under them, the horizon was turning from black to gray. Not far below that horizon hung the sun. Soon it would climb forth, inexorable. Day.

I realized that my chest was gripped with pain, as if something were clutching at it from within. I looked back into the house. Darkness had turned to gray, enough so that I could make out the form of Ité. She was on her side. I could see the firm and graceful thrust of her hips under the light cover.

I was about to go slip under the cover next to her when I heard a footstep beside me. My first thought was that it must be Commerson, come to fetch me. But as the figure materialized in the grayness it was not he. It was Ereti.

"Sholé," he said. "*Harre.* Go." He pointed to the eastern horizon, then down toward the anchorage. "Time to go."

I found myself thinking with surprise of how well I understood him. My ears were becoming accustomed to Tahitian words; I could pick out ones I understood, get the gist of things. Progress.

Another footfall. An old man, with silver hair. I recognized him, though I hadn't seen him since the day of our first arrival. The one I took to be Ereti's father. The one who hadn't wanted us to stay on the island at all.

He spoke. I seized only part of his long, quiet, yet emphatic speech. Putaveri wanted me. Putaveri loved me. Ité loved me, too, but Ité belonged here. Belonged to her gods. To her parents. I did not. I was a good man. But I must go.

Ereti nodded throughout the speech. It was as if we were listening to the conscience of the island. Telling me I was not wanted there. That there was no place for me there.

What could I do? I glanced in desperation and longing at the sleeping form of Ité. Then Ereti took me by one hand, the old man by the other. I did not resist. How could I? They led me back down the path, past Ereti's house, to the beach.

The pinnace was gone. So Commerson must have gone back to the ship last night. But an outrigger had been dragged down to the water's edge, and four men with paddles waited by it. A fifth figure stood apart on the beach. Ereti beckoned him to us.

"Ahutoru," he named him. His brother. Evidently, he was going with us.

Was all of this prearranged? With Commerson? With Putaveri? I was too miserable to figure it out. I let myself be placed amidships in the outrigger, with Ereti before me, Ahutoru behind. The old man remained on the shore, the palms of his raised hands held toward us as the outrigger pushed off. As the islanders laid to their paddles, the outrigger shot forward—so much lighter and swifter than our boats—and I was thrown back against Ahutoru. He cradled me gently in his arms. I pulled myself up into a sitting position, and twisted my head round.

The old man still stood on the shore, his hands upraised. As I watched, the first rays of day lit his face and his silver mane. Out on the eastern horizon, over the immensity of the violet-colored sea, the sun had just sprung free, a fiery deep orange, streaking the clouds and the water with gashes of golden light.

Before us, the spars of the *Boudeuse* were illuminated. As I watched, canvas broke lose from its stops and started up the masts. Then a billow of smoke from the foredeck, followed by a boom, sundering the air, the peace. Sundering my life. The signal for departure.

We were alongside before I had the chance to think anything coherent, to make any vows or decisions. It all just happened. Ereti and Ahutoru handed me up to the deck, then followed themselves. M. de

Bougainville was at his post. A gentle breeze had sprung up from the west. The anchors were coming in. Ereti explained to Putaveri that Ahutoru had decided to come with us, to see our homeland—here he gestured toward the west, as if he believed it lay farther down in a chain of islands—and would return when we came back. I'm sure M. de Bougainville would have done his utmost to prevent this if he had not been so all-consumed by making ready for departure. He simply didn't have the time to argue. I could see the lines of contrariety on his face. But then Commerson appeared from the companionway. He was not one to object. What better addition to his collection of specimens than a live Tahitian? He simply took Ahutoru by the hand and led him down below.

Ereti was now in tears. So was I. He embraced Putaveri, who then turned on his heel and went to stand beside Duclos-Guyot at the helm. Ereti and I clung to one another, murmuring *"tayo, tayo"* over and over. I wanted to give him a message for Ité, but I couldn't formulate anything. All her vocabulary lessons had been wiped from my mind. I just clung to Ereti.

Then he slipped from my embrace. He was gone over the side in a moment. The outrigger pulled away, the wet paddles flashing in the growing sunlight. It was gone, riding swiftly to the shore.

Our sails filled with the morning breeze. The anchors came up. The sidelines were cast off, and their anchors were fetched by the longboat. The *Boudeuse* was moving, northward. The shore began to slip by. This was really the end. And I was on board, not with Ité.

XX

LAST WEEK, I wrote my will. I stipulated that I should be buried without pomp by our local priest in Tynna, on a plot of our rich Ukrainian earth fifty feet square. I have left as a legacy a sum that will provide two dowries, each of 300 florins, to two girls of Tynna who marry each year, provided that they care for the flowers on my grave. I have stipulated that the peasant women of Tynna will choose the two girls each year on the anniversary of my death. They will choose those they esteem to be the most virtuous, who will be most faithful in caring for the flowers. I am sixty-three years old. I have a feeling that it will not be long before the girls of Tynna come into this legacy. May they do it honor.

Why have I done this? I remember that my old companion Commerson—can I call him my mentor?—told me he would leave his body to medical research for the anatomists of Paris. But I am not so brave as he. And besides, there is no university here in the depths of the Ukraine. My cadaver would have to travel many miles before it reached hands able to dissect it. So I tell myself, and it is true. But have I also fallen into superstition as death approaches? Why choose the priest of Tynna? Because any other arrangement would be too complicated in this remote and narrow-minded village. No one would understand. They would take me for the antichrist and throw me into quicklime, like a man hanged by justice. Better not to try to undo their ways.

And the dowries for the two virtuous maidens? Well, that sounds conventional enough, like some prize for virtue—these have become common in my lifetime. But I intend it as a tribute to Ité, in a round-about manner. It is so difficult for the impoverished peasant girls to make a decent marriage. Without a dowry, they can be condemned to a life of virginity or to the hands of some penniless ruffian who must be contented with what's left. With a dowry, they may be able to find a decent man. To know the pleasures of the marriage bed, to the extent they are capable. Of course they can never know what Ité knew—not in this priest-ridden and backward land—but maybe they can have the best their bare bones of a civilization can offer them.

As I drew up my will I found myself wishing I could ship two girls out to Tahiti each year. To have them experience love in Tahiti. I am sure it would do them good. But of course it's impossible. They could never understand. The very notion is ludicrous. It made me think of poor Baret, her pasty white body stripped bare in the Tahitian sunlight by the curious islanders. Her pale pink nipples and the light brown hair between her pallid thighs looking so out of place under that lion of a sun.

Yet they tell me there are now Englishwomen on Tahiti, along with Englishmen. Missionaries, they are, gone to convert the natives. My blood boils at the thought. Convert, indeed! To what? To our wretched, impoverished notion of a morality! Commerson was right, you see: they did come, a cross in one hand and a musket in the other. First the Spanish. Then the English. What could they understand, with their moral blinders on? What a travesty. What a tragedy.

The English. I have nothing against them personally. I fought against them, but I always considered them a worthy enemy. Five years ago, I left the Ukraine and travelled all the way to Paris to meet with the

Emperor at Saint-Cloud. I had a plan to present to him, a plan for the invasion of England, in a pincer movement that would have crossed the Channel from the Pas-de-Calais, and at the same time come down from the North Sea, in the manner of the Vikings so many centuries ago. It would have worked. But Napoleon never has put it into effect. Too much preoccupied with his dynastic problems in Italy and in the German States. Perhaps some day. If he intends to secure his empire for future generations of Bonapartes, he will have to invade England, the only power that can overmatch him. Especially at sea, of course. Witness Trafalgar.

But the point I wanted to make about the English is that it turned out they had discovered Tahiti before us. You remember that we found the Tahitians had a word for iron, which they called *aouri,* even though they did not produce the metal themselves and indeed were innocent of all metallurgy. Ahutoru cleared this mystery up for us on the long voyage home. There had been English on the island. When we reached France, we eventually found out that Captain Wallis, in H.M.S. *Dolphin,* had called at the island—well up the coast from where we landed—about ten months before we arrived. Since then, I have read his account. It's fairly worthless, since he spent most of their Tahitian visit sick in his ship's cabin. But it's clear that the English went about things in the wrong way. They had a sea battle with the islanders on first arriving, slaughtering a number of them with cannon and grapeshot. Absurd, and tragic. Then they set up a military-style camp on shore and engaged in trade with the islanders, but they never went inland, and never got to know them. It was the visit of a man-of-war. They never discovered the meaning of the place. To them, the islanders were a strange, dissolute, thieving bunch of natives.

I hold no particular brief for the country where I was born. You see that I have exiled myself from it. And I have witnessed the most savage acts of inhumanity committed in the very streets of the capital, running in blood from the guillotine. I have seen the French people become a beast enraged, and put to death their own King. Nonetheless, I do maintain that we comrades of the *Boudeuse* and the *Etoile* were the right people to discover Tahiti, to do it some kind of justice. Even M. de Bougainville, though bent to the ways of the sea and the hard duties of command, understood that we had found something extraordinary in the annals of discovery—in the annals of mankind's knowledge of itself. You think you know mankind, you see, and then you discover people— people like you and me—who have arranged everything differently. Who understand the pursuit of happiness in an entirely different way. And on the whole, I think, a better way. Yes. Here in the sunset of my life, I look back and I judge. Whatever the faults and the limits of that society, it was better than ours. More truly moral. Happier.

And now we—the English, at least—are destroying it, undermining precisely what was strongest and best about it, precisely what could have taught us a lesson: its morality. Because the Tahitians don't prostrate themselves before a dead man racked on a cross, because they do not believe in the three persons of our god, because they do not kneel at the altar rail before they make love, they are judged wicked and immoral and must be converted. Converted! I am reduced to impotent rage just thinking about it. And at least we French understood that we should not interfere in this way. If there was to be conversion, it should be worked on us, not on the islanders. Even M. de Bougainville understood this. He kept his distance. I don't even know to this day whether or not he took any of the Tahitian women to bed. Hard to imagine that he didn't—but how then did he succeed in keeping it so private? The mystery of command. He managed to maintain the commander's dignity. But he treated Ereti and Tuteha and the rest with respect.

But as soon as we were back in France, he published his first relation of our discovery. Thus knowledge of our island paradise spread through Europe, and the kings and the corsairs, the adventurers and the missionaries all entered it on their charts. Not that suppressing what we had discovered would have made any difference. There was Wallis in the *Dolphin,* as I mentioned already, then after us there was Cook in the *Endeavour,* then Cook again in the *Resolution.* It's as Commerson said it would be. Progress, if that's the right word. In any event, the coming of an age where our old world is no longer alone, but in constant communication with other worlds. Which is bound to mean that the weaker will be forced to take on the ways of the stronger. That differences will be wiped out. A dreary sameness will come to reign throughout the world.

Yet, need it be so? Do we really want everything to be the same? Do we want the children of Ité dressed in the gray muslin of English Puritan maidens? Why can we not revel in the different ways that mankind has invented to be human? I suppose it is that original curse described by M. Rousseau—the curse of the mine and the thine, the curse of property. I recall the act of possession that M. de Bougainville buried on the Tahitian shore. Ludicrous. By what right? And to think that some Europeans call the Tahitians thieves! When you add to exploration of the world the notion of property, the result is very clear. It's theft.

When I got back to France, one morning I sat down at the old marquetry desk in my uncle's house in the rue de Bourgogne and wrote out my impressions of our voyage. Not an account for publication, like M. de Bougainville's. I am not a writer. These were just some thoughts that came to me one morning. The few pages I covered ended with a noble peroration. I said that the new spirit of discovery would mark a departure for mankind, which would finally arrive at full knowledge of its planet. I wrote: "These new Columbus and Cortez have just as broad fields of glory to cover as the old, but now we are in the century of humanity, and we must at least hope that Europeans want to become acquainted with their brothers of the southern hemisphere only to teach them the truth, and to make them happy." The fond illusions of youth. I think that even as I wrote those words I knew my hope would be in vain. Truth? Why did I suppose we possessed it? And if we did, that we would want to teach it to them? I was succumbing to European arrogance again. The root error may lie in believing that our truth can be anything but oppression when taken to the ends of the earth.

But I digress. I need to finish my story. That can be quickly done.

* * *

That fateful April morning we sailed through the lagoon to the north, until we reached the passage through the reef to the northeast. Then we moved out to the open sea, joining the *Etoile,* which was waiting offshore. All this time, I hung over the port rail, my eyes riveted on the shore, as the early morning sun warmed my neck and shoulders and gilded the island sands. Ereti's outrigger had been beached; he had disappeared with his oarsmen into the grove. No one was visible on the beach. It wasn't until we reached the promontory to port, and began to open up the reach that would lead to the northeast passage, that I saw figures begin to collect on the beach. First a handful, then a score. There were women in this group. They ran the length of the beach, in the direction of our sailing. Was Ité among them? D'Oraison passed me his spyglass without a word. But I couldn't make out their identities. The ship was now beginning to heel to the freshening breeze, and the figures on the beach were moving. It was very difficult to get a fix on any one figure for long enough. I asked d'Oraison to fetch La Porte's more powerful spyglass.

Then, while he was gone, I saw her. I couldn't really see her face, but the figure, in its light, graceful carriage, was instantly recognizable. She wasn't with the group of other women; she had outdistanced them and had placed herself at the very tip of the promontory, standing atop a flat boulder. In a moment, d'Oraison was at my side, and passed me La Porte's glass. I crouched to steady it on the rail. There, finally. Circled in the spyglass was the faced of my beloved. Her brows were contracted in grief; tears stood on her cheeks. She looked utterly forlorn. I rose carefully to my full height, keeping the glass focused on her. I waved and waved. Then she saw me. She waved back, and that radiant smile spread across her face, under the tears.

But now scores more islanders were emerging from the groves, overrunning the promontory. It looked as if the whole island had turned out to see us sail. In another moment, it was just a crowd scene. Then we were past the promontory, and the figures on shore became an indistinct mass.

*   *   *

During that interminable voyage back, I found some solace with
Ahutoru, and I think he with me. For several days, he wanted M. de
Bougainville to stop at each island we came to. He knew about
them—even claimed to have a wife on one of them—and assured us
that we would be welcomed as warmly as on Tahiti. But M. de
Bougainville, having made his water and his provisions, had no intention of making port again. Ahutoru then took up the belief that France
was the next island we would encounter. He was sorely deceived in
this. Our voyage westward was more arduous than anything we had
known so far. Off the uncharted coasts of New Britain and New
Guinea, we suffered horribly, our passage blocked, our food reduced
to almost nothing, our water supplies dwindling. We dined off rats
from the ship's hold. Two men died of scurvy, including poor
Bouchage. When finally we reached Batavia, we were ghosts of ourselves. Thanks to the ministrations of the Dutch Governor General we
were restored to health, and made our passage back round the Cape of
Good Hope, reaching Saint-Malo on March 16, 1769.

Ahutoru taught me much about his fellow islanders—their habits,
their beliefs, their language. Thanks to him, I began to speak Tahitian
passably. If only I had had his instruction at the start of our stay in the
island, I would have been able to communicate so much better with
Ereti, with Ité, with everyone. Once, when we had consigned the
body of poor Bouchage to the sea, I asked Ahutoru if he believed the
body would be resurrected the following day, perhaps in France. He
scoffed at me. The body, he told me, would be eaten by sharks.
Clearly, he didn't believe in the bodily resurrection. I couldn't get him
to give me any very clear notion of an afterlife for the spirit. It appears
that the lucky ones enter into Rohutu-noanoa, Rohutu-of-sweet-odor,
where life is a continual bliss of the senses. But why and how certain
spirits reach this paradise, I could not tell. Virtue in the sense the missionaries would proclaim it certainly had nothing to do with the case.
It sounded as if what they hoped for after death was simply another

Tahiti, chanced upon by the spirit in its journey, much as it had been chanced upon by us French in our ships.

Ahutoru survived to visit the French court and to become the most sought-after dinner guest in Paris. A year later, M. de Bougainville, at his own expense, shipped him out on the *Brisson,* bound back to Tahiti. He died of a fever during the voyage. He never was able to play that role M. de Bougainville had designed for him, as intermediary between two peoples and two civilizations. Maybe it was an impossible role, in any case. He might have ended his days a man between two worlds, belonging to neither. Still, I take no consolation in this. The death of Ahutoru strikes me as just one more of the depredations we Europeans worked on these once happy islanders.

The best times of that arduous journey home were evenings following the Captain's mess, when I sat with Ahutoru and Commerson, d'Oraison and sometimes La Porte, and talked about Tahiti. Commerson was kind. That old voluptuary understood my state of deprivation; he had some sense of how my body ached for Ité's and how my soul was in mourning. He would hold out the promise of a return to the island by an older and wiser Prince. And he would urge me to put my experience in Tahiti to use for the good of mankind—to create a society free of prejudice and devoted to a proper understanding of happiness. I can't claim I ever really achieved this—but what was to be done in a France shipwrecked in revolution, and a Europe consumed by war? I did not live in the best of times. I could only make my modest contribution, later on, in a corner of the Ukraine.

One evening, he interrupted my thoughts by asking, "What do you think you learned from Ité? Or doesn't the question make sense?"

"Learned?" The question at first seemed almost as offensive as some of those he'd asked during our last hours on Tahiti. Then I said, "Learned is right. I learned that you can communicate without words. That there is a knowledge in the body. That we can love without furtiveness. That women can be as free in lovemaking as men. And much more I can't talk about."

"Good," said Commerson. "Very good. What we all need to do is set that kind of knowledge against the superstitions that continue to plague our continent. Show them that M. Rousseau is right—literally right, in a way not even he could know. That natural morality is the great thing. We must tear down the walls of prejudice, stamp out the black-robed hypocrites who would keep us in a state of servile infancy."

He was getting wound up again.

"Yet, who knows," murmured La Porte, "whether a new and enlightened government for men would really solve the problem. The problem of man's unhappiness, his restlessness. Those demons imprisoned within."

"But surely," said Commerson, "men could be governed in a way that does not suppress and pervert their natural goodness. In a way that recognizes that everyone was created equal, that they simply need to be free to pursue life, liberty, and happiness as they understand it."

La Porte was not convinced. "Perhaps that's all it would take. But I'm not so sure. Men can reinvent government all they want—they're bound to do so, over and over—but it doesn't get to the heart of the matter. It's not clear to me that Jean-Jacques' natural man is really so good after all. The state of nature may just be the war of each against each. As we civilize we suppress, because we have to."

"Jean-Jacques isn't writing encomiums to the state of nature. It's the first, uncorrupted society that interests him," replied Commerson.

"To be sure. But uncorrupted only if primitive man is naturally good."

"Don't our Tahitians at least tell us that could be so?"

I found myself thinking of those two trussed corpses at the *marae*.

La Porte hesitated a moment, then he said, "If you mean that different ways of organizing humankind result in placing the rules and *tabus* in different places, with variable results for our happiness in different domains of life, I agree with you. But if you mean that a simple change in the form of government—in our own France, for instance—is going to change human nature, I think you're wrong. It goes deeper than that."

"The war within us," said d'Oraison in an undertone. "That's what you're talking about, isn't it. It's not just the rack and the torture chamber and the Bastille used by the rulers. It's the rack and the Bastille inside us."

La Porte nodded. "Our unease in civilization. The toll exacted for not devouring one another."

Commerson snorted. "As if we didn't devour one another. Cannibalism barely held in check. That's your basic European society."

"I know," said La Porte. "My point is simply that cannibalism is lurking everywhere. It just takes different forms in different places. You stamp it out in one form; it raises its head somewhere else. Because it refuses to be eradicated."

"But," I said, "surely some forms of cannibalism are to be preferred to others? I mean, Tahiti was not perfect. It had its gods and superstitions and priests and even human sacrifice. But still, its main principle was love."

"And not the impossible love of the Christian man-god," struck in Commerson. "Real love. Human love."

I nodded. Then fell into a revery.

Another evening, Commerson, seeing me in a dreamy lethargy and guessing that I was thinking of Ité, suddenly asked me if I thought I had left her pregnant. I flushed at this and said I had no idea. After all, we had been there too short a time.

"Long enough for her to have been fertile, with the usual results."
This was true.

"I wonder what will become of your child. Perhaps he will become a great chief in Tahiti. The tallest, with the fairest skin. A leader in battle. A wise man."

We turned to Ahutoru to ask him what would be the destiny of a child born to Ité from her love with Sholé. His response was doubtful, and troubling. First he said that probably Ité's parents would have it strangled as soon as it was born. It appeared this happened often. An unwanted child was simply killed. Immediately. And the mother didn't necessarily have any say in the matter.

We were horror-struck. Commerson bit his lip, evidently regretting having raised so uncomfortable a subject.

But then Ahutoru told us that the child would not be killed if the mother looked at it with love the moment it was born. Then it was saved.

Commerson looked at me anxiously. I bowed my head.

After a moment, I said, "It could be. She could look at it with love. She was, after all, so full of love. It simply cascaded out of her. And she must have known from the start that one day I would leave, go away in those hulking black ships."

"True," said Commerson. "And I'm sure she wanted your child even so. She'll love it; she'll be proud of it."

"And it will live an incredibly healthy life," put in La Porte. "Without decayed teeth."

I appreciated their wish to comfort me, but I ceased to listen. My mind had fixed on that last vision of Ité standing at the point of the promontory, her smile radiant through her tears.

XXI

Back in France, I felt bored and empty. It wasn't long before I let Frascati drag me back to Sophie's, where I found myself something of a celebrity. She had now left Lauraguais for the more magnificent protection of the Prince d'Hénin, captain in the personal guard of the Dauphin's brother, the Comte d'Artois. She promptly complimented me on my adventures—M. de Bougainville's circumnavigation was the talk of all Paris, and the happy life of the Tahitians was the subject of the day.

"Fair Prince," Sophie said, her face a picture of pleasant mockery, "need I ask how well you made the acquaintance of these savage maidens? Not savage to you, I wager."

"Mademoiselle Sophie, that is a question I will answer only in my memoirs, which you can read after my death."

"I won't have the patience to wait till then, I'm sure. Give at least the advertisement for that notable tome."

"No, Sophie. It would take too long to try to make you understand. To see it all, to smell it, to recreate that atmosphere, so that you would feel its dreamlike quality. But know that it was not a dream.

Tahiti is real. You wouldn't understand. The whole island really believes in the Venus you figure on the stage."

"Is it possible? Should I pack my whole salon into the *Boudeuse* to go and see?"

"No, since these ladies and gentlemen, and others"—my glance swept the exceptional mixture of company in her drawingroom—"would at once destroy what they went to seek. In fact, we've already begun that destruction."

"Correct, Prince." A voice spoke from over my shoulder. I turned to see the round and smiling face of M. Diderot. "No offense, sir, since you've so cleverly stated it yourself. You have planted the seed of corruption in those happy isles. The Tahitians will learn to curse the *Boudeuse* and all she brought."

I drew myself up. "No doubt. And yet, can discovery be a bad thing? We have extended our knowledge of the human family." I hesitated, trying to get it right before this fierce logician. "We have discovered new possibilities of humanity. We did not know all of mankind before."

"Yes, of course. 'Tis not I who will deny our need for universal knowledge. But that is for us, for the makers of reports and newsletters and encyclopedias. It does the discovered no good."

This put my thoughts as concisely as possible. "And yet," I tried to object, "surely there could be a benign discovery—one that would not interfere? And certainly not enslave, like the Spanish?"

"Degrees of the benign and the malign, certainly. But the principal fact remains: the coming of the outside observer alters and corrupts that which is observed. As we murder in order to dissect under our microscopes."

I considered. "So natural man is condemned, the world over?"

"Yes," he replied. "The war in the cavern, as I call it. Natural man constantly wrestled to the earth by moral man—so called. What's been imposed on us, to keep us from paradise on earth. To keep us enchained. To ensure the domination of those that have power."

"If you gentlemen are going to be so solemn, you'll hardly be in the mood for Pantin." Sophie's mouth was drawn into a perfect figure of mockery.

"Pantin?" I asked. "What does that mean?"

"Come see. We set out in ten minutes."

M. Diderot had turned away. So I let myself be packed into a coach with five others, and seven coaches set off across Paris to arrive, close to midnight, at Mlle Guimard's private theatre in her apartments at Pantin, an improvised shoebox of a stage before which we sat on chairs pushed so close together there was no room for elbows or knees, while Sophie and Mlle Guimard and a dozen new recruits to the Opera went backstage with a certain young Chevalier de Malte whom I had never seen before, and whose claims to his title struck me as extremely dubious. Then the curtain parted on a pantomime set on the Isle of Paphos "in the year 40,000 of the Reign of Love."

The action was too trivial to describe. Sophie played a nymph who wished to seduce the Chevalier de Malte. But to do so, she needed to become a virgin again, to be worthy of his untried manhood. This meant bathing in the Fount of Venus, a kind of tub made up to look like a vast seashell set at the center of the stage on which scalloped pieces of cardboard represented waves. The Fount was surrounded by the Maidens of Paphos, a dozen young dancers draped only in light gauzy veils through which you could see everything. Here Sophie was found immersed by the bare-chested Chevalier, who approached escorted by two charming disheveled nereids. After peeking coyly over the edge of the shell at her discoverer, Sophie slowly rose. She was perfectly naked, her hair loose, her arms raised above her head, in a kind of figuration of those births of Venus that so many artists have painted. The Chevalier fell back in astonishment and admiration. They held the pose for a moment in a kind of *tableau vivant*.

The men on either side of me were breathing heavily. The air in the room was oppressive, charged with the heat of crude desire. On the stage, poorly lit by a row of flickering candles, Sophie and her attendant nymphs were a rousing spectacle. Her body was still adorably voluptuous, with its full breasts held high by the movement of her arms, her tousled curly brown hair falling over her shoulders, her rich fleece between her magnificently generous thighs. Yes, that was the Sophie I had known, the body with which I was so familiar. The Sophie who still had the self-confidence to strip naked among a group of girls ten years younger.

The curtain fell; the audience applauded and whistled. Then the curtain parted again, and Sophie and the other nymphs stepped forward to curtsey. The Chevalier de Malte, stripped to his breeches, stood behind Sophie, his arms encircling her naked waist. Chairs were pushed aside as the spectators moved onto the stage. Each nymph soon had an arm round her waist. Some very grand personages began seeking the dimly lighted recesses of Mlle Guimard's apartments with their nymphs.

There was some discrepancy in numbers between the nymphs and the gentlemen, even if you counted in the women in the audience—mostly, I think, from Sophie's world rather than mine, though I couldn't swear there wasn't a real countess or two among the ambitiously turned out actresses and dancers. The shortage of women gave me an excuse for slipping out. I walked through the silent streets to the square, where I found a cab.

I sank back on the greasy cushions as the cab moved swiftly through the Faubourg Saint-Laurent into Paris, through the sleeping city. It was not really because there weren't enough nymphs to go around that I had left. I knew I could have pressed my claim successfully. Maybe even replaced that doubtful Chevalier de Malte with Sophie. No, as the orgy was preparing my decision had been instinctive and immediate, even though I was quite aroused by Sophie's spectacle. Had I become a prude? I mused, as the cab rocked over the cobblestones. It was the contrast of those pretend nymphs in their cardboard waves with the real thing in that far Pacific island that was fast becoming something of a dream. Sophie's foolish Isle of Paphos could not help but bring back that April morning when the *Boudeuse* was surrounded by those glowing, healthy bodies. And that pool where Ité and her friends had played with me one glorious unforgettable morning. The contrast was too much.

There was a sudden jolt as the cab turned into the rue du Carrousel. Then a moment later it careened onto its right side and scraped to a halt. Of all the bores. I crawled upwards to the door on the left and let myself out, unhurt. The driver was swearing at his horse for what was clearly his own fault—he had swerved too close to the corner post at the intersection, and knocked lose the right-hand wheel. Where he was going to find a wheelwright at this hour I could not imagine. I paid him and set out on foot for the Pont Royal and home.

It was on one of the obscure side alleys off the rue de Grenelle that the woman appeared as from nowhere. She was tall, wrapped in a long cloak that fell from her shoulders to her feet and hooded her face. She looked at first glance almost distinguished—there was something elegant in her stature—until I saw that her cloak was ragged, torn, and splotched with all the filth of the Paris gutters, and her face gaunt and anguished beneath the hood. The hand she held toward me was somehow refined, with long, pointed fingers, though dirty enough. A beggar, I thought, though a strange hour at which to think one could find alms. I made to quicken my pace, when she laid her hand on my arm, with a whispered but agonized call: "Seigneur!"

Arrested in my stride, I spun on my heel to get away from her. Then from the deeper shadow behind her emerged an apparition. A girl, a young woman, maybe fifteen years old, maybe younger even. As I paused, both annoyed and intrigued, the older woman, still holding me with one hand, reached with the other to the girl and pulled the cloak from her shoulders.

There she stood, shivering in the night air. A gorgeous young creature, fully formed in the first bloom of youth, tall and supple, with dark hair falling to her shoulders in wanton curls, a high firm bosom visible through the thin material of her simple cotton frock, which was clean though faded and worn. Her dark eyes flashed in a kind of defiant pride.

"Seigneur! My daughter. Untouched, a virgin. Yours."

I stood staring. This had never happened to me before, but it was common enough. Frascati had told me about a mother who made her way into his very antechamber in the attempt to sell him her daughter—though he claimed the "daughter" was probably as old as the would-be seller and clearly didn't belong to the race of virgins. It happened all the time: maidenhoods for sale, the start of a career. With good luck, you ended up like the women in Sophie's entourage. With worse luck, in the Palais-Royal. Now three years of bad harvests meant that peasant women were coming into Paris to sell their daughters. But neither mother nor daughter here looked like a peasant. On the contrary, the daughter was a morsel fit for a prince. As I gazed I found my appetite was aroused.

"Just one hundred écus, Seigneur. Yours to keep." Her voice seemed to have the accent of good breeding, though it was staccato, broken. Her face was distorted with anxiety.

A hundred écus for a bedmate. Expensive for one night's entertainment to be sure, but for the vacant nights ahead? Of course I didn't have that much in my purse. But no doubt she'd come down in price if I bargained.

"A hundred écus!" I began. "What do you think of?"

Her hand twitched on my arm with a febrile grasp. I turned from the girl's bewitching form to the mother's face. Tears had begun to make their way down her ravaged cheeks.

"My only daughter," she said, choking on the words. "Only because it's the only way. To a good man like yourself. She will be better off." Her words trailed off. She was suffocating.

What a mudhole of a world, I thought. From nowhere Commerson's figure arose before me; I heard his voice speaking in denunciation of our corrupt societies. No, I couldn't do this. A man of pleasure I might be, and I would never be a prude. But not this.

With my free hand I drew my purse from under my cloak. The woman dropped my arm and stood silent, tears now coursing down her cheeks. The girl had wrapped herself again in her cloak, and stood with downcast eyes. I poured out what I had into my left hand, some thirty écus. Enough for two weeks or so of my ordinary pleasures. I placed the coins back in the purse, and handed it to the woman.

"Here is thirty écus. When that is gone, call at my house in the rue de Bourgogne." I took out my tablet and scribbled the address. "There will be more, within reason. And keep your daughter. She deserves better than to become a whore."

She clutched the purse to her side. She looked at me with astonishment and anguish. Then she began sobbing. She wanted to say something, but nothing came. I turned on my heel and walked away as fast as I could.

Yes, she came to the rue de Bourgogne a month later, where Lejeune on my instructions gave her another thirty écus—but only once. She didn't reappear after that. A blessing, I thought, though this relief was superseded by doubt. I should have given her some continuing pension, something like what I would later do for the virtuous maidens of Tynna in my will. But I wasn't possessed of Charlotte's fortune at that time. I was only capable of this muddled act of virtue, which probably only delayed the day of reckoning for the girl I was offered.

I can't find much consistency in my behavior. I remained a man of pleasure, and love came to me in several different forms before I settled down with Charlotte. It didn't have to resemble love with Ité— how could it? But still it couldn't fall too far short of some incurable idealism she had inculcated in me. Not prudishness, that was never my line. But nothing too cynical or matter-of-fact. And nothing that clearly went against the free will of the woman offered me. No sold bodies. Thus, Ité had the strange effect of making me chaste for periods of my life. She was there in my mind as an ideal. A heathen maiden with no idea of morality as a moral guide in my life! I know this will be hard to understand, yet it was so.

So that night I went to bed alone in the rue de Bourgogne, imagining the orgy under way in Pantin. Lascivious images slipped across my mind as in the magic lantern. Here a breast, its nipple raised to an avid mouth. Sophie's voluptuous thighs parting. Young lips painted red, open in an ecstatic smile, teeth glinting. Then the dark ringlets framing the virginal face in the shadowy alleyway. Then these images were blotted out by a loving golden body on the straw mat of an open hut, by the memory of grave and generous eyes, a luminous smile, and a gentle voice murmuring words I couldn't understand.

The cold, fetid air of Paris made me shiver as I tossed restlessly. I could hear in my mind, I could almost feel the soft breeze playing in the palm fronds over that hut that had been the home of my greatest happiness, on that island that had changed me forever. I longed to go back. As I writhed in sleeplessness I vowed to ship out on the next voyage to the Pacific—surely there would be one soon?

But of course I never went.

A Note on Sources

My story is freely based on a number of contemporary sources, especially Louis-Antoine de Bougainville's *Voyage autour du monde,* first published in 1771; and the journal he kept during the voyage; and also the journals and notes by Philbert de Commerson, Louis-Antoine Starot de Saint-Germain, Charles-Félix Fesche, François Vivez. The Prince of Nassau-Siegen wrote a brief account following the voyage, preserved in three manuscript copies. I consulted that in the Archives of the Ministry of Foreign Affairs, Quai d'Orsay. Most of the material concerning the voyage can be found in the lavishly illustrated and annotated *Bougainville et ses compagnons autour du monde, 1766–1769,* edited by Etienne Taillemite (2 vols., Paris: Imprimerie Nationale, 1977). I have sought to remain faithful to the contemporary accounts while permitting myself to supplement the historical record with the play of the imagination.

PB